PROVIDENCE

Visit us at www.boldstrokesbooks.com

PROVIDENCE

by
Leigh Hays

2020

This Trade Paperback Original Is Published By
Bold Strokes Books, Inc.
P.O. Box 249
Valley Falls, NY 12185

First Edition: February 2020

Credits
Editors: Barbara Ann Wright and Stacia Seaman
Production Design: Stacia Seaman
Cover Design by Tammy Seidick

Acknowledgments

I wrote the first draft of this story over ten years ago, so there are a lot of people to thank.

Barbara, Sandy, Radclyffe, Ruth, and the small army of people who make the books happen at BSB. I can't wait to see what happens next.

My two writing groups, both past and present. NORWIG, who encouraged and nurtured early versions of this story through thoughtful and generous criticism. Splendid Tribe, who supported me in the process of revising. It's a solitary job, and it helps to have coworkers along the way.

My coworkers both past and present who've supported me through this process.

Aurora Rey for keeping me honest by kicking my ass when I needed it. I continue to grow as a professional with your friendship and guidance.

My family, in particular, my mother, and my family of choice. My life is richer with you in it.

My wife for finding space in our life for me to write and reading all the drafts. Not bad for a wet noodle.

My son. Because you make everything better.

For H. Here's a love story for you.

CHAPTER ONE

Enjoying the last bit of summer, Rebekiah Kearns lounged on a green canvas camp chair, watching the orange sunset filter through the buildings of downtown Providence. A moving sea of college students and tourists strolled past the art booth she shared with Neil Marguiles. The last rays brushed across Neil's oil prints, echoing the rich reds and bright oranges lingering in the August sky. The colors pulled people toward their booth and resulted in a couple of purchases.

Neil thanked the last customer before he turned to Rebekiah with a wink and a grin. "Works every time."

Rolling her eyes, Rebekiah shook her head. His paintings were good but not his best work. He deliberately chose the sunset prints for this time of year. "I don't know why you waste your time painting. You have a gift for marketing."

Neil shuddered and clutched his chest. "Perish the thought."

Night settled over the city, and a warm breeze blew in, bringing the scent of grilled meat and salt water. Rebekiah stood and shaded her eyes against the last bit of glare off the Providence River. During the summer months and early fall, Providence's downtown hosted Waterfire, a festival of arts, food, and music centered around eighty-plus floating metal braziers anchored down the middle of the Woonasquatucket, Moshassuck, and Providence Rivers.

"I'm going to take a few shots of the lights." She waved toward the photographic prints on the side walls of their tent. An assortment of historic buildings and street scenes hung on metal wires mixed in with a seascape or two. "I need more material."

He grinned. "I see that. Bring some food back."

She slung her bag over her shoulder. "Anything in particular?"

"Whatever that smell is."

She tilted her head. "Probably Atomic Bomb Barbecue." A local favorite for authentic Southern pit barbecue.

His handsome face wrinkled. "Why can't it ever be tofu?"

Rebekiah laughed. "Because soybean doesn't grill like real meat."

He waved her off. She ducked into the crowd and toward the river. She weaved through the foot traffic, following the flow across the bridge and toward the Riverwalk. To her right, rowboats pushed through the water, oars slapping and splashing into the current as they carried torch bearers, their passage lighting the black braziers installed down the middle of the river. She found a relatively open spot and pulled her camera from her bag.

Flames rippled along the surface and converged into the shadows. She focused on that shimmering display, taking a shot, adjusting the shutter speed again and again until her legs started to cramp and her stomach started to rumble. Tucking the camera close to her side, she stood and resumed her walk toward the center basin. The wind shifted and a plume of woodsmoke crossed her path. It reminded her of bonfires on the cape.

She wandered through the crowd. Her hands itched to take more shots, but she forced herself to stay in the moment. She passed a stage where the crowd density increased and the noise level grew. She paused for a moment but continued on and found the line for Atomic Barbecue halfway down the block. She groaned at the length and looked for another shop. A Greek vendor a couple booths away provided meat and vegetarian options. Armed with falafel and lamb gyros, she headed back to their booth.

Neil stood with open arms and plucked the food from her hands. "You are a savior. I'm famished." He stuffed a loose tomato into his mouth. Nodding across the tent, he said, "There was someone here asking about that picture."

Rebekiah turned and knew immediately which one, tucked into the far corner where it wouldn't catch the eye of a casual observer but forward enough that it would pull someone in if they were interested. A black-and-white composition that looked like an orchid until you got up close and saw that it was actually two women fucking.

"Man or woman?"

"Woman. Mid-twenties, maybe a little younger or older. Grad student written all over her." He bit into his sandwich, chewed, and swallowed. "She took your card."

"Really?" Rebekiah smiled. A few of the pictures were hooks designed to pull in potential customers. Like Neil, she sold touristy photos during Waterfire, but her main business was boudoir photography, sexy shots in pinup styles, and she used the event as a marketing tool. But the orchid photo showcased a different approach, grounded in fine art. She'd put it up as a whim to see if it would catch anyone's eye.

She unwrapped her gyro and started eating. The music went into full swing, and the bass line made its way to them a few streets down. She continued watching people ebb and flow, thinking about Neil's comment. This woman was the first person to notice it, and she needed to think about her approach if and when the woman returned.

Another hour passed, and Neil sidled up behind her as she finished talking with a customer. "That's her."

Rebekiah looked in the direction he was pointing. An eclectic group of twentysomething women, men, and gender nonconforming people gathered around a set of tables, laughing and chatting. One looked up, and Neil waved. She looked down. Something in her look, the defiant tilt of her jaw and the shuttered vulnerability in her eyes, was intriguing.

She lifted her camera and snapped a few shots. One of the woman's friends leaned over and said something in her ear that made her cock her head toward Rebekiah. Rebekiah shook her short red hair out of her eyes and looked right at her. She kept taking pictures, catching a half-smile or calculated look as her subject tried to ignore the attention while simultaneously preening under it. She waited until the woman finally walked over.

She hefted the camera and asked, "You don't mind?"

The woman shook her head. "No." She shrugged. "It's kind of flattering."

"I'm Rebekiah." She reached out.

"Nicole." She barely squeezed it.

Rebekiah strengthened her grip for just the fraction of an instant, enough to let Nicole know she was there but not enough to be a jerk. Nicole squeezed back before letting go. Rebekiah smiled, pleased by her response. "Neil said you liked my pictures."

Nicole nodded. "Yeah, I do." She pointed toward the picture in the back. "Especially that one."

Leaning in to study it, Rebekiah turned back. "Interesting. What draws you to it?" She stared at Nicole's profile. A tiny scar traced along the corner of her eye toward her ear. It crinkled when she squinted.

"It's not what it seems." Nicole reached out and traced the air in front of the picture. "It's not until you're up close that you see through the flower to the women underneath. But once you see them you can't see the orchid anymore." She cleared her throat. "Is that a stock image, or did you take that picture?"

"Which one?" Rebekiah knew exactly what she was asking, but she wanted to hear her say it.

Nicole's face brightened. "The women. Were you there when they were…" She rolled her hand.

Rebekiah raised an eyebrow. "Fucking?"

Nicole giggled. "Yeah."

"Yes, I was."

"Did they know?"

Rebekiah folded her arms. "That I was there or that I would use the image?"

"Both?"

Rebekiah glanced at the pair in the picture, remembering the day she took it. Genuine affection suffused her body, and she smiled. "They knew."

"How did you convince them to do that?"

She shrugged. "I asked." She touched Nicole's forearm. "Nicole, are you a photographer?"

She held up her hands, dislodging Rebekiah's, and shook her head. "Oh no. I'm just...curious."

One of Nicole's friends leaned into the tent and said, "Hey, Nic! We're heading up to the stage. Are you coming? Laura's getting tired of waiting."

Rebekiah glanced over to Nicole's friends and then back. Shit, she needed more time. "Why don't you call me? I'd love to shoot you." She passed her a business card.

Nicole accepted it and let herself be pulled out of the tent with a backward glance or two before the crowd closed behind her. Rebekiah maintained eye contact the whole time. She caught one last look from her and smiled, not sure if she'd be hearing from her again but hoping she would.

Neil whistled. "You are a fucking pussy magnet."

Rebekiah chuckled and collapsed into her chair. "You're just jealous."

"You're damn right I am. She didn't even look at me."

"Neil, you fuck men."

"So? It hurts to be ignored."

Rebekiah rolled her eyes. "Oh, the fragile white male ego."

"That's right, sister." He touched her hand. "Smooth and stroke it, baby."

Rebekiah snatched her hand back. "Ew. Gross." She glanced at her watch. "Shit. I got to go soon. Sera's going to be wondering where I am."

Neil laughed. "You and that dog. Who knew she'd be such a perfect companion for you?"

Rebekiah smiled. "I know." Sera's original owner had left Providence for London and asked Rebekiah to look after her, *until I get back.* That was two years ago, and no one had heard from her since.

Neil shook his head. "I'm surprised you didn't bring her."

"She's not fond of crowds." Rebekiah sighed. "Do you need me to help pack up?"

Neil shook his head. "Nah. I'm pretty butch. I can handle it." He nodded across the way. "Or have that guy in the black shirt help me. It'll give me an excuse to ask him out."

Rebekiah laughed and stood. "See, you still got game." She collected her stuff and patted him on the back before heading home.

❖

Lindsey Blackwell adjusted her messenger bag across her chest, leaving New Harvest Coffee and heading east on Westminster Street. Pushing through the morning commute, she walked toward Providence's financial district. At the corner of Exchange and Westminster stood the five-story brick building where she worked. Sandwiched amid the modern concrete and glass office buildings and a few turn-of-the-century high rises, the Queen Anne style—with its bay windows, patterned masonry, and recessed entrance—was one of the shortest buildings in the district. Lindsey's business partner, a former Morgan Stanley investment banker, preferred buildings with less than twenty floors. Cathryn wanted something with stairs she could "run down in less than a minute."

Inside, the noise of the street stopped, and Lindsey bypassed the granite and oak reception area where two women policed the ebb and flow of the building. She pushed the up button for the elevator with her knuckle while balancing two cups in her hands. A group of young professionals dressed in banker chic gathered around her. She listened to them tap on their phones and talk about the latest merger deal until someone nudged the loudest pair and nodded in her direction. The shop talk dried up, and Lindsey shook her head.

One of two women in the group looked her up and down and smiled. She nodded toward the cups. "I hope your boss appreciates you."

Lindsey grinned. "She does."

"I'm Vanessa." Clear green eyes, brown skin, black hair, and just enough bravado coming off her to pique Lindsey's interest.

"Lindsey."

"I haven't seen you before. Do you work for Traveler's?" Lindsey's firm shared the building with three other businesses, including the bank on the first three floors.

Lindsey shook her head. "Wexler Blackwell." The doors dinged, and she led the way into the elevator.

Vanessa followed and turned to face her. "Oh, the big money."

Lindsey shrugged.

More people got on the elevator, and they moved closer together. She glanced around and lowered her voice. "If there's an opening, let me know. I'm a forensic accountant."

Lindsey matched her tone. "Not satisfied?"

Vanessa's professional veneer cracked, and she gave Lindsey a once-over before she said, "I could do better."

Lindsey laughed. "Yes, you could."

The doors opened on the third floor; everyone except Lindsey walked out. She pushed her floor and heard one of Vanessa's colleagues say, "That's Lindsey Blackwell, the other partner of Wexler Blackwell." Vanessa glanced over her shoulder in shock, and Lindsey offered her best *what can I say* look before the doors closed.

Lindsey walked into the Wexler Blackwell suite to the sound of a Bloomberg anchor reporting on the monitor behind the front desk. "Yesterday, Nasdaq took a hit, and the Asia markets are down this morning." She already knew that the market had been rough for the past few weeks. Floods in China and a decline in global spending were killing consumer confidence.

The suite boasted an open floor plan with a mix of glass walls, exposed brick, and high-end office furniture. She moved through the inner ring of workstations toward her office. Quiet clicking and soft conversations floated through the space. A couple employees glanced up and nodded as she walked past. Her director of research, Sabine Fiorenza, stood at her approach and said, "Welcome back."

Lindsey had spent the last six weeks traveling to India, China, Hong Kong, South Korea, and Tokyo. She smiled and passed Sabine the second cup of coffee. "Good morning."

Sabine smiled. "Thank you. I missed this." She took a sip and hummed appreciatively. Nodding toward the far side of the suite, she said, "Cathryn wants to see you."

"Now?"

Sabine's face grew serious. "Now."

Lindsey gave her a look and motioned toward her office. Sabine followed. Natural sunlight poured through a wall of windows and onto the long credenza behind her desk. Various objects d'art, a couple glass awards, and other gifts from clients sat along the credenza.

"I'll go see what she wants. But then I want to get the team together. I have a couple prospects I want full workups on. And Jason Huang is ready to make some real decisions with his father's foundation. I've already started a write-up, but I'm going to want more information about the green energy market here and in Europe."

Sabine smiled and looked up. "And how was Jason?"

Lindsey shook her head and grinned. "Charming. Irreverent. Extravagant."

PROVIDENCE

"Where did he take you this time?"
"Tibet. Potala Palace. The Dalai Lama's winter palace. By private train car."
Sabine rolled her eyes. "Of course."
She shrugged. "He got free publicity out of it." Jason Huang was in his mid-twenties; Lindsey, her mid-thirties. She'd worked for years with his father—Li Jie Huang or, more accurately, Huang Li Jie—a Hong Kong billionaire who successfully integrated his large holdings in China after the handover. The Huangs followed Lindsey when she left Goldman Sachs for her own company.
Sabine waved her off. "Go."
Lindsey left her and walked back across the open space. More people ducked in and out of her way with a greeting here and a check-in there, so it took her twice as long to walk the same distance back to the elevators and beyond to Cathryn's office. She paused at the edge of Cathryn's work area and nodded at the admin assistant who motioned her through. She knocked on the half-open door.
"Come in," Cathryn shouted.
Cathryn's office was cut in clean lines. Modern furniture mixed with glass tables and neutral colors gave off a sterile feel. There were no pictures on her wall, just a bank of clocks on one side and a large screen TV on another. Floor to ceiling windows behind her looked down at Westminster Street and across to the Turk's Head building. Reaching down, she pointed her remote at the TV and shut it off. She shook her head and said, "We're getting crushed in Asia."
Lindsey nodded and took a seat on one of the armless couches. "I know." Lindsey's local institutional clients—Brown University and Rhode Island School of Design—had portions of their endowments tied into the Asian markets. She'd already placed a few calls to the brokerage firms she worked with in Tokyo and Shanghai. If the trend continued, she'd need to move quickly to minimize any losses.

Cathryn walked past her and shut the door. She settled across from her and said, "I fired Roger."

Lindsey's mind snapped back to Providence. "What? Why?" Roger handled estates and trusts for their firm.

"Our auditors came back with irregularities in his department."

"Irregularities? What kind of irregularities?" Stunned, Lindsey leaned back and shook her head. Roger was the third partner and the last person she expected they'd have to fire, especially for financial reasons. She'd known him her entire professional life.

Cathryn sighed. "A few accounts didn't add up. Nothing I can prove but enough to make me think he's been stealing from us for the past two years."

Lindsey leaned back and exhaled. Roger. Damn. "Jesus. Does the staff know?"

Cathryn stood and headed over to her credenza. She poured herself a cup of coffee and offered one to Lindsey. She declined. "Not yet. Let's keep the details between us, but I need you to look over his clients. Delegate what you can and meet with any new prospects until we get someone in." She sat back down. "I'm sorry to do this to you."

"It's fine." Lindsey nodded. "Do we have anyone internally that you're thinking about?"

Cathryn shook her head. "No. Not yet." She drank her coffee and sighed. Her phone chirped, and she stood. "That's my conference call with New York. Do what you can."

Lindsey went back to her office. Sabine stopped her on the way. "Your mother's office called to remind you about tonight's fundraiser."

Lindsey groaned and hung her head. "I swear that woman has an RFID chip in my head. I just got back. How does she know when I'm in town?"

Sabine gave her a sympathetic look.

She'd call her mother's press secretary later. She walked into her office and paused. "Sabine, can you come in?" She headed over to the windows in her sitting area and looked out at the view. She watched the pedestrian traffic and a russet dog chase a pigeon across Burnside Park before she heard Sabine close the door behind her.

Taking a deep breath, Lindsey focused inward and spun around. "Okay, change of plans. Roger's been let go, and we need to focus on his stuff before we get to ours."

Sabine gasped and glanced up from her tablet.

Lindsey nodded. "I know. Me, too." She headed over to her desk and sat down in the black Aero chair. "Let's get everyone together in half an hour." Picking up her coffee, she hauled her iPad and laptop out of her bag and set to work.

CHAPTER TWO

Rebekiah had been pleasantly surprised when Nicole emailed her a few days ago, asking for more details. They'd met for coffee, and after a few minutes of casual flirting, got right to the point. "Just to be clear, this is not a boudoir shoot. You're willing to have sex on camera."

Nicole had flushed. "Well, not on video."

Rebekiah had frowned. Did she think she was doing porn? Her initial confusion turned to irritation. "This isn't porn."

Nicole had held up her hands. "I didn't think it was."

Whoops, she must have sounded as irritated as she felt. Well, whatever her reasons, she needed to trust Nicole's intentions if she wanted to shoot her, so she'd outlined her general approach and ended with, "I'm not sure what I'm looking for. Are you willing to take my lead?"

"Yes."

Now, a few days later, Rebekiah called, "How's it going?" over her shoulder as she tucked a piece of paper into Nicole's file. It was a standard consent and release form that allowed her to display and alter images from the signee. She was pleased Nicole had the foresight to read and sign it before coming. Having it out of the way beforehand set the mood earlier. As far as Rebekiah was concerned, nothing happened until it was signed. She'd been around the art world and worked in it long enough to know how to protect herself.

"Good." Nicole's voice emanated from behind the deep blue drape hung on an L-shaped rod in the corner.

"Are you warm enough?" Rebekiah asked as she paused at the thermostat. Sera snorted and snuffled in her bed behind Rebekiah's desk. "Not you," she whispered. The russet American Staffordshire terrier twirled and turned her butt toward her owner. "Really?" Rebekiah rolled her eyes and glanced toward the dressing area. Raising her voice, she said, "Nicole?"

Nicole pushed back the heavy curtain with a muted whoosh. She crossed her arms over her chest and shuffled her feet.

Rebekiah studied her, a grad student standing in expensive black lingerie in her studio. She wasn't built like those skinny girls starving their bodies until every single bone stuck out, defined and prominent under their skin. Nicole's breasts were average size with a bit of droop, not perky but not saggy. The stomach above her pubis bulged slightly but in a way that gave her curves a sensuality lacking in the current definition of mainstream feminine beauty. Rebekiah turned the thermostat up another degree and crossed to her.

"May I?" She slowly pulled Nicole's arms away from her chest, smiled, and said, "You look lovely."

Nicole blushed and ducked her head.

Rebekiah felt a slight tug on her hands and stepped back. "This is about you, Nicole. If you're not comfortable, you need to let me know."

Nicole nodded. "I'm okay."

"Good. Then let's get started." Rebekiah backed up into the open floor plan of her photography studio. Sunlight filtered through arched windows and bounced off the pale hardwood floors and bright white paint that bookended the studio's long end. Brick walls and heavy black shades provided contrast in the room. Her current work area was centered around a low bed covered with a white sheet and a collection of gray cushions. A couple of white and gray light umbrellas surrounded the bed.

Rebekiah gestured toward the cushions. "Why don't you get

settled?" She stopped behind a camera on a tripod and took a few shots to test the exposure settings. She adjusted the aperture for more light and made sure the shutter speed and the ISO matched the aperture change. Then she started grabbing the light umbrellas by their black stands and positioning them.

While she worked, Nicole sat down and shifted, moving a pillow here and there. She fumbled with her hands, looking unsure about covering up or not. Rebekiah took a few more shots. She had no intention of using them, but she needed to get Nicole into the space of being photographed. "Why don't you move your hands away from your chest?"

Nicole stared at her. "Where do I put them?"

Rebekiah kept her eye against the camera and gestured above her head. "Put one across your stomach...right there... good. And the other...yeah just a little...perfect. Okay, now why don't you lean back?"

"Like this?"

Rebekiah pulled the camera from the tripod and cradled it in her hand. She nodded. "Yeah. Perfect. Pull your leg up. Chin on your knee." She brought the camera up and bent back to her work.

Nicole nodded and situated herself. The position opened her legs a bit more, and her face changed.

Rebekiah lifted her head away from the camera and knelt in front of her. "Are you okay with this?"

Nicole picked at the fabric on the pillow next to her. She gave a quick nod. "Yeah, yeah of course."

This approach was all wrong. There was too much distance between them. She felt no connection with her. Rebekiah took a deep breath and said, "Your body language says otherwise." She clapped her hands and held them against her lips before she asked, "How can I help you here?"

"Can I wear some more clothes?"

Rebekiah smiled and rocked back on her heels. "Of course."

She jumped up and walked away. She came back with a white dress shirt and held it out for her.

Nicole got up and put it on. The tails came down to mid-thigh and the sleeves went four inches past her hand. She quickly buttoned it up and then struggled with rolling the sleeves up.

Rebekiah stepped in and adjusted them into neat folds that draped against her mid-forearm. She stepped back and surveyed the final look. Pursing her lips, she cocked her head to the side. She moved in, unbuttoned the top two buttons and the bottom one. It gave Nicole just the right ratio between revealing and on display. She gave a quick decisive nod and backed away. "Better?"

Nicole glanced at the billowing fabric held together by two buttons instead of five and smiled. "Yeah. This is better." She sat back down and kept shifting her position.

"Just relax." Rebekiah reached out and moved her hand along her thigh. "Like this." She pushed her thigh outward so that just a hint of her lace appeared. Nicole sighed and leaned back. Finally. So much work to get her here. It was easier doing this with friends. "Perfect."

Determined to make the best of it, Rebekiah picked up her camera. "You're doing great, Nicole." She centered her subject in the viewfinder and started clicking off a round of shots. "Just great." She adjusted for light, focus, and distance, getting a range of long and short shots. "Move your hand." She stood on a stool and shot down. "A little higher. Right there. Catch your nipple… yeah, you got it." She stepped off the stool and circled the bed. She crouched down next to her and smoothed her hand along her calf. "It's just you and me here. No one else."

With her mind working on logistics, Rebekiah kept her hand on Nicole's leg. "I want you to close your eyes. Think about the way you like your body to be touched."

Nicole smiled.

Rebekiah moved back. "Good. Now I want you to show

me." Nicole's hand moved down her body, caressing her skin and slipping into her shirt. "That's right. Tease yourself. Now slowly." Nicole's entire demeanor changed. Her face flushed, her body uncoiled, and her legs spread. "That's good. I want you to touch yourself."

Nicole's eyes closed, and she moved her hand down her stomach and toward her underwear. "That's it." Her fingers brushed against the fabric. "Nice." Rebekiah crab-walked to the side to switch angles and lifted her camera again. "You're gorgeous. Just a little...oh, yes."

Nicole's hand slipped into her underwear.

"Just like that. So good, darling. So good." The more she spoke to her, the more aroused she became. What started as stilted and off-putting was becoming sexier by the moment. She moved closer. Her hand rested on Nicole's upper thigh, and the tips of her fingers brushed along her. She wanted to touch her but held back. "Take those off and open your legs so I can see how good you make yourself feel."

Nicole swallowed hard and stared into Rebekiah's eyes as she slid her underwear off. She never broke eye contact as her left hand slid across the dip in her hip and toward her dark patch of hair. Rebekiah's breath quickened and her hands shook, and still she eased back and lifted her camera again.

"Just you and me. You're gorgeous. Do you know how much I want to fuck you right now?" The words slipped out of her mouth before she had a chance to censor them.

Nicole gasped.

Giving into the mood, Rebekiah grinned. "So good. So good," she murmured. Nicole's finger brushed a sensitive spot—her eyes snapped shut, and her hips rolled. Rebekiah focused on that open-mouthed vulnerability when she whispered, "Come for me, Nicole. Come for me."

After Nicole's climax, she took a few more shots before the afterglow wore off. She put the camera down and, tamping down her desire, asked, "Thirsty?"

Nicole started to sit up and nodded. Rebekiah handed her a glass of water and wrapped a blanket around her shoulders. Nicole sank into the soft cotton and took a long drink.

"That was…" Nicole shook her head. "Amazing."

Rebekiah smiled. Despite the rough start, Nicole had given her exactly what she wanted. "I'm glad you liked it."

Nicole set the glass down, then glanced up at Rebekiah. "Do you still want to fuck me?"

Her desire returned full force, she knelt down on the edge of the bed. "Absolutely."

Nicole dropped the blanket, and Rebekiah crawled forward.

❖

Lindsey looked up as Sabine knocked on her door and ducked inside her office. "Jennifer Winslow is here to see you."

Lindsey glanced at her calendar and cursed. "I forgot." Jen worked for Brown University Alumni Affairs and Development, but her relationship with Lindsey predated her current job. The pair were both children of prominent Rhode Island families and spent their childhood in the same social circles. They figured out quickly they had both queer and social connections. Jen helped Lindsey forge relationships with her first clients, and as Lindsey's business acumen grew, she returned the favor, introducing Jen to major donors along the way.

Sabine shook her head. "Do you want me to send her away?"

Lindsey hit save and pushed away from her desk. "No. I'll go talk with her."

Sabine followed her out of her office and settled back at her desk. Lindsey continued toward the reception area. She spotted Jen lounging on the leather couch idly flipping through a magazine. In her early forties, she wore tailored black pants, a red shell, and a matching suit jacket. Her brown hair framed a serious face with minimal makeup and a slightly less corporate version of Lindsey's heels and skirt.

Jen tossed the magazine back on the pile and stood. "Welcome back. You almost look rested." Her serious demeanor evaporated with her smile.

"So do you." Lindsey matched her smile and stepped into her open arms. She always forgot how much taller Jen was until she stood next to her. A master of projection, Jen could make herself smaller or larger if the situation called for it. Lindsey pulled back and took a deep breath.

Jen eyed her before crossing her arms. "You're canceling."

Lindsey winced. Now that Jen was here, she didn't want to cancel. "*Yeah.*"

Jen leaned in. "It better be a meeting."

Lindsey knew she meant an AA meeting. She shook her head. "No. Just work."

Jen rolled her eyes. "Have you had lunch?"

"No."

"Let's go and grab takeout." She held up her hand. "You can bring it back and eat at your desk."

She had a client meeting in a half hour. She didn't really have time to go, but when she opened her mouth to protest, the look on Jen's face said no excuses. She smiled. "Let me get my wallet."

Jen waved. "It's on me. Let's go." She nodded toward the elevators and called over her shoulder, "If I let you get away, there's no telling how long it'll take to get you back."

Lindsey laughed and followed. The doors closed, and Jen punched the bottom floor. "So, what's got you so busy you can't eat today?"

Lindsey sighed and leaned against the wall. Her work moved at breakneck pace at times, but she was still reeling from Roger's dismissal. Her instinct was to protect the firm and her reputation, so she hesitated. She almost didn't say, but Jen had always kept her secrets for her. "Cathryn fired Roger."

Jen's eyes widened. "What? Why?"

Now that the seal was broken, she relaxed and let it all out. "Audit found something. She thinks he was stealing from the company."

Jen exhaled. "Shit. Are you pressing charges?"

Lindsey shook her head. "There's nothing concrete." The elevator opened, and she glanced around to make sure no one would hear. "But I'm going through his files today."

"Shouldn't audit do that?"

"Not those files. Client files. I'm picking up where he left off." When they got outside the building, she paused. "Which way?"

"Left." Jen pointed. "The Thai Palace."

Lindsey nodded and continued her conversation. "It sucks. I've known Roger since B-school." She exhaled. "Hell, I brought him into this business."

Jen shook her head. "You can never tell. A few years ago, this woman retired—well-liked and respected—but six months after she left, we start getting these calls from people wanting to know where their money went. Turns out she was running a pyramid scheme out of the office and using university funds to bankroll it."

"Want happened to her?"

Jen shrugged. "Last I heard, she's living on one of the Caribbean islands that doesn't extradite to the US. You just never know." They ducked in and out of the lunch-hour pedestrian traffic until they came up the restaurant.

After they ordered, Jen paid, and they shuffled to the side. "Are you going to talk to him?"

"Roger? I don't know. I'm not sure what I'm going to do."

Jen snagged an empty table and they sat. "Are you still with Karen?"

Lindsey made a diving jet plane with her hand, crash and burn. She'd known from the start that it wasn't a forever thing. In fact, it never should have been a thing at all, but she'd been lonely and distracted, so she allowed the whole relationship to go on too long. "She moved out six months ago while I was in London."

Jen grimaced. "Ouch."

Lindsey shook her head. She'd been relieved to come home to an empty apartment. "No, I'm just glad she didn't take anything that wasn't hers." She leaned forward. "Remember Kelly?" In a long list of poor choices, Kelly had been the worst of those choices. The sex had been phenomenal but nothing else was.

"Just barely."

"Yeah. She was crazy. Took all the electronics. I came home just as she was making another sweep."

"Why didn't you have her arrested?"

Lindsey groaned. "And keep her in my life for the next six months? No, thank you. I can afford new equipment." She switched topics. "How's work?"

Jen opened her hands in a half shrug. "It's good."

Lindsey stared. It wasn't like Jen to be so off. "That's some enthusiasm you've got going on there."

"Brian's retiring. My boss." She shook her head. "He's been grooming me for the last three years to take his place, but I can feel the wagons circling. They're going to hire another man into that position."

"Is there anything you can do?"

"Quit." She shook her head. "I can't, though. Carter's finally settled at Hutchinson's. Rachel and I are still sharing the house." Rachel was Jen's ex-wife and the co-parent of her son, Carter. "I'm kind of trapped here."

Lindsey reached over. "I've got some money. I could help."

Jen shook her head. "Nah. I'll figure it out. If and when it happens." She smiled. "Who knows, I could get lucky."

"I can't believe you're still living with Rachel." Jen and Rachel rotated visitations so that one of them stayed with their son in the house, and the other lived elsewhere.

"Ugh. I know." Jen stood up as their order was called. "It's great for Carter." She handed an iced coffee to Lindsey, and they headed back to the street. "But I think I might kill Rachel before the end of the year."

Lindsey admired Jen's devotion to her son and patience with her ex. But she'd never make the compromises Jen did to make her relationships work. She just didn't have that kind of stamina for that level of commitment. "I don't know how you do it."

Jen sighed. "I just think of it as having two kids instead of one."

They talked back and forth about mutual acquaintances until they stopped in front of Lindsey's building. Jen fished Lindsey's containers out of the bag and handed them off. "At least you'll eat."

Lindsey smiled. "Thanks." She leaned in to give her a half hug as they juggled their meals and drinks. Pulling back, she asked, "Hey, are you going to my mom's fundraiser?"

Jen grinned. "Going? I made that happen. What about you?"

"Well, I was on the fence, but now that you'll be there..."

Jen laughed. "Then I'll see you there."

Lindsey left with a quick hug and a promise to reschedule. Sitting at her desk, she opened her lunch and tapped her mouse to check her email. A calendar reminder popped up. She had ten minutes to get to her next appointment, just enough time to wolf down her lunch and review the client folder. She flipped it open and quickly read up on Rebekiah Kearns.

CHAPTER THREE

A re you sure you want to do this? It's a lot of money." Elena pulled out a chair and sat in the conference room with her back to the windows.

Rebekiah glanced out toward Kennedy Plaza and the multitude of buses coming and going before she shrugged out of her jacket and settled into the chair next to her. The burden of Emma's money weighed on her. It was their last connection, and after four years, she was ready to let go. The protracted court battle with Emma's siblings was the only reason she'd held on to it for so long. "It's not like I'd had it before."

Elena nodded. "But you also don't have to give it away."

Rebekiah put her hand on Elena's forearm. They'd had this conversation before, and she was in no mood to have it again. "Thanks for coming. You didn't have to do this."

"She was my friend, too. Besides, it's always nice to have a lawyer present when you're signing contracts."

Rebekiah didn't comment on the fact that Elena was a defense attorney, and they were not waiting in a courthouse.

The glass doors opened, and three people entered, two women and one man. Rebekiah's eyes slid past the first woman and landed on the second one. A few inches shorter than Rebekiah, she was still tall for a woman, most of it in her legs. She wore her dark hair in a short business style, neither butch nor femme. Her business suit was expensive, tailored to fit her torso and accentuate her shoulders and breasts. And when they made eye contact, her dark gray eyes and smile said that she'd caught Rebekiah checking her out.

Every nerve in her body took notice, and all she could think to say was, "You're not Roger."

The woman reached across the table. "Lindsey Blackwell."

Rebekiah half stood and shook her hand. Lindsey's grip was firm and dry. She felt every point where they touched before she let go and sat back down. She suppressed her reaction and focused on the matter at hand. "Rebekiah Kearns. Elena Travada. Where's Roger?" He had handled her accounts since Emma's estate had left probate six months ago.

Lindsey sat in the chair across from her. "Roger no longer works for us. I've taken over his accounts." She scanned the document in front of her before she looked up and held Rebekiah's gaze. "All of it?"

Rebekiah steeled herself and nodded. This was not the first time she'd had to convince someone she wanted to do this. Before Roger and Elena, Emma had tried, but Rebekiah had been angry and adamant. "I don't want it," Rebekiah had said.

Emma had been unfazed. "Well, you're taking it." They'd argued for hours, and later, Rebekiah had broken down in Emma's arms. "It's a shit trade for you."

"It's all I have left to give you."

Four years later, she was still angry and adamant that the money was no substitute for her best friend. "All of it."

Lindsey stared, and Rebekiah felt the full weight of her personality in those intelligent and calculating eyes. This was a woman accustomed to being the smartest person in the room and working that to her advantage. Lindsey didn't lose.

Giving her the win, Rebekiah glanced away, and Lindsey said, "You have thirty-two million in assets. Is that correct?"

More than she thought. Rebekiah hid her surprise and decided to play along. "You would know."

Lindsey gave a curt nod and scanned the room. "Yes. You make fifty-five to sixty thousand a year?"

Rebekiah glanced around, trying to see where Lindsey picked up that number. "A little closer to seventy. What's your point?"

Lindsey steepled her fingers and tapped them against her mouth. "This kind of money changes things. Most people get an inheritance like this and blow it away in ten years. They buy things that cost too much to maintain, and it chips away."

Rebekiah almost lost focus, too transfixed on Lindsey's fingers, remembering their strength and wondering what they'd feel like touching more intimate places, before she wrenched her attention back. She didn't care about the money chipping away. She'd never wanted it in the first place but felt obligated to take it. She shrugged, unmoved by the argument. "But not if I give it all away."

Lindsey tilted her head, and a slight smile played on her lips. "True, but I could make this money work for you. Have you ever wanted to do something more? We could get this money to do that for you. Give me six months, and let me prove it."

Emma had said something similar when she told her she didn't want it. Something deep inside her stirred, and for the first time, she considered what she'd do with that kind of money. She'd never have to work again. No more bills. Giddy relief bubbled inside her that evaporated into guilt. She shouldn't want this.

Elena's full-on lawyer voice emerged. "That's not why we're here today."

Nodding, Lindsey held up her hand. "I know. You want to give it all away. And I'd be the first person to help you do that, but I think I can make your money do more good than a one-time donation. Do you trust me?"

Rebekiah perked up at the challenge. Did she trust her? Rebekiah suppressed the laugh that threatened to escape. "Trust is a funny thing. It takes time to build." She paused and leaned in. "Are you willing to put in the time?"

Lindsey held her gaze.

Rebekiah reveled in that intensity, wondering what it would be like elsewhere. That look, those eyes, the passion below the surface. She had an urge to capture that passion with her camera. Lindsey's focus never wavered. "Absolutely."

But her answer didn't matter. For the chance to see her again, Rebekiah would hang on to the money a little bit longer.

❖

Lindsey waited outside the conference room while Rebekiah and her lawyer looked over the contract; both Brian and Sabine had already left. Lindsey took her time studying Rebekiah. Small nose, small lips, bright blue eyes, and curly brown hair styled into a long pixie that stopped just below her ears. Shave off a few years, tousle her hair, downgrade her clothes, and she'd be the poster child for "starving artist." But her smile and poise conveyed a warmth and confidence that her looks were just catching up to. Rebekiah was a woman who would physically come into her own in her late thirties; she was a few years away but starting to look the part.

Black pants, pale blue dress shirt, brown oxfords. Her leather jacket slung on the chair next to her. She was dressed for comfort with a nod toward business casual. Her friend, Elena, wore gray pinstripes, a red blouse, and a tailored suit coat. She was dressed for court. There was an aura of protectiveness in her stance toward Rebekiah. Friend, family, lover?

Rebekiah met her look through the glass wall and offered her a slight smile. Lindsey responded in kind before she realized what she was doing. She dismissed the warmth that suffused her body as the byproduct of signing an attractive client. Rebekiah was not the first client she'd landed with sexual overtones. She'd defuse that smolder easily enough. She'd turned away more than one suitor with cold professionalism and solid business acumen.

Sabine came back with another folder. "How do you want me to handle her follow-up?"

With barely a sideways glance, Lindsey tucked the folder under her arm. "I've got it."

"Really? Are you sure?"

Lindsey pulled her gaze away from Rebekiah. She had already begun off-loading Roger's accounts to Sabine. It was more work for the junior analyst, but it was also a promotion of sorts. However, it was a delicate balance, and she'd have to hold on to a few people. Rebekiah's net worth was a little below her normal range and slightly outside her area of expertise. She specialized in institutional investments, but she had experience with family wealth management. Besides, Rebekiah was hard to read, and she liked a challenge. "I'll run with it for a bit. I have a couple ideas that might make sense for me to work with her."

Sabine nodded, and Lindsey glanced back toward the conference room. She'd been surprised that she landed her so quickly, but she was too concerned about Roger's exit to let a thirty-two-million-dollar client walk out the door to spend too much time analyzing it. Once Rebekiah left, it would be twice as hard to bring her back in. And who knew how much money Roger had cost them?

Taking a deep breath, she opened the door and asked, "How are we doing here? Any questions?"

Rebekiah glanced at Elena, who shook her head. Whoever Elena was, she held sway in Rebekiah's life. Lindsey would have to account for that later. Rebekiah slid the contract over. "What's our next step?"

Lindsey paused half a beat. Not *your* but *our*. Interesting. She adjusted her pitch accordingly. "I'm going to take a hard look at your portfolio and look for areas of growth. But then we're going to talk. Most people have a personal relationship to money. We need to figure out what yours is and develop a plan to suit it."

Rebekiah chuckled. "That's easy. I earn it, and then I spend it."

Lindsey held her gaze, meeting Rebekiah's blue eyes head-on. She couldn't get a read, and it bothered her. A piece of the puzzle was missing, and it had to do with the inheritance. "That's not what I meant. Can I be blunt?"

Rebekiah nodded.

"Most of my clients are accustomed to great wealth. There's a shared culture that I draw upon with them. But with you…" She paused for a moment and considered her next words, wishing she'd had more time to do research before meeting her. "There's something tied up in this money—something emotional—that made you want to give it all away. Yes?"

Another curt nod. She saw Rebekiah tensing, so she switched tactics. "We're going to have to talk about that."

Silence stretched between them. Lindsey's gaze never wavered while Rebekiah sized her up. Elena rested her hand on Rebekiah's forearm. Lindsey felt an odd tinge of jealousy at their easy intimacy that she pushed aside.

"And if I don't want to?"

"Then you can either live off the interest or give it all away. I'd prefer you did the latter. If I know the reasons why, I might be able to make your money work in a different way." Why was she still so resistant? She'd already signed the contract. What had her so tied up in knots about this money?

There was a cat-and-mouse feel to this conversation that bugged her. Not the give-and-take so much as the thought that just this once she might be the mouse and not the cat.

Rebekiah's body language loosened up, and she stood. Elena followed.

Lindsey scrambled to her feet. Had she pushed too hard? She hated being so blind in negotiations. She glanced at the signed contract.

Rebekiah dropped a business card on the table. "When you're done with my portfolio, come see me at my studio, and we'll talk."

She picked up the card, but Rebekiah was already out the door. What just happened? Did it really matter? She'd salvaged one deal. Time to make another one. But without Rebekiah's presence, the room felt small. Lindsey fumbled with the card. *Rebekiah Kearns, Boudoir Photography.* Rebekiah specialized in pinup pictures. A nervous laugh escaped her lips. No wonder she felt so exposed.

CHAPTER FOUR

L indsey came home to her loft. Dark cherry hardwood floors, white walls, and black iron trim combined with leather and brightly colored Ikea furniture lent the space a warm but utilitarian look. She slipped off her heels and dropped onto her couch. Rubbing her foot, she closed her eyes. Twenty minutes later, she woke up disoriented with her shoe in her hand and her phone vibrating across the room.

She got up and dug around for her phone. Hitting the home button, she glanced at the display. A text from her mother. *Nice to see you tonight.*

Lindsey rolled her eyes. They'd spoken for less than ten minutes total, and most of that in the company of other people. She typed back, *Same.*

You slipped out early.

Of course she noticed. It was always about optics with her mother. It didn't look good when her daughter wasn't around. Jen had picked her up straight from work, where she'd pulled her emergency cocktail dress from its garment bag off the back of her door. She spent an hour working the room, just long enough to make her presence known, before the last few weeks caught up with her, and she made a quiet exit. *Jetlagged.* She hit enter, stood, and walked to the kitchen.

China or London?

China. Pouring a glass of water, she headed up the stairs to change. She walked past her bathroom—a blue tile, glass, and porcelain affair—and into her bedroom. Another vibration.

Your father's in town next week. Dinner?

She smiled. It would be good to see him again. He was always their buffer. *Okay. Text me details.*

Will do. Gotta go. Good night.

Good night. She tossed her phone aside and snorted. Typical. Perfunctory emotion, cursory check-in, followed by familial logistics. She'd adjusted to this level of communication long ago. She checked the time; she didn't want to be late.

Slipping out of her dress, she changed into a pair of NYU sweats and a blue T-shirt. She moved through her apartment, grabbing water and checking the thermostat before settling down on her couch. Pulling out her laptop, she found the online conference room she was looking for, tucked the earbuds into place, and logged in.

Adam was the first to appear on video. "Hey there."

"I didn't expect to see you tonight." She glanced at the time. "Isn't it still early in Vancouver?"

"I'm in Toronto this week." His Canadian accent bled out on the *t*'s in Toronto. "Where are you?"

Lindsey leaned back and to the side so he could see the Providence skyline behind her. "Home."

He clutched at his chest. "Be still my beating heart. What's brought you back?"

More people started to ding into the call. She recognized several faces, other business people who traveled the world.

After the meeting began, Lindsey listened with half an ear, mulling over her meeting with Rebekiah. From the moment she shook her hand, she knew that she'd have to fight for every inch of ground with her. She had a couple ideas for keeping Rebekiah on board. If she could get a jump on Rebekiah's buy-in, she could pass along the detail work to Sabine. At the time, it made sense to keep Rebekiah's account with her, but she was beginning to feel the pressure of the extra workload. A weird possessiveness sparked inside her at the thought of passing her off to Sabine. Although she had her favorites, she didn't get turfy with clients. Something about Rebekiah was different.

She didn't have time to suss that out as the introductions worked their way around to her. "My name's Lindsey, and I'm an alcoholic." After six years, that phrase almost rolled off her tongue. The next person spoke, and she quashed her thoughts as the discussion began in earnest.

"Today we're going to talk about step three: Make a decision to entrust our will and our lives to the care of the collective wisdom and resources of those who have searched before us." The facilitator leaned forward. "Would anyone like to begin?"

Lindsey smiled and spoke up. She introduced herself again, and a round of hellos came back from the men and women on her screen. "I call this the God clause."

The group smiled back, and a few laughed. They were a self-selected group of freethinkers, agnostics, and atheists. Until this group, Lindsey's experience with AA and the higher power had been mixed. Giving in and surrendering her actions to a higher power was always a stretch for her. The implication in both tone and interaction from members who embraced a higher power were twofold. One, that she would eventually fall off the wagon; or two, that she would come to her senses and accept the higher power. "And that was the problem with my first attempt at sobriety. I just couldn't reconcile my values and beliefs to a being outside myself."

More than one person nodded, so she continued. "So I started to attend other meetings, and I found another version of this step. We committed ourselves to lifelong abstinence, staying away from the first drink for a day at a time. And I got it. I cannot drink casually, socially, at all. I cannot control the consequences, and there are always consequences. That is a fact and one that I cannot shove aside or control but that I must accept if I want to live sober. And I cannot do that alone. Once I understood that, staying sober was easier; not easy but doable." Losing Monica had been the biggest of those consequences, and understanding her role in that breakup had been the hardest thing she'd ever done sober.

She finished and sipped her water. A wave of thank-yous greeted her. A few other people shared their thoughts—one woman also admitted her struggle with her agnosticism and the third step in particular—and then the meeting wrapped up with the closing business and the final group statement in unison, "Keep coming back. It works if you work it."

Lindsey logged out of the session, and Adam initiated a video call.

With a click, his face appeared on her screen. "Thanks for speaking." Seven years ago, Adam had brought her to her first AA meeting, but it took a whole year before she admitted her addiction. Six months after that, he offered to become her sponsor. He worked in wealth management for the Bank of Canada. They shared the same schedules and the same issues. After Jen, there was no one she trusted more. "How's work?"

Lindsey sighed. "We let go of one of the original partners."

Adam made a face. "That sucks."

"Yeah. I get his workload, and there's some complications about what was going on." She shook her head, pushing away her concerns over Roger's misdeeds. "Anyway, what about you?"

He gave her the broad strokes of his life—family and work—before launching into a story of a client meeting gone terribly wrong.

Lindsey wiped her eyes, she laughed so hard. "That beats my week." She yawned, and Adam mirrored her. They wrapped up the call, and Lindsey closed down the window. She lingered online for a bit, checking her email and skimming a few articles she'd saved. Her thoughts ran back to Rebekiah and why she would want to give her money away.

She opened their client database. Designed in-house but with other commercial add-ons, it allowed her to search several public and private sources for biographical data, assets, and corporate holdings. She typed in Rebekiah's name and got her asset information. The money was an inheritance from an Emma Strahan—no familial relationship—and had just come out of probate in the last six months.

The money itself was reasonably well managed and diversified. She could do better, but it would do well without much work. The bio data said she was single, no kids, no siblings, parents deceased. Both several years ago. However, Emma's death was more recent, and her birth date put her at the same age as Rebekiah. A lover? If so, that could explain her desire to get rid of the money. She could only imagine her grief. She paused for a moment, uncertain how hard she wanted to push. She'd already got her to keep the money, so why was she hesitating now? In the span of one meeting, Rebekiah had moved from a deal to a person with a past. How did that happen? Only one way to find out.

Suppressing her nerves, she opened an email and considered her words. She wanted to be firm but sensitive. After all, Rebekiah did invite her to her studio. She'd take that opening.

Hi Rebekiah,

I've looked over your assets. There are a couple options I want to discuss in person. When can I swing by your studio?

Lindsey Blackwell

She hit send.

❖

Rebekiah and Sera left her studio shortly after six and walked home. Her encounter with Lindsey had replayed in her head for most of the day. Elena had been shocked that she agreed to keep the money.

"I've waited this long. What's a few more months?"

What she hadn't said was that Lindsey herself had been the real reason she'd held off. Lindsey. Contained, confident Lindsey. She was hard and forthright with something softer simmering underneath. Rebekiah didn't want to walk away from that right now. If Roger had shown up, she was sure she'd be a few million dollars poorer.

Large windows dominated the open floor plan of her one-bedroom corner apartment. Ambient street light filtered through the windows, landing on the hardwood floors. She flipped a switch, and a series of spotlights flooded the kitchen counter set along the length of the wall. Her phone rang just as she put her bag down on the kitchen island amid the bowl of fruit and assorted papers. She checked the caller ID. Collette. She frowned. Collette never called her. "Hello?"

"Hi." Collette was Thea's longtime companion, not that Thea called her that. Given Rebekiah's pseudo parental relationship with Thea, it meant that Collette was her stepmother of a sort. At least, Rebekiah treated her as such.

"Hey, what's up?"

Sera plopped down and stared up at her.

"I wanted to check in and see how things are going."

"Good." Rebekiah's eyes narrowed and focused on the invitation to Thea's retrospective that sat unopened in her pile of mail. "Work's good." She waited a beat and added, "I finally won the case." Emma's older siblings had fought Rebekiah's inheritance since the reading of the will.

Collette's smile came through the line. "That's good news. How are you feeling?"

Rebekiah stood and headed toward the windows along the far wall of her apartment. Sera padded after her. The evening rush hour was over, and people were ducking in and out of the restaurants below. "I'm not sure." She fingered the curtains. "It doesn't feel real yet. At least the money part." Sera bumped her legs, and she reached down to pat her head before she turned away from the window. "It's a lot of money."

"Have you given any thought to what you are going to do with it?"

Rebekiah shook her head even though Collette couldn't see her. "I didn't want to think too much about it until it was final. Michelle and David were pretty rabid until the end."

Emma's parents made their fortune in New York City real estate and left each of their three children a sizable trust. David and Michelle ran through their money quickly; Emma did not. And after college, she became a model, where she doubled her inheritance before being diagnosed with ALS.

They'd met at Rhode Island School of Design and recognized in each other a kindred spirit. Both children of absent parents and awkward familial arrangements, they and their circle of friends created a family of their own. And when Emma traveled the world for various fashion shows and photography shoots, she always came home to Providence, not New York. So when she discovered her illness, she came home to die.

"I imagine they are still grieving as well."

Rebekiah sputtered. "Yeah, if you say so."

They spent a few more minutes talking about Rebekiah's work and the young artists she worked with. "There's this one girl...well, woman, but she's young. Her eye's excellent, but she's got nothing to say. I keep trying to get her to think about what she's looking at, but she's stuck on the technique."

"Huh. That sounds familiar." Collette's tone gently teased.

Rebekiah laughed, all too aware of her own struggles with her voice and Thea's frustration with her over it. "Yeah, I guess it does."

The last fight between Thea and her happened two weeks before Emma's death. Rebekiah's boudoir business had started taking off, and she was getting steady income. At the same time, she was taking shots of Emma and their circle of friends. Thea had found one such photo and asked her why she wasn't displaying it. "This is where you live, Rebekiah. Not in these pinup pictures." Thea had gestured to the few display shots she had on her studio walls.

"Not everyone wants their life on display."

"You're not everyone." Thea had grabbed her hands. "You could be so much more."

Rebekiah had yanked her hands away. "I already am." The rest of the words faded into anger and remembered bits of conversation. "I never asked you to be my mother" might have come out at some point. As well as "I never asked your mother for this. She knew I wasn't prepared to raise you." And more, like "You never listen to what I say" and "You never hear me when I speak." Finally ending with Rebekiah saying, "You've never seen me for who I am."

Rebekiah pulled back from the memory, so raw and still fresh, before she took a deep breath. "You're calling about the reception." A gallery in NYC was honoring Thea's work as a fine arts photographer with an exhibition and a retrospective.

Collette took a deep breath. "You haven't RSVPed. It's next week."

"Does she want me there?"

"Of course she does."

"Did she ask for me specifically?"

Collette sighed. "Honey, she's never going to ask."

"Then I'm not coming."

"Rebekiah."

Rebekiah clenched her jaw and remained silent.

Collette waited and then blew out a breath. "You are both so fucking stubborn."

"Well, as she's so fond of saying, she taught me everything I know." Her bitterness made the words terse.

Collette inhaled. "I'm sorry she hurt you. I wish…"

Rebekiah closed her eyes. "Don't. I can't. Not today."

Collette let it go, and they wrapped up the conversation.

Rebekiah hung up and sank into her couch. Sera walked over and leaned against her thigh. She scratched her ears. Sera moved into the motion and pushed hard against her. She sighed and kept petting her. "Thanks, bud, I needed that."

The conversation with Collette had put her in a sour mood. Her evening thwarted, she got off the couch to feed Sera. Thoughts of Emma and Thea swirled in her head. Wanting to avoid the maudlin mind trip, she turned on the TV across the way and listened to *The Daily Show* and Samantha Bee while she cooked.

As she sat down with her meal, Sera made to jump on the couch, and Rebekiah glared at her. Sera huffed and settled at her feet. Scrolling through the list of shows, she paused on *The Walking Dead*. Not her normal fare; she preferred documentaries to science fiction, but something about the show had appealed to Emma during her final months, and Rebekiah found herself bingeing it with her. She tried watching after Emma died, but it felt too hard. As the opening scene came on, she felt herself dragged into the narrative and embraced the feeling of comfort she'd shared the first time she started watching.

CHAPTER FIVE

Lindsey checked the time. Four minutes to seven. She was a little bit early. Hefting the messenger bag, she knocked on the door. A scuffle sounded, followed by a muffled curse, and the door swung open. Rebekiah caught herself on the door as a russet pit bull pushed past her and banged into Lindsey's knees. Lindsey yelped and rocked back on her heels; Rebekiah grabbed her before she fell.

Rebekiah steadied her while she regained her equilibrium. She let go and wrapped her hand around the dog's collar. "Sera, what the fuck?"

Recovered from her run-in, Lindsey crouched down and offered her hand. Sera leaned in and took a sniff. "What a beautiful dog. Pit bull?"

Rebekiah was still scowling. "American Staffordshire terrier. Close relative to the pit bull."

Sera finished her inspection and licked Lindsey's wrist before she butted her head against her knee. Lindsey laughed and landed backward on her butt. She settled back and stroked Sera's head. Sera basked in the attention and encouraged the love for a few minutes. "Not very fierce, are you?"

Rebekiah patted Sera's stomach. "Not particularly."

Sera snorted and started to dig her nose between Lindsey's legs.

Rebekiah stepped forward and tugged on her dog's collar. "Really, Sera. You just met her. Get out of her pants."

Lindsey laughed. "It's true that I like a little more romance in my relationships."

Rebekiah smiled, and Sera settled in front of her. "You should give her a chance. She's a little out of practice." She offered Lindsey a hand. "Come on in."

Lindsey hesitated, a slight warmth spreading through her body as she remembered the feel of her palm at their last meeting, before she grabbed Rebekiah's hand and followed her into the studio.

Rebekiah let go, and Lindsey felt a loss. "Take a look around. Would you like a cup of tea?"

"Sure." Lindsey put her messenger bag on the coffee table and stepped into the larger part of the studio. The reception area bisected a huge, well-lit room. To her left against a white backdrop stood a huge bed draped in white sheets with blue and black accent pillows. Umbrellas in stands surrounded it at various heights. A camera and tripod pointed toward the bed. Photography equipment lined the opposite wall in wire racks. Brickwork mixed with white walls filled in the rest of the space, and windows lined the exterior wall across from the recessed reception area. Another couch sat under the last of the windows with a small bookshelf beside it.

Along the walls were several framed pictures. Most of the pictures were women engaged in various erotic poses—alone, in pairs, or multiples—and they showcased a singular style that Lindsey assumed was Rebekiah's. The sex didn't bother her. She consumed her fair share of pornography. But this was not porn: It was different. It was intimate and welcoming.

She paused in front of a picture of a dark-skinned woman whose open legs occupied the full bottom third of the picture. It was shot in such a way that her ample breasts, large curves, and half-lidded eyes pulled the viewer in and down toward the V of her legs. It was a pose straight out of *Playboy* but lacking the blatant objectification. Was it the angle or the photographer? Lindsey leaned back and glanced at the other photos. All similar pinup styles but devoid of that dehumanizing gaze. It was brilliant.

The level of trust these women had in Rebekiah blew her mind. How did she get them to open up so intimately? Lindsey shook her head and smiled, in awe of her talent and a little envious of the connection she had with these women to be able to earn that kind of trust and receive that careful attention.

"I hope orange pekoe is okay." Rebekiah handed her a mug.

Shaking off her thoughts, Lindsey wrapped her hands around it and took a deep breath. "Perfect." She took a tentative sip. Too hot. She turned to Rebekiah and said, "These are really good. Do you have shows?"

Rebekiah wiggled her hand. "Occasionally. When I've got something to say." She pointed at the picture. "You know she told me she was fat."

"She's gorgeous."

Rebekiah moved closer. "I know. Actually, I have an idea that I'm working on that might be a show. I'm still taking shots. If you're interested?"

Lindsey's eyes widened as the implication struck home. She touched her hand to her chest. "Me?"

Rebekiah smiled. "Why not?"

"Why do you want to take pictures of me?" For just a moment, she imagined what it would be like to have that intensity focused on her. Would she want her to be naked? Her cheeks flushed, and to her surprise, she found the idea appealing.

Rebekiah waved her hand as if to encompass Lindsey's head and shoulders. "There's something…restless and yet still about you. It's a contrast that I can use."

And just as quickly, reality crashed around her. Rebekiah wasn't looking at her but rather her perception of her. It made her wonder who the women in the other pictures were outside of Rebekiah's gaze. Lindsey cocked an eyebrow. "Use?"

Rebekiah shrugged with a half grin. "Poor word choice?"

"Just a little. But honest, so there's that." Lindsey frowned. She got the feeling that Rebekiah was toying with her. That if she really wanted to take shots, she would pursue a different tack. Or maybe not. She felt completely out of her depth.

Rebekiah shifted. All pretense left her voice. "Since we're being honest, what would it take for you to say yes?"

Lindsey frowned. There was no way she was having this conversation with a client and yet she asked, "Clothes on or off?"

Rebekiah opened her hands. "Whatever you're comfortable with."

She swallowed. "Does this really work?"

"What?" Rebekiah cocked her head.

Lindsey gestured at Rebekiah's body language and approach. "The whole earnest appeal."

"Sometimes." Rebekiah grinned. "Is it working now?"

Lindsey laughed, relieved that Rebekiah had switched tactics and moved from hard sell to self-deprecating. She wasn't sure if she could resist the hard sell, but there was no way she was going to tell her. "Not really. I'm flattered, but I don't think I could do that." She hooked her thumb behind her to indicate one of the more sexual poses.

Rebekiah shrugged. "I'm sure you already do. The camera's less intrusive than you think."

Lindsey stared. With Rebekiah behind it, she had no doubt that it was. She represented an interesting mix of bravado and genuine confidence, and if Lindsey could figure out which one was real, she might actually have said yes. Instead she said, "Why don't you tell me why you want to give your money away?"

"Let me show you." She walked across the studio and flipped through a few frames along the wall. She pulled one out and set it on the floor. "Here."

Lindsey stared at the photograph in front of them. The woman in the frame lay bare amid white and blue fabric, her eyes open and her mouth twisted in a grimace of pleasure. Her hands covered the V of her legs, the edge of her fingers drawing across her pubic hair, her vulva exposed, and her clit centered in the curl between her thumb and index finger. The shot was made starker by the subtle use of color; without the blue fabric and her hazel eyes, the picture would seem to be black and white. The effect was striking, the woman's vulnerability in that moment captured and encapsulated. But this picture was different from the pictures around the room, rawer, with less technique, almost a candid. Without knowing how, Lindsey knew Rebekiah loved this woman.

Lindsey's hand ghosted along her face. "She's beautiful."

Rebekiah's body brushed up beside her. "She was." She slid the picture back into place and pulled out another slightly smaller frame.

The same woman stared out, her eyes open and her features slack. She was dead. The black and white hues enhanced the effect, but the framing, the blue fabric, even her hazel eyes called back to the other photo, but it was a pale echo. The same sensual care appeared in both photographs, but this one lacked the warmth of Rebekiah's other shots.

"She wanted me to take that shot. She made me promise to do it. It's her money, not mine." Rebekiah tucked the photo away and stared at the wall.

Lindsey stepped back. So that was Emma. There was no doubt in her mind that they were lovers. She wondered what it took for Rebekiah to take that picture. Pose those limbs, stare into those eyes, press the button. She'd dealt with people's grief as they worked through their inherited wealth but nothing so vivid and visceral as that photograph. So voyeuristic and open. Every fiber of her professional body said to walk away. This money was a hot mess wrapped up in an emotional landmine.

"I think I can help you." The words left her mouth before she realized it.

Rebekiah turned toward her with a look that said she doubted it.

Lindsey held up her hand. She had no idea what to expect when she'd showed up. She'd been hoping to buy a little more time to diversify Rebekiah's investments and get a longer commitment from her, but now that she was here and knowing what she did, she knew which way to go. "Hear me out. I get it. I know you'd still like to give it away, but I think we can carve out a sizable portion of this money and turn it into a foundation." She pulled back, but her eyes stayed connected to Rebekiah. Keeping her as a client was no longer the goal. She was hurting, and Lindsey knew how to fix that.

Rebekiah frowned. "I don't want to manage that kind of business."

"It would be self-sustaining." She paused and chose her next words carefully. "You loved her enough to watch her die. Now you have a chance to create a lasting legacy for her. Let me show you how."

Rebekiah folded her arms. "You're asking me to trust you with something very personal."

Lindsey knew what she was going to say before she even said it. "You can take pictures of me." She didn't need to meet her halfway. She'd already signed the contracts. But she wanted her trust. The brief vulnerability opened the door. No harm in it as long as she controlled the terms. Her stomach fluttered. She could do this.

Rebekiah moved closer. "Are you sure?"

Lindsey knew what she was asking. She'd never done anything like this in her professional life, even when she was drinking. It was risky and exciting. But she wanted it. More than the contract itself, she wanted to feel like those women on Rebekiah's walls. "I'm sure. How about you?"

"I'm in your hands."

Lindsey was pretty sure it was the other way around, or at least it would be, but for now, she said, "Are you up for some trips?"

CHAPTER SIX

Rebekiah parked her white Lexus on a side street off North Main. She opened the back door, and Sera scrambled out, the blanket covering the leather falling on the floor in her wake. They walked past an upscale framing shop and into a recessed entryway. Etched in black letters and accompanying a thin solid vertical line were the words Cohen Gallery. She pressed the doorbell and waited. Seconds ticked by, and she shoved her hands in her pockets to keep from fidgeting. Did she get the time right? After a month of deliberation, she had finally sent Aldina a couple of mock-ups only to wake up to a terse email: *11 a.m. tomorrow.*

The door buzzed, and Rebekiah headed upstairs.

Sunlight poured in through the windows and bounced off the white interior. Subtle hints of color—gray, cream, and a splash of red—added warmth to the bright white. An unoccupied desk sat in the far right corner, and a white oak table dominated the front half of the room. Aldina Cohen, a small wiry woman in her mid-fifties, leaned over the table, resting her elbows on it and staring at the photos strewn across her workspace. She stood, and her bracelets jingled together. Her smile softened her severe looks as she took in her two guests.

She crouched, designer dress and all. Sera's wagging tail slapped Rebekiah's leg on the way by. "Come here, beautiful. I can't believe Dahlia left you behind." She ran both hands up and down Sera's flanks and scratched right behind the ears. Sera soaked it all in, leaning toward each touch. Aldina stood, and Sera cleaved to her leg. She petted her one last time before she said, "Go lie down." Then she turned to Rebekiah and wiggled her hands. "Come here."

Rebekiah laughed and stepped into the hug. Something tight inside her relaxed. "You give the best hugs."

"So I've been told." Aldina pulled back and kissed her cheek. She maneuvered around Sera and motioned toward the table. "I was looking through your portfolio."

Rebekiah was mildly surprised to see several of her pictures on display. She spun one of them toward her. Taken several years ago, it was a shot of Emma and Elena shortly after college. "She looks so young."

Aldina leaned over and hummed agreement.

Rebekiah brushed Emma's features. Nostalgia flowed through her, quickly consumed by something bittersweet and hollow. She pushed it away along with her emotions. "I forgot she looked like that."

"That's because seventy percent of your pictures show her dying a slow and agonizing death." Aldina had never liked Emma. Among the many terms she used to describe her, *vapid* and *self-centered* were her favorites. She tolerated her for Rebekiah's sake. Even in the end, Aldina couldn't muster a shred of empathy for the woman who'd dominated Rebekiah's last four years. She narrowed her eyes. "She never should have asked you to take those pictures. You still have the last one tucked away, don't you?"

Rebekiah ducked her head. It was an answer by omission. It had surprised and stung her when Aldina had rejected her show for Emma. She'd never brought it up again, but now she wanted to know. Even if she didn't like the answer. "Why wouldn't you show it? Because she's dead?"

"Like that matters. Have you seen some of these shows?" She rolled her eyes and scoffed. "I've got one guy who molds shit into sculpture and then shellacs it. You think a corpse is going to shock my clientele? No. I'm not showing it under your name because it's not your work. That's her vision. Her style." She swiped her finger across her chest. "Not in my gallery."

Rebekiah's mouth dropped, and her anger flared. Sera's head popped up, and she made a guttural noise—not a growl and not a bark—but a noise of attentiveness. "How come you never told me that?"

"Like you'd listen to me. You were grieving. Nothing gets through in that state." She rummaged through the photos, collected them, and spun them toward Rebekiah in slow motion. "These are you."

Rebekiah stared at the photos one by one, aware that even if she didn't remember taking them—which with a few she didn't—stylistically, they were all hers.

Aldina walked to her desk and shook the mouse to wake her computer. She opened a preview pane and scrolled through the images of Nicole, Renee and Dawn, and Meghan: her flower portraits. Pointing, she said, "I want more of that. This is you. A different you, a deeper you. But this is what I've been waiting for. When do you want to show them?"

"I wasn't…I'm not really ready to show." She'd sent them to Aldina to critique them, not show them.

Aldina tilted her head and put her hands on her hips. "It's been five years. I'll give you six months to finish the idea that's starting here. Then we'll set up a showing. I think two or three more subjects, and you'll be good to go. I might have a model or two that you could use." She turned around and wrote a note to herself. "I'll send them to you. You decide."

Rebekiah just stared. She'd been prepared to talk technique, not a show. She wasn't sure she could do it. The deadlines, the pressure. Her creative drive had been dormant for so long that she was worried she couldn't access it on demand. What if she pushed too hard, and it went silent again?

Aldina smiled and stepped forward. Cupping her cheeks, she

held Rebekiah's stare. "Why do you think I called you? You're ready. Come back."

Rebekiah left with a few more details in hand and led Sera to the car. She was going to have a show. The same woman who'd given her first show was going to get her back up and into the scene again. She chirped the key fob and ushered Sera into the back seat, forgetting to put the blanket up. What did it matter? It was Emma's car, and she was dead.

Four years. She promised Emma that she'd make those pictures count, but she just couldn't do it. Aldina would never show those pictures, and knowing why made it clear to her that no one else would. Aldina was right; those pictures were not hers. She was done trying to make it work. She'd lost the will to create once, and now that the spark was back, she didn't want to lose it again.

But there was another promise she could keep, the money. Emma's final request, both verbal and written, said the same thing: *Do something good with it. Live off it. But don't let them squander it on stupid shit.* Rebekiah had been about to give up on that promise, too, but then Lindsey had stepped into that room, telling her she could do something more. And for the first time, when she thought about Emma and the money, she felt hope. This time she'd keep her word.

CHAPTER SEVEN

C an I get you anything to drink?" Rebekiah breezed past her fridge while Lindsey trailed behind her. She checked her clock—just after six. "Did you want to get dinner first?"

Lindsey shook her head. "I'm good."

Lindsey had contacted her a week ago to arrange a trip to Philadelphia. After their business was settled, Rebekiah asked if she still wanted to sit for her. Lindsey said yes immediately, and Rebekiah had spent the last seven days considering how she wanted to shoot her. But now that she was here, all the plans evaporated. She moved around the studio and shifted yet another piece of equipment before she realized that she had no idea what she was doing. Something about Lindsey knocked her off-kilter. Not wanting to explore the reasons why, she gave up all pretense of working and turned to her guest. "Do you have any questions?"

"How does this work?"

Glad for the distraction, Rebekiah slid into professional mode and explained the process. At the end of her spiel, Lindsey took a deep breath and looked around. "Where do you want me?"

The word want triggered a flash of arousal so strong that she stamped down the urge to answer that question honestly and brought her professional persona to bear. "Come here."

She led Lindsey toward the white backdrop where a wooden chair sat angled to face the windows surrounded by lighting equipment. Rebekiah guided Lindsey into the chair and resisted the urge to linger. "Sit there. I'll be right back."

Stepping back, Rebekiah picked up her tripod and placed it a couple feet away. She leaned in and adjusted the settings for the light, angle, and distance. Looking through the viewfinder, Rebekiah centered Lindsey in the shot. She sat with her hands in her lap, her face angled away. Rebekiah pressed the button.

Lindsey jerked at the sudden sound and turned her head. "Wh—"

Rebekiah paused. "Sorry. I didn't mean to startle you."

Lindsey crossed her arms. "I'm not sure how to do this."

"All right. Would it be easier if I sort of arranged you?"

Lindsey bit her lip and shrugged. "Maybe."

Rebekiah walked over. "Okay. Stand up." Lindsey did as she was told. "Let's take off your jacket. Yeah, just put it there. And the scarf." Lindsey let it drop to the ground. She toed her boots off without prompting. Bright green socks peeked out from the bottom of her pants. Rebekiah smiled; those would make a great shot.

Rebekiah glanced around and pulled another chair into the frame. She pulled the straight-back chair away and pointed toward the plushy chair with arms. "Sit here."

Lindsey sat down and perched on the edge of the chair.

That wasn't going to work. Rebekiah suppressed a smile. "Turn sideways."

"Like this?" Lindsey threw her legs over the left arm and leaned back against the other arm.

Rebekiah picked up her camera. "Good. Now turn your head."

Lindsey moved. "How's that?"

"Perfect." Rebekiah took a few more shots before she leaned forward and fanned Lindsey's hair in front of her face.

Lindsey closed her eyes at the touch, and the sight made Rebekiah warm inside. She leaned in so close her lips almost brushed her ear. "Keep your eyes closed."

Lindsey took a shuddering breath, and Rebekiah took another series of shots.

"Open your eyes and look right at me." Gray eyes stared and caught Rebekiah in their depth. Her stomach flip-flopped, and she hesitated, unnerved. She felt naked before her.

"Rebekiah?"

Realizing that she paused too long, she shook off her feelings and smiled. "You have gorgeous eyes, Lindsey. So much feeling in them and so cold, too. Like winter in January. Snow clouds in November." Lindsey blushed, and Rebekiah caught that, too. Rebekiah continued to talk about her eyes, getting the reaction she wanted, her mouth on verbal autopilot. Most of what she said she promptly forgot, focused on getting the next shot and what she needed to do to get there.

❖

Lindsey relaxed as Rebekiah spoke. Something in her voice soothed her, and she found herself drifting in a warm, safe space, not hearing the words. Rebekiah pulled one of her legs off the side. Lindsey shifted so that she could accommodate the wider stance. Rebekiah leaned down, a camera in her hand, her legs brushing against Lindsey's hanging leg. Lindsey shuddered at the unexpected touch, and when she moved, Rebekiah leaned forward. "Like this."

Lindsey swallowed hard and kept her pose. She relished both the attention and the quiet commands. The seductive pull of Rebekiah's fleeting touches and soft voice lowered her inhibitions.

"Now look up."

Rebekiah took a few more shots and then pulled the camera away. She winked, her eyes inviting intimacy. "Perfect."

Lindsey lost track of time while Rebekiah continued to move her body. Like her voice, Rebekiah's hands felt safe and secure. Lindsey's mind unspooled. Her thoughts, feelings, concerns drifted away. Her entire world shrank down to a hand here, an arm there, open this, close that. She'd had attentive lovers before but nothing quite like this. She wanted more. It would be so easy to take off her shirt.

"Is that your phone?"

Lindsey woke and cocked her head to the side. A ring called from inside her jacket. She stood too quickly and overbalanced.

"Careful." Rebekiah held her steady. She motioned for her to sit again. "I'll get it."

Lindsey sat on the edge of the chair, slowly reacclimating to her surroundings. By the time Rebekiah gathered her jacket, the call had gone to voice mail. "Sorry about that."

Rebekiah waved her off. "It's okay. We're all set for today."

Lindsey straightened, still in the half-fuzzy state. "That was it?"

Rebekiah crossed her arms and smiled. "Were you expecting more?"

"I don't know." Maybe she was.

"Are you hungry? We can eat here or go out."

Lindsey glanced at her watch. She'd sat for an hour; it felt like twenty minutes. "Sure. Let's go out." She stood and winced, sore from the awkward arrangements.

Rebekiah smiled. "Stiff?"

Lindsey shrugged into her coat and nodded. Her phone buzzed again. She spoke while she reached for it. "I want to run a couple ideas by you. I'm thinking there's a person I want you to meet in Philly."

She glanced down at the number. Tokyo. She groaned internally. She was working a deal that was on the edge of coming together or blowing up. A mix of relief and disappointment washed over her. For the first time in a long while, she wished she didn't have to work. "Sorry. I have to take this."

She answered and listened to her Japanese counterpart talk about the latest snags in their project. As he relayed the details, his voice got higher and higher, and any hope for dinner with

Rebekiah disappeared. Holding up her hand, she said, "Okay, hold on, hold on. I'm in the middle of something. I'll call you back in ten minutes." She pulled the phone away from her ear and ended the call.

Rebekiah stood in the middle of the room and said, "You have to go."

"I'm sorry." Lindsey looked at her. She couldn't get a read off Rebekiah. A different mask had fallen into place, and the early connection had faded. She put on her boots and slipped into her jacket. Grabbing her bag, she moved to the door.

Rebekiah beat her to it and held it open. Leaning her head against it, she said, "Don't worry. I've got your number."

Rebekiah's tone brought that closeness back, and Lindsey paused, aware of the weird intimacy of the last hour and the close proximity now. She felt an urge to brush a kiss against her cheek. Instead, she nodded vehemently. "Right, right. See you in Philly."

Rebekiah winked. "Good night."

Afraid that Rebekiah had read her intent, Lindsey said, "Good night," and turned on her heel. It wasn't until she hit the street that she realized she'd forgotten her scarf.

CHAPTER EIGHT

Lindsey watched the night settle over Victoria Harbour from the rooftop restaurant of the Hong Kong Four Seasons. Listening to the mix of English, Cantonese, and Mandarin around her, her mind wandered from one conversation to the next, picking up bits and pieces in all three languages. Looking out the window, she saw ghostly gray clouds lit up by the moon with patches of blackness below where the South China Sea looked like glass.

Two months had passed since Roger's firing, and she was still dealing with the aftermath. She needed to move on Rebekiah's portfolio; a whole month had passed since she'd seen her in person. But business wasn't the only driving force for Lindsey. She'd liked the way Rebekiah made her feel when she took pictures. And honestly, she wouldn't mind being in the spotlight again. But their schedules seemed to clash.

She stood when the waiter pulled the other chair out, and Li Jing settled across from her. With a flick of her wrist, she waved Lindsey down and said in Cantonese, "Sit."

Lindsey sat and pulled her napkin back on her lap.

"Sorry I'm late." Li Jing waved the waiter off and leaned forward, switching to English. "I can't end a meeting on time these days." Lindsey had worked with her for close to ten years and valued her insight and knowledge. An investment banker, Li Jing navigated disparate cultures and saw many perspectives, especially when her male counterparts weren't paying attention.

She had worked out of two of the three biggest banks in Southeast Asia before opening her own boutique investment shop three years ago. "Were you waiting long?"

"Not long."

"I'm starved." She caught the waiter's eye and pulled him over. They ordered quickly before he left. "Your Cantonese is getting rusty."

Lindsey shrugged. "Too much time in Beijing."

"Yes, I hear more Mandarin these days, too." In her late fifties, Li Jing came of age in the years before the handover. She pursed her lips. "I see you went on holiday with Jason Huang." She raised an eyebrow and smiled. "Isn't he a little...masculine for your tastes?"

Lindsey thanked the waiter as he refilled her tea. Li Jing held her hand up to tell him no. Li Jing knew she preferred women. Among the many business traditions Li Jing observed, procuring companions for her business associates was still one of them. After she stopped sending eligible men Lindsey's way, Li Jing started sending women instead. Lindsey only slept with one of them, an event she only knew about the morning after. It was at the height of her drinking. Now, Lindsey just smiled.

Li Jing narrowed her eyes and asked, "How's your mother?"

Lindsey nodded. "Senator Blackwell is good. She sends her well-wishes." Lindsey's mother wouldn't be able to pick Li Jing out of a lineup, but her connection to Lindsey served Li Jing's interests.

Their food arrived, and they ate with a minimum of small talk. They tended toward the larger debates: politics, economics, and current events. Lindsey enjoyed it. She liked someone who kept up and actually outplayed her on more than one occasion. Only after their meal was swept away and they were left with tea and oranges did the topic shift toward their business together. Li Jing wanted Lindsey's investment contacts for a project in Seoul. They discussed options for another hour before coming to an agreement. No handshake, no contract, just a deal made over tea and Japanese whiskey.

Li Jing leaned back and asked, "How long has it been since you last drank?"

Lindsey sucked in a breath. Her sobriety was a well-kept secret; Cathryn didn't even know she was in recovery. She often paid bartenders and waitstaff beforehand to keep her drinks nonalcoholic. The whiskey next to her was the real deal, but she hadn't taken it in hand. No sense denying it. She pushed the drink across the table. "How long have you known?"

"I've had my suspicions for a few months."

"It's been several years."

Li Jing sipped her drink and put it down. "I thought so. You don't have to pretend with me." She called the waiter over and told him in Cantonese to take the drinks away.

Lindsey shrugged. "I didn't want to offend you."

"Do you know why I make time in my schedule for you?"

"Because I always have something to offer you."

Li Jing nodded. "Yes, but not what you think." She waved her hand around. "I'm surrounded by sycophants and opportunists. You offer honesty and integrity. I can trust you. You can trust me. Let's not have secrets between us. Let me know when you're back in town, and I'll have you out to my house instead."

Lindsey left the restaurant a few minutes after Li Jing, still stunned by her personal offer. She took the elevator to her room and entered her suite. Ten years and they'd never set foot in each other's personal space. Always a public location. For a moment, she considered that the offer might be a romantic overture before she pushed it aside. Li Jing had never indicated that she liked women that way. She followed the same professional code as Lindsey. But tonight, Li Jing had opened the door for her, and as a result, Lindsey had revealed her alcoholism. Only two people outside AA knew she was in recovery. She had drawn a line between public and private for so long that it felt weird to mix the two. Mixing her worlds wouldn't kill her. She needed to accept the gesture as is and stop overthinking.

Tomorrow, she returned to Providence and another personal-professional dilemma. Rebekiah. Irene had gotten back to her about the Philadelphia trip. She grabbed her laptop and looked at her calendar. She sent off a series of emails and received confirmation from both Irene and Rebekiah within minutes of each other. Rebekiah's email was brief and to the point: *Sounds good. See you there.*

She was halfway through an itinerary when Rebekiah's second email arrived with the subject line *Picture*, and the body said *I'd like to do more*, with a link. She clicked on the link and was stunned at the image. Her headshots had never looked so good. Rebekiah had caught her mid-smile and captured a part of herself that she'd never seen before. It was almost as if it wasn't her.

She smiled and typed back, *If they all come out like that, then sure*" The speed with which Rebekiah replied to her work email gave her pause. Could she have tried to connect with her earlier? Was she avoiding her without knowing it?

A third email arrived a few minutes later. *After Philly? I can procure food afterward. Attached is my consent form. Like you, I don't work without a contract. RK.*

It was a standard contract giving Rebekiah rights to her image. She considered sending it along to her lawyer but didn't want her business lawyer involved with a personal deal. Which was what it was, a deal. Nothing stood out. No indication that there might be something more. But then why did her breath catch or her face flush when she thought about the way Rebekiah touched her, so confident and calm with such careful intimacy? Was she like that with everyone or just her? She wanted to find out, so she'd reread them in the morning and send them back signed.

She stood up and stretched, then got ready for bed. Flipping on the TV, she found a Korean drama that turned off most of her work brain but did nothing for her personal thoughts. Sleep eluded her as her mind churned through scenes of Rebekiah taking pictures of her followed by other scenes where Rebekiah convinced her to take other pictures. A pleasant thrum of arousal spread through her body and relaxed her until she fell asleep clutching the remote and dreaming of black chemises and spreadsheets.

CHAPTER NINE

Rebekiah arrived in Philadelphia midmorning to a text message from Lindsey saying her flight was delayed and that a driver was waiting to take her to their hotel. Her ambivalence toward her inheritance took a back seat to her desire to see Lindsey again, and she had agreed to a business trip in mid-November.

She'd managed only one photo shoot with Lindsey, and the pictures were not what she was expecting. Doubly impressive considering she'd been so involved in her own reactions to Lindsey's presence, she thought they'd be all over the map. But the final results were breathtaking. She'd barely done any touch-up; Lindsey's personality had come through so easily. She'd thought they'd be distant and engaging, the dual qualities that drew her in, but they revealed another facet, an honest vulnerability that she found herself coming back to again and again.

Rebekiah checked into the Ritz-Carlton near Rittenhouse Square, reminded of the surreal experience of traveling with Emma in the company of the world's rich and famous. Nothing about Lindsey suggested that level of financial wealth, but Rebekiah assumed her proximity to it must open the same doors.

Her room—suite, actually—had two separate spaces divided by a pocket door that shared the same view of downtown. Marble and stone buildings stared back at her against the gray sky. Low clouds hugged the horizon, signaling snow.

She turned on the TV and flopped on the couch. She

considered going out and seeing the sights, but Lindsey had given no real timeline, and she was here to meet people, not sightsee. Besides, the wind was much colder than the jacket she'd brought. She listened to the slightly urgent talk about the latest winter storm heading straight toward Philadelphia. She glanced out the window and saw tiny flakes blowing around like bits of white ash in the wind. Giving up on the apocalyptic weather forecast, she flipped to the Food Network. She dozed through a second cooking show and startled awake to a text from Lindsey.

Just checked in. Want to meet in the lobby?

Rebekiah glanced outside. A steady sideways stream of snow blew across the buildings, but no accumulation yet. She grabbed her camera bag and headed downstairs.

Lindsey waited by the marble arch between the lobby and the restaurant, checking her phone with that same remote intensity Rebekiah had seen through her lens. She almost pulled out her camera, but Lindsey looked up and hefted her phone, forcing her to be present. "Irene just texted. How about a late lunch?"

Rebekiah glanced out the window and once again wished for a heavier jacket. "Sure."

"I hope you don't mind staying an extra day. The airport's closed. I might have been the last flight in." Lindsey nodded toward the windows where snowflakes had started to accumulate along the window well. The possibly of extra time with Lindsey caused a slight surge of excitement.

Halfway across the lobby, Rebekiah mentioned her jacket in an offhand joke, and Lindsey made a beeline toward one of the many boutique shops built into the hotel. She started to protest, but Lindsey held firm. Surprised by her thoughtfulness, Rebekiah followed and subjected herself to various coats until Lindsey nodded her approval. Lindsey thanked the sales rep and said, "Put it on my tab. Room 536."

Rebekiah glanced at the price tag and shook her head. Thoughtfulness was one thing. This next-level generosity made her squirm. "Oh, no. I'm not letting you pay for this."

Lindsey tucked her hand into her elbow and pulled her away from the counter. "It's a business expense."

Rebekiah frowned and stopped near the revolving door. "It is not. I do have money for this, you know."

Lindsey took her in with a look and said, "I do. But you're here as my guest. I take care of my clients."

Client. Rebekiah hid her disappointment at being grouped in with everyone else. For a brief moment she'd felt special. She rolled her eyes and turned toward the door. "Of course you do." Apparently, Lindsey had picked up the same cavalier attitude toward money as the people she represented. Emma would be pleased. Rebekiah smiled, knowing Emma would have liked how Lindsey made the cost of the coat easier to swallow.

Lindsey took Rebekiah to lunch at the Cooper Inn where they met Irene Talbot, the chief development officer of the Reiher Finance Fund. Irene's discussion was frank and eye opening. Her foundation allowed her to seed a variety of projects and provide grant support to several nonprofits, creating a web of social justice financing. Listening to her speak, Rebekiah realized that giving it all away had less and less appeal. Lindsey, and now Irene, had a point. Managing it seemed like a better option to do long-term good. Emma's words, "do something good with it," kept rolling around in her head.

After lunch, Irene took them on a tour and spoke at length about the challenges facing the fund. By the time they left, Rebekiah had a newfound perspective of her wealth and the enormity of it as well. She'd never really understood just how much money Emma had left her; it had felt so abstract. No wonder she didn't want to see it go to waste. Seeing the ways small donations stacked on others opened her eyes, yet the amount was so insignificant compared to what needed to be done. Overwhelmed, she couldn't imagine trying to navigate it all without Lindsey beside her.

They parted ways at the hotel. Lindsey had a conference call she needed to take, but they agreed to meet for dinner. Back in her room, Rebekiah stepped out of the shower and wrapped a towel around her before collapsing on her bed.

She awoke a few hours later with her stomach rumbling. She rolled over and glanced at her phone. No text from Lindsey.

Standing, she tossed her towel in the bathroom and rummaged in her suitcase for clothes, settling on blue jeans and a black Henley. She touched up her hair, getting rid of the slept-in look before slipping on her black boots and grabbing her camera bag. She palmed her key card and left her room.

She knocked on the door to Lindsey's suite and waited. She fidgeted with her camera bag before the door swung open, and Lindsey motioned for her to enter. She wore jeans and a button-down, her hair loose around her face. She held her finger up to her lips and tapped the Bluetooth headset in her left ear. "Have a seat. I'll be done in a few minutes." She swung away and said, "Well, if you look at the figures on page fifteen, you'll see the numbers we're talking about."

Rebekiah walked into the suite and glanced around. Her own room down the hall boasted the same features. She settled on the couch and looked out the window. Lindsey's suite looked down into a park that Rebekiah assumed was Rittenhouse Square. But her eyes tracked back to Lindsey.

"No, the number above. Yes, that one." Lindsey sat at the large, glass topped desk with her red-clad feet propped up on the table. One hand swiped across her iPad while the other twirled an expensive-looking pen.

The juxtaposition of professional tone and relaxed posture called to Rebekiah. She gave into her urge and started shooting.

Lindsey glanced up at the quiet click. For just an instant, her entire presence stared into the lens. Then her face changed, and it was gone. "No, Robert, that's not what it's saying. Yes, that's true, but the research indicates…"

Rebekiah tuned her out and slipped into wallpaper mode. She moved around the room, making herself a part of the furniture so she could take the shots she wanted. Lindsey ignored her for the most part and spent the next twenty minutes mildly chiding and gently educating the other caller. Something about Lindsey's work demeanor struck her, and she zeroed in on that strength and determination. The set of her jaw while she spoke, the way she articulated her point with her hands even though her colleagues couldn't see her, the intense focus while she listened to understand their point, and finally, the smile that spoke of her pleasure in the work. Rebekiah watched her body language start to wrap up the conversation and settled on the couch just as Lindsey disconnected the call.

Pulling the headset out of her ear, she tossed the tiny gadget on her desk with a clink. She leaned back, rubbed her hands across her face, and sighed. "That was too much work for such a simple concept."

Rebekiah set her camera down.

Lindsey dropped her hands into her lap and turned toward her. She smiled. "Sorry to keep you waiting." She nodded toward the camera. "Is this part of our deal?"

Rebekiah stilled. She'd pulled her camera out almost automatically, with no thought to art or technique. She'd just wanted a couple photos of her. When had she stopped taking pictures for fun? She shook her head and tucked that thought away. "No." She cocked her head to the side and hefted the camera. "Do you mind? I can delete them."

Lindsey paused for the briefest of moments and shook her head. "If you can use them, by all means, keep them."

Rebekiah smiled, knowing they'd never go into a show. Lindsey only saw the work and not the way she interacted with the work. Her facial expressions, her gestures, even her posture shared pieces of her that Rebekiah found fascinating. No, these pictures were for her alone. Rebekiah clapped her hands against her knees and got to her feet. "Are you hungry?"

❖

"How long have you lived in Providence?" Rebekiah asked.

Lindsey plucked a mussel from its shell and popped it in her mouth. She chewed and swallowed while she counted in her head. "Six years."

Rebekiah's eyes shot up. "Really?"

Not the reaction she was expecting, but still, she welcomed the back and forth of conversation. She didn't mind being photographed. In fact, it felt good to be seen as picture worthy. It unnerved her just how much she liked it. "Why does that surprise you?"

Rebekiah took a piece of cheese off the cheese board and shook her head. "I assumed you'd just moved here."

"How come?" She dipped a crostino in the mussel broth and tried to ignore the way Rebekiah's hands moved from plate to mouth. Talking was definitely safer.

"Providence is a small town once you take away the students. And the queer community is big but not that big."

Lindsey swallowed and took a sip of her ginger ale, a poor substitute for the dry martini she craved. With three fat olives. She sighed and put her drink down. "I spend a lot of time on the road. I actually grew up in Barrington."

"You grew up in Rhode Island?"

Lindsey nodded. She usually didn't share that last part, but her craving distracted her. "Here and DC," she added. "My grandparents lived in Jamestown. My mother has a house in Barrington."

Rebekiah whistled. "Old money or new?"

Lindsey wiggled her hand. It was a question a fellow Rhode Islander would know to ask. "More like political legacy. My great-grandfather was a US senator. He married well but not wealthy. We've all worked for a living. Most of the money's in real estate and long-term investments. No trust fund for me." She stabbed the soft mussel meat and ate it whole to buy some time. Growing up with, but not part of, the wealthy elites had been hard as a child, worse as a teenager, but she had parlayed that cultural knowledge into her career.

"Blackwell?" Rebekiah's eyes narrowed. "As in Senator Paula Blackwell?"

Lindsey nodded and offered a small smile. "Ayup. That's my mother."

Rebekiah leaned her head in her hand. "I didn't know she had kids."

Lindsey snorted. It wasn't the first time she'd heard that. "That's deliberate. The senator likes to keep her personal life…personal." Unfortunately, that public invisibility had bled into personal invisibility. Lindsey's reactions to not being seen had changed over the years. She'd stopped looking for acknowledgment and started pulling away. These days, she tended toward public appearances over personal visits with her mother. She shrugged. "Let's just say the holidays are a little less about us and more about the constituents." She nodded toward the last mussel. Rebekiah gave her the go-ahead. She speared the last one and changed the subject. "What about you? Are you from Providence?"

"More or less."

Hoping to keep the topic of conversation on Rebekiah, she asked, "Where was the less?"

"My parents had a house in Wellfleet. We split our time between here and the cape. Do you go to Barrington often?"

Lindsey shook her head. Rebekiah was proving to be a deft deflector. "Not really. My mom lives in Barrington. It's an election year, so she's in Rhode Island more this year. I tend to come home when I know my dad will be there."

"So you're closer to your dad than your mom?"

Lindsey scowled. "Close is not a word I'd use to describe my family, but yes." Why was she sharing this? Her clients only knew surface details at most. Where did her small-talk skills go?

Rebekiah looked up as the server picked up their empty plates and left. "Beats the alternative."

Lindsey processed that information without comment. She knew Rebekiah's parents were dead; the biographical dossier said so, but still. The reality of it was much different in person than on paper. "I read that your parents passed away when you were young." Rebekiah's face questioned her. "I have a basic dossier on you."

"So you knew."

"Yes, but not the specifics. I'm sorry." And she was. Not just for her loss but because she'd shifted the conversation. She could feel Rebekiah closing off, and it bothered her. The slight buzz of attraction was still there, popping up when Rebekiah moved a certain way, but the subject had gotten very heavy.

Rebekiah waved her off. "Don't be. It was a long time ago." Rebekiah looked up. "People get weird. I've had therapy, and I'm fine." She rolled her eyes. "I have abandonment issues. Who doesn't?"

Lindsey laughed at her poor joke, not sure how else to respond and getting no clues from Rebekiah. Even though she made light of it, Lindsey wanted to stick with the emotions. "I wasn't getting weird. I was just trying to reconcile the facts with the reality. How'd they die?" She'd stopped her research before she got into too much detail.

"My mother died from HIV complications when I was in college, and my father overdosed when I was nine." Rebekiah shrugged. "They were junkies." She tilted her head. "How much research do you do on your clients?"

Again, Rebekiah tried to steer the conversation away from her, and this time, Lindsey let her. She had no words for her, and it was obvious Rebekiah didn't want to talk about it in-depth. It was an old wound but a wound nonetheless. And a little too close to her own issues with recovery. "It depends." She opened her palm. "On the money involved, the time I have to prep, the information available."

"So, what else do you know about me?"

Lindsey glanced toward the ceiling, wondering how far

this conversation had moved in such a short span of time. "You graduated from RISD about ten years ago with a degree in photography and an illustration minor. I have addresses for you in New York City, the cape, and Providence."

Rebekiah nodded. "That sounds about right. Anything else?"

"There's a ton of reviews for several shows. Some in Providence and some in New York City." She looked over and shrugged. "I skimmed them enough to know you're a well-regarded artist." If she had more time, she would have had Sabine research the galleries and get a sense of Rebekiah's real status in the art world.

"All that from your database in the sky?" Rebekiah sipped her water.

Lindsey grinned. "Well, all that and you inherited your money from Emma Strahan with no legal or familial relationship to you." She met Rebekiah's eyes. "Along with biographical details, place of birth, age, etcetera, that's about it."

Rebekiah frowned. "If you know all that, why pretend not to?"

Lindsey considered her answer. Something about Rebekiah demanded honesty. "There's a certain biographical context that helps me figure out what people want or need to do with their money. Plus, the facts don't always tell the whole story." She glanced out the window. The night sky was filled with the orange glow of falling snow. The snowflakes had switched from heavy drops to tiny pinpricks and had significantly slowed down. If it stayed that way, her chances of getting out tomorrow looked good. She wasn't sure she wanted to go.

"Can I interest you in a nightcap?"

Up until this point, she could dismiss the evening as a meal between close colleagues. She'd already shared more about her family than she had with her last two, or was it three, girlfriends. She suspected it had to do with Rebekiah's ability to put people at ease and her own comfortableness with total strangers. Going up to Rebekiah's room represented a different boundary that she should not accept, but she didn't want the night to end. She felt a closeness with Rebekiah that went beyond the professional. However, the offer of a drink presented its own problems. She hesitated, not wanting Rebekiah to think her no was about her but a little afraid to share her issues with alcohol. "Uh, I don't drink."

Rebekiah set her napkin on the table and stood. "Oh, okay."

Whatever rapport they had was slipping away. Lindsey felt the need to clarify. "No, I don't drink because I'm an alcoholic."

Rebekiah smiled and offered her a hand. "Well, then, how about a Coke and some company?"

Rebekiah's ease with her confession made up her mind for her. Tossing her reservations aside, Lindsey took her hand and said, "I'd love that."

Lindsey mentally rolled her eyes at her words. "Love that"? Why would she even say that? For a moment, she realized what she looked like from the outside. One woman holding the hand of another woman heading up to their room. Was that what was happening here? Did she want that? Did Rebekiah? She was so involved in her thoughts that she almost missed Rebekiah telling her that she needed to pick up her camera in Lindsey's suite.

Lindsey gave her a look and unlocked her room. "I've got soda. Why don't you come inside?" With that simple shift in rooms, Lindsey's control of the situation returned.

Rebekiah paused and said, "I'll be right back." She came back hefting a bucket of ice. "It felt weird showing up empty-handed."

Closing the door, Lindsey smiled and said, "I could use the ice." She grabbed a couple of glasses from the kitchenette and two cans of Coke from the fridge.

Rebekiah grinned and put the bucket on the table. "See? Not so random." She doled out some ice and helped Lindsey pour the drinks.

"Was it worth the trip?" Better to start out professional than too personal.

Collecting her camera, Rebekiah took her Coke and sat on

the couch. "Yes. Definitely. And I think you're right. I can do a lot of good with the money."

Lindsey sat across from her and smiled. She could do this. "Good. I have one more person I want you to meet."

Rebekiah took a sip of Coke and pointed. "Here?"

Lindsey shook her head. "No, New York City. Probably early December. Does that work for you?"

"I think so." Rebekiah watched her for a minute. "How long have you known Irene?"

"Her younger sister and I were roommates in high school."

"Roommates?"

Lindsey gave a lopsided grin. "Boarding school."

"That makes sense."

"How so?" Lindsey's smile faded, and she tilted her head.

Rebekiah spoke with her hands. "That you're so contained."

"Contained?" She'd never heard that word used to describe herself. Independent, stubborn, aloof, yes, but contained was new. She didn't know how she felt about it.

"Self-sufficient. Polished."

Lindsey knew that she gave off that façade. Years of recovery left her with more self-awareness than she wanted. Curious, she asked, "Is that what you saw when you took my picture?"

"Among other things." Rebekiah smiled.

"Such as?" Lindsey directed a look at her. It was Rebekiah's turn to divulge details.

"It's hard to describe."

Lindsey leaned in, curious to know how much Rebekiah saw. "Try me."

Rebekiah took a deep breath. "You have an intensity that sort of defies explanation. It stays with you at all times. But when you're relaxed, it disappears, and there's a softness, a vulnerability. The person behind the mask appears."

A pleasant warmth suffused her insides. She felt both seen and desired in a way that hadn't happened in many years. She found it disconcerting and tried to deflect the attention. "Is that what you're looking for when you're taking pictures?"

"Depends on the pictures. My paid work is a collaboration between myself and the client. They tell me what they're looking for, and I try to capture that. My art is different. I might be looking for themes, but each model presents a different landscape to explore."

"What theme are you working on now?"

"Strength, vulnerability, hidden potentials really." She laughed. "And sex."

Lindsey laughed with her. She couldn't tell if Rebekiah was trying to seduce her or really believed what she was saying.

Rebekiah held up her hand and grew serious. "No, really, I tend to gravitate toward sex and all the baggage that comes with it. There's a moment when women come that their eyes and their faces become vulnerable and exposed. All pretense stripped away." Rebekiah leaned forward. "People use sex to connect. I just want to facilitate that."

Matching her tone, Lindsey leaned in. "And there's no ulterior motive in it for you?"

Rebekiah grinned and moved closer. "Are you asking, does it turn me on?"

She considered pulling back, but she wanted to know. She nodded. "I am."

"Sometimes. With the right person."

She swallowed. And there it was. Her intentions laid bare. Rebekiah wanted her. "I see."

"Do you?" She shifted closer.

Lindsey leaned toward her. "Yes."

She closed her eyes as Rebekiah's lips brushed hers. She gave in to the feeling of connection and opened her mouth when Rebekiah's hands slipped behind her head, deepening the kiss. She moaned as her tongue slid inside. She felt her smile against her lips and echoed it.

Rebekiah stood and pulled Lindsey with her. Lindsey stumbled against her, breaking their kiss. Reality tamped down her arousal. She was on a business trip kissing a client. "Fuck." She backed up, and Rebekiah released her. She covered her mouth and shook her head. "I'm sorry. That was inappropriate."

Rebekiah reached out. "There's nothing to be sorry about. We're consenting adults."

She kept shaking her head. "It's not professional. I don't do this anymore." Not since she stopped drinking.

Rebekiah waited and then nodded. "Okay. I'll go." She headed toward the door.

Lindsey groaned internally. "Rebekiah?"

She turned at the door.

"Does this change anything?" She motioned between them.

Rebekiah grinned. "Of course it does."

Disappointed, Lindsey closed her eyes.

"But not professionally. I'll still work with you."

She opened her eyes and watched Rebekiah close the door behind her. This time, she groaned audibly and dropped to the couch. Throwing her hand over her eyes, she muttered, "What've I done?"

She thanked the universe that she had an early flight in the morning.

CHAPTER TEN

True to her word, Rebekiah continued to work with Lindsey. But that kiss threw her for a loop. Despite her bravado with "this changes everything," she wasn't prepared for the mix of emotions it stirred up, the giddiness, the anxiety, and finally, the fear. She used Lindsey's busy schedule to quietly back off. Still, they arranged to meet during the first week of December in New York City. She'd arrived in New York yesterday evening, expecting to meet Lindsey at the hotel, but she'd gotten no texts. Checking in, she texted again and sent an email. Maybe Lindsey was starting to back off, too. She ignored the pang of disappointment that came with that thought.

By the next morning, she was more worried than disappointed. Lindsey rarely left a text unanswered for more than an hour, so she called her assistant and then called her room. "Hello?"

"Lindsey?" The voice didn't sound like her.

"Rebekiah?" She sounded terrible. "Why are you calling me on this phone?"

"You're not answering your other phone."

"I'm not?" She heard rustling along the line. "What time is it?"

Lindsey's confusion kicked her worry into anxiety. "Ten seventeen. Lindsey, can you open your door?"

"I don't understand."

She knocked gently. "Please. I'm just outside."

She pocketed her phone as Lindsey opened the door in just her underwear. Her anxiety faded at the sight of her, and her desire flared only to switch into concern as she got a good look at the haggard woman in front of her. She gently pushed past and closed the door. Lindsey swayed; Rebekiah caught her.

"Let's get you back to bed." Lindsey offered no resistance, and Rebekiah frowned at the heat coming off her body. "Have you been here since you landed?"

Lindsey nodded while Rebekiah helped pull the blankets up. She shivered. "I'm so cold."

Switching into automatic caregiver, Rebekiah searched the closets for another blanket. She snapped it open and let it drape across the bed. Spotting the mini-fridge, she pulled a water from it, broke the seal, and helped Lindsey to a sitting position. "Here."

Lindsey took a big sip and leaned back. Then her face contorted, and she threw the covers off before rushing toward the bathroom. Rebekiah grimaced at the retching sound from the other room. She picked up the phone and dialed reception. A pleasant voice greeted her by Lindsey's name.

"This is actually another guest, Rebekiah Kearns, in Lindsey's room. Do you have medical staff on call?"

"We have a nurse practitioner. Would you like us to send her up?"

A brief feeling of déjà vu settled over her, recalling another time with another sick woman. Rebekiah glanced toward the bathroom. "Please do." She hung up and walked toward the bathroom. Tapping on the half-open door, she tentatively swung it open. "Lindsey?"

Lindsey sprawled with her head over the toilet and her cheek resting on the seat.

Ignoring the flood of memories, Rebekiah took a deep breath and walked all the way in. She crouched and gently touched Lindsey's arm. Lindsey looked at her without recognition. Red splotches dotted her neck, arms, and hands.

"I called the doctor."

Lindsey stared, her usually expressive eyes flat and faded.

"Do you feel like you're going to be sick again?" She smoothed her hand along her back.

Lindsey shook her head a fraction of an inch as if she knew any sudden movements would send her back to the bowl.

She reached down and offered a hand. "Let's get you cleaned up." She pulled her toward the sink and wetted a wash cloth. She rummaged through the drawers and found a toothbrush and toothpaste. Apparently, the seven hundred a night rate offered all the amenities. She got it ready and helped Lindsey stand in front of the mirror while she brushed her teeth.

She was helping her pull a T-shirt over her head when she heard a sharp knock on the door. "That's the nurse."

"I'm fine," Lindsey muttered as she crawled back into bed with an audible hiss.

Rebekiah refrained from rolling her eyes and opened the door. She thanked the nurse for coming and rattled off the symptoms before moving toward the far end of the suite to give Lindsey as much privacy as possible. She stood when the nurse crossed the room.

"I want to send her to the hospital."

Rebekiah nodded. "Did you call an ambulance?"

"She's refusing." Her expression said the rest. She needed Rebekiah to convince her.

Slightly uncomfortable shouldering that responsibility, Rebekiah exhaled and walked to the bed. She sat down on the edge. Lindsey's eyes were closed. Considering her options, she decided to bypass negotiation and just tell her that she was going. Since Lindsey seemed like the type who won most negotiations, the odds were in Rebekiah's favor that she could score a quick victory by not even allowing wiggle room. She leaned down, and Lindsey opened her eyes. "It's time to go. Did you want to go by ambulance or cab?"

Lindsey's eyes narrowed. "I just need to sleep it off."

Rebekiah found Lindsey's hand and held it. "That's not what the nurse thinks, and I don't think you're a good judge of what you need right now." Rebekiah squeezed her hand. "You've asked me to trust you, and now I'm asking you to trust me."

Lindsey stared, and Rebekiah felt that willpower push and pull against her before she finally nodded. "Cab, please."

"Thank you." Relieved at her agreement, she squeezed her hand and leaned down to brush a kiss against her sweaty forehead. She helped her bundle up, and they headed downstairs to wait.

A black and yellow cab pulled up in the lobby circle. Lindsey turned. She tried a smile, but it didn't quite get there. "It's okay. I've got it from here."

Rebekiah nodded. She'd already violated Lindsey's privacy enough for one day. "Okay." She stepped back but jumped forward as Lindsey wobbled. Wrapping an arm around her waist, she whispered, "Let me help you."

Lindsey gave a slight nod, and Rebekiah helped her into the cab.

They rode in silence. Rebekiah tried to think of something to say, but the awkward intimacy made it hard. She had avoided mentioning the kiss in the few emails and texts they exchanged setting up this trip. She was paralyzed by indecision, something that was new to her.

Lindsey reached out and squeezed her hand. "Thank you."

Startled by her touch, Rebekiah barely heard her over the Indian hip-hop playing into the back seat of the cab. She smiled. "You're welcome."

Lindsey's head rested against the smudged window while she watched the traffic move through Times Square. "I'm so tired."

Rebekiah held her hand until the taxi pulled up in front of the ER. Lindsey opened the door and stepped out. Rebekiah slid over and handed the cabbie the fare before getting out.

Lindsey stood on the curb. "You don't have to pay."

Rebekiah shut the door and turned around. "I know." She followed Lindsey into the hospital toward reception.

The woman at the desk glanced up. "Can I help you?"

Rebekiah spoke up first, Lindsey supplying medical cards and other identification as needed. She collected the clipboard and helped Lindsey to the chairs at the far end of the room. She filled out the questionnaire with what little information she had while they waited to be seen.

Lindsey spent most of it semiconscious while Rebekiah tried to suppress the memories of the last time she'd visited an ER. It was a few days before Emma's death. Emma could barely stand, and Rebekiah had to fight to get her released to hospice. She died three days later. Lindsey's condition triggered her anxiety, but her rational mind refused to go there. However, the longer she sat there, the worse it got. She closed her eyes and tried taking deep breaths. She could feel her heart racing. She practically jumped to her feet when they called for Lindsey.

Lindsey lifted her head. Rebekiah reached down. "That's you."

Lindsey groaned and got to her feet. The nurse came forward and slipped an arm around her waist. "Let's get you checked out." She looked over her shoulder. "Are you coming?"

"Uh…" Rebekiah's anxiety, coupled with her reluctance to intrude, rooted her tongue to the roof of her mouth.

"I'll come back and brief you." The nurse smiled and kept walking.

Rebekiah sank down in the chairs and wished that she still smoked.

❖

Lindsey woke up disoriented and soaked in sweat. She felt more alert than she had in days. The fever must have broken. She moved, and her arm tugged on the IV. The past few days came back to her a bit hazy. Not even her worst hangovers left her feeling so wrung out.

She scanned the room—a nylon curtain split her from the other occupant—to the tiny TV on the wall and back around to the window, and that was where she found Rebekiah fast asleep, curled up in a chair by her bed with her feet propped up along the windowsill and her hands tucked under her armpits. She flushed thinking about Rebekiah helping her get dressed, cleaning her up, and just sitting with her. So much for professional boundaries.

Nothing about Rebekiah followed her normal script either professionally or personally. Watching her sleep, she realized she didn't care. She was still here, and that counted for something.

She dozed off until the nurse walked in to check her vitals and hand her a glass of ice. When he left, Lindsey looked over and saw Rebekiah covering a yawn.

Taking a small sip of the ice chips, she said, "You didn't have to sleep here."

Rebekiah shrugged. "I didn't want you to be alone."

Her stomach fluttered, and she smiled to take the sting out of her words. "I would have been okay."

"I know."

"You don't have to do this," she said, even though she wanted her to stay.

Rebekiah smiled. "No, I don't. But I'm here."

"Did they tell you what's wrong with me?"

Rebekiah nodded. "Dengue fever." She nodded toward the IV. "There's no treatment other than pain relief and fluids. All they did was hook you up to an IV and pump you full of fluids." She gave a half grin. "And some Tylenol."

"Isn't that some tropical disease?"

A grim smile graced Rebekiah's face. "Sort of. It's mosquito borne, like malaria."

She took a deep breath. "Probably picked it up in Beijing."

She took another deep breath. "I got sick last week and thought the worst was over until yesterday." She sagged against her pillow.

Rebekiah cocked her head to the side. "How often do you travel?"

She shrugged. "About two weeks out of the month."

"So, you spend about six months out of the year somewhere else?"

Lindsey paused. "Yeah. I guess so. Why?"

Rebekiah's voice gentled. "Who takes care of you when you're sick?"

Somewhat confused, Lindsey considered her question. Other than a few memorable childhood illnesses, the answer was no one. "I do."

Rebekiah took a deep breath. "Okay." She glanced at her hands and then at Lindsey. "I called your work." She clarified. "When you didn't answer your phone. I spoke with Sabrina."

"Sabine."

"Right. Anyway, she called back while you were getting checked out. She cleared your schedule and spoke with Gordon at the Four Point Foundation." She waved her hand. "She said to tell you to check your email for details but that she's put everything on hold for two days and took care of anything that couldn't wait."

Lindsey smiled. "Good." She closed her eyes. Her thoughts drifted and she spoke before her filter came back on. "You're very good at this." She opened her eyes and stared.

Rebekiah tilted her head and raised an eyebrow. "Relaying messages?"

Lindsey smiled. "No. Taking care of me." Even though she didn't need to be taken care of, she had to admit it felt good to have someone look out for her.

Rebekiah returned her smile. "I've had practice."

"Emma. I'm sorry." Of course. She should have known.

Rebekiah waved her off. "It's fine. But I know my way around a hospital." She leaned in and said, "I may have stretched the truth about our relationship a bit to get things done quicker."

"How much?"

Rebekiah grimaced. "They think we're married."

Lindsey rolled her eyes and chuckled, thinking she'd heard worse ideas. "Well, sweetie, how about you work on getting me out of this place?"

CHAPTER ELEVEN

Lindsey spent the morning working through the general office workload and then moved on to her specific workload. With a week before Christmas, the year-end business was in full swing. But thoughts of Rebekiah crept in between breaks in the work. The NYC trip loomed large. What was she doing? Was she pursuing Rebekiah? Was Rebekiah pursuing her? Was it business or personal?

The kiss felt pretty personal, but Rebekiah hadn't made a single mention of it. And the way she took care of her when she was sick, no one did that for her. Lindsey understood the ebb and flow of macro relationships, but the nuances of romantic relationships left her confused. Either way, she didn't have time for romance or sex; she never did. Work always came first. Right? Right. Then why was she having such a hard time concentrating?

She looked at her watch. Taking a deep breath, she exhaled and turned back to her laptop with a muttered, "Suck it up and get back to work."

"Can I see some identification?" An hour later, Sabine's voice cut through her thoughts. She stood up to see a woman standing with another man next to Sabine's cubicle.

Sabine stood with her arms folded while the woman flashed her badge. Sabine glanced at it before eyeing the man. He showed her his ID, too. Sabine said, "Follow me."

Lindsey stood up just as the pair walked into her office.

The woman flashed her badge. "Agent Gail Travers. DOJ." Department of Justice. Lindsey reached out and shook hands. "Agent Travers. And?"

Sabine lingered by the door, waiting until Lindsey let her know it was okay to go.

"Agent Feldon."

She shook his hand; it was damp. She resisted the urge to wipe her hand down her pants and decided to sit behind her desk rather than in her sitting area. "What can I do for you?"

Travers sat down, and Feldon followed suit, reaching out and shutting the door first. "We're following up with Roger Stross's associates." Felton pulled out a pen and pad and leaned forward. Travers asked, "When was the last time you spoke with Roger Stross?"

Lindsey leaned back, irked. Roger. Of course. Her schedule had been so hectic that she'd never reached out to him, and it weighed on her. Considering that the feds were here now, she was glad she didn't. Cathryn was right to fire him. "Sometime in July."

"And nothing since?"

Lindsey shook her head. "No, nothing."

Travers asked, "How well do you know Yevgen Kharitonov?"

She recognized the name, one of Cathryn's people. She shrugged. "Not well. I've met him twice."

"When was the last time you saw him?"

Lindsey shook her head. "I don't know. A few months ago." She tapped her desk. "Here. At the office." She frowned. "He's just a third-party contact for Cathryn. She works with him more often." She reached for her phone. "I can get Cathryn in here."

Travers put her hand on the phone. "That's okay. We've already spoken with Ms. Wexler." She moved her hand. "Were you aware that your firm made three separate payments to the Kharitonov Group totaling 1.4 million during the last year?"

"No." Her stomach dropped. Was this the irregularity Cathryn found? She kicked herself for not pressing for details.

Travers folded her arms. "Does that seem high to you?"

Lindsey held back her yes. 1.4 million in one year? Not significant by itself but significant because it was a third-party vendor and not a direct client. What was Roger doing with Cathryn's clients? "It depends."

"On?"

"The type of business we're doing with them." She remembered a conversation she had with Cathryn a few years ago around federal regulations. "How many times have you paid for dinner, bought hotel rooms, purchased tickets?" Cathryn had said. "That's not a bribe. That's the cost of doing business."

Lindsey chose her next words carefully. "We pay a variety of local third-party vendors to help us seek business opportunities in their home countries. Some of those deals can be quite expensive." What was Cathryn doing with Yevgen?

"Let's cut the business jargon. They're bribes."

Lindsey shook her head. "No. They're not. We're fully compliant with the FCPA." She reached for her phone again. "I can bring up documentation to support that."

Travers smiled. "Thank you. We appreciate your willingness to open your books to us."

Lindsey felt the trap snap. There was no way to say no without looking guilty, but with Roger's recent and unreported embezzlement, there was no way in hell she was going to give the feds her books. Not before she looked at them. She plastered a smile on her face and said, "Of course. It'll take a few weeks with the holidays and all."

Travers grinned. "Of course. We can always get a court order." She knew Lindsey was on to her.

Lindsey hedged her bets and gave her best regretful look. "You might have to. I can provide you with our FCPA documentation. But I'm not authorized to release our corporate accounts to you. I'll need to consult with my partners first." She picked up her phone and dialed Sabine's number. Sabine's curt yes was met with an equally brief, "Can you make a copy of our FCPA procedures and bring them in?" She hung up and made a point of pulling her keyboard toward her. "Sabine will have the paperwork for you in just a few minutes." She nodded toward the door.

Travers tipped her head. "Thanks for your help."

Lindsey smiled. "Anytime." She kept her eyes on the door and watched Sabine hand them a manila folder.

The payments worried her. They were much larger than they normally doled out, but Cathryn was right. The federal corruption law interfered with legitimate and quasi-legitimate business. And with so many other multinational corporations engaging in far more obvious and illegal activities, it didn't seem fair that the DOJ were singling them out. It wasn't her first time dealing with federal interference. However, it was possible that Roger's misdeeds had led the feds to investigate other avenues in their firm. They'd need something substantial to subpoena the firm's accounts, and she doubted they had it. Agent Travers wouldn't have bothered with the cat and mouse if she had something on their business. But they were easy prey if they rolled over. Lindsey had no intention of doing that.

❖

Rebekiah watched through the lens as Elena circled the young submissive bent over the Queen Anne writing desk. Her posture made a perfect L across the wood; naked but unbound, she wore only fishnet stockings—a single side garter to hold them up—and glossy four-inch pumps. Her feet sat perfectly centered on the white squares amid the black diamond tiles. Her labia stood out, cupped between her lemon-shaped ass and bare upper thighs.

"Do you know why you're here?" A close-up of Elena

in her black leather dress. Another of her face, both stern and compassionate.

"Yes, Elena."

Rebekiah remembered the last time she asked Elena why she didn't use mistress as a title. Elena had laughed. "It's too fucking silly. It knocks me right out of dom space."

"What about Ms. or ma'am?"

"Oh, Jesus, Rebekiah. Ma'am? I am not an old lady; I get enough of that word from the young kid at the coffee shop. And Ms. I sound like a school teacher. Well, hmm. Maybe Ms. isn't so bad after all. I'll have to keep that in mind for my subs with a teacher fetish."

Elena dragged the leather straps of the flail along the woman's back and down her thighs. "I want you to count off each stroke for me. We'll go to twenty-five." Her hand rose, the strips brushing back against her wrist.

"Yes, Elena."

Swoosh, snap. "One, Elena." Swoosh, snap. "Two, Elena." Swoosh, snap, snap. "Three, four, Elena." The sub's voice shook, and she took a deep breath just as another swoosh, snap resonated in the room. "Five, Elena." Swoosh, snap. "Six, Elena..."

Rebekiah slipped into her own world of watching and wanting. She slid to the floor and lay on her back with her camera pointed toward the woman's face. She listened to the rhythm and watched the sub's face change as the leather slapped her bare ass. Her eyes opened and closed with each slap. A silent O formed on her lips before she took a deep breath and uttered "Eleven, Elena." Her eyes stayed open. And for one second, she turned her head, looked Rebekiah in the eyes and said, "Twelve, Elena." Her face twisted in a grimace of pleasure and pain on the edge of both and neither. Rebekiah smiled; anticipation thrummed through her body.

She kept going, moving around on the floor until Elena reached the last stroke and stopped. Stepping away from her sub, Elena ran a hand along the woman's heated ass. Rebekiah watched the sub try to suppress a flinch, her own excitement rising. She looked up through the lens and snapped off a couple more shots of Elena with her hands on her hips and an expression of command and attitude on her face. A hand descended into view, and Elena pulled the camera away from her.

"Wait…I'm not done."

Elena lifted Rebekiah's chin. "Tonight you are." She kissed her on the forehead and handed her back the camera before ushering her out the door.

Somewhat disappointed and definitely aroused, Rebekiah left the room and wandered the event. Various scenes played out in the expansive warehouse setting. She'd been informally documenting the Rhode Island BDSM community for a little over ten years. As Elena's involvement grew, so did hers. Over the years, she'd joined in, taking on secondary roles, an active observer and passive participant. But she preferred words over props.

Her comfort level with diverse sexuality tapped into a niche market, and she'd become one of a handful of photographers taking queer portraits both in and out of scene. She charged reasonable rates, and as a result, she often had a plethora of willing models for her fine art projects and a venue to expand her boudoir techniques.

In the far corner, someone caught her eye, just a glimpse, but she could have sworn it was Lindsey. Intrigued and still aroused, she shifted closer and saw the woman sink to her knees in front of a leather-clad woman sprawled on a settee. She was too far away to hear the words but watched her crawl toward her dom and bury her face between her legs. A potent mix of jealousy and desire surged up, and Rebekiah moved closer.

The dom—Diane—looked up and extended a hand. "Want a taste?"

"Lindsey's" head came up, and Rebekiah's arousal vanished. Up close, she looked nothing like her. Attractive in that same sort of way, but the features were all wrong.

Stepping back, Rebekiah lifted her camera and said, "I'm good with this."

Diane shrugged and said, "Suit yourself."

She stayed with them for a couple more minutes, taking a few shots she'd never use. It felt rude to see her face and turn tail, but her mood was gone. She wandered away, on the cusp of leaving when Neil's voice cut through the cacophony of music and various sex acts. He waved her over to a grouping of old couches and chairs where about a dozen people sat and talked. She let him introduce her to the mostly male group.

"And this is…" He paused at the only woman and tilted his head.

She reached across and shook Rebekiah's hand. "Sabine."

Rebekiah grabbed her hand and smiled. She looked and sounded familiar, but Rebekiah couldn't place her. "Nice to meet you."

They talked art and then music before the talk turned personal, and they splintered into smaller and smaller groups. Sabine kept looking at her as if she knew her, and that was when it hit her. Lindsey's assistant. She reviewed her actions for the past hour. Her mind stumbled on the Lindsey look-alike. Did she see her and make the connection? She felt embarrassed and exposed, as if she had been caught cheating.

They'd left New York City two weeks ago on the same flight to Providence a few hours after Lindsey had been discharged from the hospital. She dropped her off at her apartment and then nothing but a few texts since. Not that she'd expected much. They'd shared an unexpected intimacy going from first kiss to hospital support in the span of a few weeks. Rebekiah suspected Lindsey needed time to build her defenses again, and she was willing to give her that. After the hospital visit, she wasn't sure that she was ready to dive back in either. But seeing her clone here tonight had stirred up that original desire.

Sabine moved over and leaned in. "Did you figure it out?"

Her perfume pressed into Rebekiah's nostrils, and she stared down the lace corset. The line of her breasts matched the seam and drew her eyes even lower.

Rebekiah swallowed, suddenly more nervous than she was expecting. "What?"

"Where you know me from?"

Rebekiah nodded. "Oh. Yeah, that." She coughed and shifted away. "Lindsey's assistant."

Sabine leaned back. "More like her associate."

"I see." Rebekiah didn't know the difference, but she didn't say anything. "How's she doing?"

Sabine ran a hand through her long black hair. She shifted sideways and propped her head in her hand. "You haven't heard from her?"

"Just a couple texts."

"Really." She pursed her lips. "Interesting."

"How so?"

"Lindsey doesn't usually work with clients like you."

"Yeah, she told me." Rebekiah tried to figure out where the conversation was going.

"She should have passed you along to me once she signed you. She didn't."

"I'm sorry?"

Sabine laughed. "Me, too." She straightened and said, "I've worked with her for six years. She's very predictable. It's good. I like it." She waved her arms around the room. "I like structure, rules. Lindsey does, too." She waved a finger. "But you…You do not."

Why was she telling her this? An image of Lindsey on her knees, willing and wanting, flashed through her head. Rebekiah shrugged and played it cool. "What can I say?"

Sabine glanced across the room, and Rebekiah followed her line of sight. A handsome woman smiled at Sabine, and she smiled back. She reached across and patted Rebekiah's hand. "Be careful with her." She stood up and left.

Rebekiah sagged against the couch, surprised at how tense

she was talking with Sabine. The constant up and down of her arousal left her exhausted and unfulfilled. Time to call it a night.

She didn't bother to find Elena or Neil to say good-bye before shrugging into her winter coat and stepping outside. Snow covered everything in a fine layer, and the powder absorbed her footfalls across the parking lot. Slipping into her car, she closed the door and swiped open her phone. She found the chat history with Lindsey and reread her last text the day after they got back from Providence.

Just checking in.

Hey. I'm good. Tired, Lindsey had replied.

If you need anything...

Thanks. I'll keep that in mind. And thanks for the help in NYC.

No problem. Glad I could help, Rebekiah had answered.

I owe you.

No, you don't.

We'll reschedule with Gordon. Probably after the New Year. End of the year is his busy season. Text with details?

Sure. Rebekiah remembered waiting for a reply, but no dots appeared, and she'd put the conversation aside.

Nothing. For two weeks. At the time, she'd wanted to reach out, but didn't know what to say. The hospital trip brought up unpleasant memories that she didn't want associated with Lindsey. But the desire to see Lindsey was intense. She hadn't forgotten the kiss, although she'd let Lindsey think she had. The vulnerability Rebekiah saw in New York only underscored her original interest in peeling back her layers to the person hiding underneath. Still, she couldn't bring herself to call her.

A knock on her passenger window made her jump. Neil stood shivering with his arms wrapped around his torso. She started the car, rolled down the window, and leaned over the console. "Where's your jacket?"

He shrugged. "Can't find it. Open the door. I'm freezing my nuts off."

She hit the automatic locks. He crawled in and slammed the door. His teeth chattered, and he sagged against the seat. "Brr. How long have you been sitting here?"

Rebekiah didn't answer him. "What are you doing?"

Neil yawned. "I need a ride."

Rebekiah shook her head. "I almost left without you." She slipped her phone between the seats.

He nodded. "Who's on the phone?"

"No one."

He scooped it up and swiped it open. "Who's Lindsey?"

She flipped the wipers on, sloughed off the snow, and backed out. "No one." She changed the subject and pulled out of the parking lot. "No takers tonight?"

He put her phone back and shrugged. "A couple, but it's a little too close to the holidays for me." He adjusted the vents and fiddled with the temperature settings on his side. The Lexus had the extras. "Desperation sex is not really my gig."

Rebekiah exhaled. Maybe that was it. These feelings with Lindsey. The seasonal push to connect.

"How's your show coming?"

Rebekiah merged onto 95. Traffic moved smoothly—the snow was not sticking to the road. "Almost done." She thought of the two finished sets. She'd taken the original shot of Meghan on her wall, shrunk it down, and blended it into another shot she took of a red gold marigold and then blew the whole picture up to a four-by-four semi-gloss print. She'd surrounded the warm tone with an off-white matte in a rust-orange frame. For the couple, Renee and Dawn, she'd arranged nine pictures in three horizontal triptychs mounted in a vertical series mirroring and mimicking their sexual images with the stems and petals of orchids. She chose black lacquer frames and metallic finish to accentuate the contrast and colors. She gave him the broad outlines of those two sets.

He clapped his hands. "I can't wait. It's been too long."

Rebekiah murmured her agreement. Despite her initial reluctance, she'd really warmed to the idea and was looking forward to it. Out of the corner of her eye, she saw him shift and stare. She let him until he finally spoke.

"You okay?"

Rebekiah debated how much to reveal. "Yeah. I'm just worried about this last photograph."

"What's wrong with it?"

"I can't get her to sit for it." That wasn't entirely true. She hadn't asked, and after the kiss and then New York, she wasn't sure what she wanted.

Neil clutched his chest. "Oh my God. Pick someone else." He waved behind him. "There was a whole warehouse full of exhibitionists back there."

Rebekiah chuckled. "I know, but…"

Neil hummed and leaned back. "I'm going to assume that you've already cataloged all the things about her that you could find in someone else and found them lacking."

"Mm-hmm." But it was so much more than that.

"Then you have two options. Honesty or manipulation. If you already have a consent form, you could just work the situation with remotes and not tell her. But that shit'll backfire quick. If it's the sex part, is there a way you could work so she would feel less exposed?"

"Maybe, but I want to see her face when she comes." Did she? Yes, but she knew there was more to it than that.

"See, this is the problem with the way you do art. Your ego gets involved, and you have to be a part of it."

"It's not that."

It sounded weak to her ears. Even before Emma's death, she'd needed an emotional connection to her subjects, and that desire for depth had intensified in the last few years. Since then, the number of times where she'd used her art to fuck someone was alarmingly high.

"I need to connect with my subjects." Lindsey was no different. It didn't matter that she was seeing her places or thinking about her all the time. She'd take the shots, and the feelings would stop. They always did.

Rolling his eyes, Neil snorted. "That's some fucked-up shit from Thea." Rebekiah's hands tightened on the wheel. "Look, I'm just saying. Talk to her. She might say yes."

CHAPTER TWELVE

Lindsey logged in to Rebekiah's account, clicked on the link that brought her into the JP Morgan site, and received an access denied. She tried again with the same result. She wanted to move money over to another account before year end. Frustrated, she called to Sabine's desk, "Did you send the paperwork to JP Morgan for the Kearns account?"

Sabine glanced up from her monitor and nodded. "About two months ago." She clicked a few keys. "Yep. October thirty-first. There's a confirmation number."

Lindsey frowned. She wasn't this careless with her clients. She knew better. She should have followed up before now. Two months was a long time. Roger, Rebekiah, that stupid fever, she'd let them throw her off her game.

"You can't get in?"

Lindsey shook her head.

Sabine glanced at her computer clock. "Let me give them a call before they leave for the day."

"I can do it. It's my fault." Lindsey reached for her phone.

"No. I've got it."

"Thanks." She went back to work and glanced up when Sabine knocked on the door. Her expression said it all.

"They don't have any record of receiving it."

Lindsey wagged a finger at her. "And that's why I don't want them managing her money." She stretched her shoulders.

"So, we need another form. Signed." Lindsey ran through the logistics in her head. Almost three weeks had passed since New York. She'd spent a week recuperating, which really meant no traveling and shorter work days, even working from home for the first few days.

After a brief text exchange after she got back, there was nothing. She wasn't sure what to expect, and she wasn't sure what she wanted. Rebekiah was a client, after all. But New York felt different. Rebekiah had seen her with her guard down. Even before New York, she'd let her see behind the mask. The line between their professional and personal relationship was fading.

But she still worked for her, so she picked up her phone and typed a short and apologetic text. "Tomorrow's Christmas Eve," she said aloud, "so if I want to do any of this before the holidays, I need to do it now."

"I could drop it off if you'd like," Sabine said.

Lindsey waved her off. "No, go home. Finish your shopping. I'll track her down." She wanted to see her and get a sense of where they stood.

Sabine left half an hour later with a "See you tomorrow." Lindsey started wrapping up another hour later when her phone dinged.

Really? What kind of an operation are you running over there?

Relieved that their banter was intact, Lindsey smiled and typed back, *Apparently, a half-ass one. I'll compensate and bring dinner?* A slight warning bell dinged in the back of her head that she quickly squashed.

Sounds good. Still at studio. Okay to meet there?

Sure. Any requests?

Surprise me.

Lindsey shook her head and packed up. She left work and walked home. She called in her order to the souvlaki house on Pine Street and changed into casual clothes before coming back down.

She didn't bother calling. She waited for a half a minute, then checked the door and found it unlocked. "Hello?" Bright lights filled the end of the room and the rest of the studio. Music played so loud that it was obvious why Rebekiah hadn't heard. She was just about to announce her presence again when Sera barked a greeting.

The music stopped, and Rebekiah popped her head around the corner. "Hey. You made it."

Lindsey brought the paper bags to the coffee table. Sera wound around her legs and sniffed at the bags. Setting her messenger bag down, she crouched on the floor and caught Sera's face in her hands for a big sloppy kiss.

Rebekiah grabbed a couple plates, and Lindsey opened up the bags and set to work putting out the meal. Greek salad with romaine leaves, big tomato wedges, black kalamatas, sprinkled with feta cheese. Aluminum wrapped gyros stuffed with lamb, lettuce, onions, tomatoes, feta cheese, and tzatziki sauce. Grilled octopus, dolmades, pita bread, olives, and a soft goat cheese emerged from the bag, and for dessert, a pair of crispy golden baklava triangles. She felt a jolt of happiness at the domesticity of the moment.

Rebekiah sank down next to her with a couple of bottled waters. "Here. It looks wonderful." She picked up her gyro, unwrapped it, and took a huge bite. "Mmm."

Lindsey smiled and speared a piece of octopus. She tapped her fork against the container. "Then try this." She held her fork aloft and tilted her head in invitation for Rebekiah to take a bite.

Rebekiah leaned over and intercepted her bite. Chewing, she grinned. "Oh…that's tender."

Expecting her to take the fork, Lindsey did not anticipate the spike of desire when Rebekiah leaned in and snapped it up. She almost dropped it as the reason she'd been avoiding her became crystal clear. She didn't trust herself to be alone with her. Before she could respond to that, she felt a nudge against her thigh. Sera glanced from her to Rebekiah with a hopeful look on her face.

Lindsey reached over and passed the dog a piece of octopus. Sera gulped it down in one bite.

Rebekiah's mouth dropped open. "Did you…you didn't just feed my dog off the table?" Her whole face registered complete disbelief.

Lindsey stopped in mid-bite and put her fork down. "Why?"

Rebekiah brought her hand to her forehead and covered her eyes. She groaned and shook her head. "Oh my God, Lindsey, you are such a sucker."

"What? She seems like she does it all the time."

Rebekiah pulled her hands away. "That's because hope springs eternal in the mind of a dog." She sighed and pointed toward the far wall and Sera's dog bed. "Go lie down." Sera looked at her and then at Lindsey. "Sera, lie down." Sera's butt twitched, but she still stared at Lindsey.

Rebekiah glanced at Lindsey, and Lindsey mirrored her gesture and tone. "Sera, lie down."

Sera's body sagged, and she crawled to her bed. She snorted and rooted around for a bit before she finally settled.

"Aww." Lindsey felt bad sending her away.

Rebekiah rolled her eyes. "Oh no, you don't."

"But she looked so sad." Someone needed to stand up for her.

"And when she throws up all over your kitchen because she's grown accustomed to human food so she knocks over the garbage can to eat it, you can remember how sad she was."

Lindsey nodded and waved her fork in the air. "Good point."

"Uh-huh," Rebekiah muttered before she bit into her gyro.

They ate in silence for a while, and Lindsey was surprised at how comfortable it was. Rebekiah engaged her in quiet nonverbal cues and smiles, and it felt good. So many people in her life took her silence the wrong way, including most of her former lovers. Conversation required work, and although she was good at it, she tended toward quiet when she let her guard down.

She finished dinner quickly—years of bolting food and running had created a speed eating habit—and Rebekiah reached for her plate. "All set?"

Lindsey smiled. "Yeah. Here, I got that." She helped clear up their meal and then held out her oily hands. "Do you have a bathroom?"

Rebekiah nodded. "Out the front door, take a right, and there's two unisex bathrooms." Rebekiah ruffled Sera's head. "I need to take this one out for a walk." Sera got up and danced around at that word. "Make yourself comfortable, and I'll be back in a few minutes."

Lindsey returned from the bathroom and wandered toward the main part of the studio. Spotting the bookshelf, she perused the titles, hoping to get a glimpse into Rebekiah's psyche. Books sometimes told a different story. Mostly coffee table and exhibition books; she idly pulled them in and out to get a better look. A picture fluttered to the floor just as Rebekiah walked in with Sera in tow.

She leaned down and picked it up. Two women lay on a wide white bed with their calves wrapped around the other, something so personal and so immediately intimate about them. "Did you take this?"

Rebekiah glanced at the photo in Lindsey's hand and shook her head. "No." She took it and tipped it toward the light. "But there's something about this one that I really like. I'm trying to figure it out."

"It's her hand. They're in love." Lindsey hid her surprise that someone who took erotic pictures could miss so obvious a connection. The larger woman cradled the other woman's lower back and upper buttocks in such a way as to suggest tenderness. Her fingertips gently brushed the skin underneath, seemingly caught in the act of stroking.

Rebekiah stared for a little bit longer and nodded slowly. "Yeah, maybe."

"Sometimes it's the way they touch that tells you." Wanting to move away from the personal, Lindsey said, "Let me grab the paperwork, and I'll get out of your hair."

"Okay, sure." Rebekiah followed her into the reception area and leaned against the wall. "I'm glad you came."

"Well, if I'd been paying attention, I wouldn't have to." She looked up and caught the slight frown on Rebekiah's face. Did she just hurt her feelings? She took a chance and smiled. "I mean, me, too." Friendships had never been her strong suit. They evolved gradually and over time. Her sexual relationships tended toward the exact opposite. They burned bright in the beginning and faded within months. Her lovers were attracted to her remoteness and then complained about it when she didn't change for them.

Rebekiah's face brightened, and she pushed off the wall. "I've been meaning to call you."

"Really?" Her insides trembled. She wasn't sure she was ready to hear what Rebekiah was going to say. Grabbing a pen, she sat down and flipped a folder open.

Rebekiah came over. "I wanted to schedule another sitting." Lindsey pointed out the places for her to sign, and Rebekiah did. When they finished, she handed her the pen, but instead of letting it go, she wrapped her hand around Lindsey's fingers, and they held the pen together.

Lindsey looked at their joined hands. Rebekiah's fingers were smooth and warm. There was a tenderness in her touch that drew her in. All their interactions had been leading up to this moment. Rebekiah was different. Every encounter Lindsey had with her did not fit into her professional or even personal pattern. She allowed Rebekiah more leeway. At first, she thought it was because of Roger and the increased workload. Everything felt more urgent and necessary. She was willing to bend her rules to get the deal. But the time to pass her off came and went, and she still worked with her. With each conversation, they revealed pieces of themselves to each other. Rebekiah saw her, and Lindsey wanted to feel that connection again. The idea of removing her clothes and letting Rebekiah watch her come undone made her insides burn. "And if I say yes, will you want me to come?"

Rebekiah's other hand covered their hands together. "Would you like that?"

Lindsey swallowed and heard the husky rasp in her voice but could do nothing to change it. Her body already acquiesced to what her mind was thinking. "Where do you want me?"

❖

Rebekiah pulled the drapes closed to shut the night out of the studio. She made sure the heat was on and finished setting up the lights for the shoot. She tested the angle and two cameras she'd set up on tripods. She wanted as little technical distraction for the shoot as possible so she could concentrate on making Lindsey comfortable. She wished she'd had more time to prepare; she felt rushed and disorganized. The last time she'd been this meticulous about a setup was Emma's final shoot. That realization brought an unexpected wave of grief. She took a deep breath and expelled all that pent-up emotion. Now that she knew where all her anxiety was coming from, she could let it go.

Sera growled as she ran under her feet with a red scarf dangling from her mouth. "What the hell?" Coming back to the present, Rebekiah turned and called, "Sera!"

Sera ignored the call and huddled into her bed, sniffing and snuffling the red wool. "What are you doing?" Rebekiah ducked in and yanked the cloth away. Sera barked at her twice. Rebekiah frowned. "Hey, don't yell at me." She held the slobbery cloth up and turned it in her hand. Lindsey's scarf. She called to the dressing room, "Lindsey, my dog chewed your scarf. Bad dog," she muttered at Sera. Sera closed her eyes and pretended to sleep.

Lindsey spoke from behind the changing screen. "Really?"

"I'll see if I can get it cleaned." She hung the soggy scarf off one of the photography racks and stared at it for a minute longer. "But if not, will you accept a substitute?"

Lindsey laughed. "You don't need to get me another one. I have tons of scarves."

Rebekiah frowned, shooting Sera one last glare before she went back to the cameras, then took a few shots to test the lighting. "How's it coming?"

"Do you have something I could wear, or should I just come out naked?"

Rebekiah's breath caught, and she choked.

"Are you okay?"

"Yeah. Just grab whatever you see hanging in there." Her mind raced through all the clothes on the rack, imagining what she would look like in each of them. Women came out of her dressing room half-naked all the time. This should be no different, right? She tried to focus and adjusted the aperture before she took another shot. The camera slid in her hands, and she wiped her palms on her pants. "Make sure your things are off the floor. Apparently, my dog has a fetish for your clothes." Lindsey's laugh came back through the space.

She emerged wearing a black kimono with cherry blossoms along the hem and up the torso. She walked past Rebekiah and sat down on the edge of the bed. "And what about her owner? What fetishes does she have?"

Rebekiah pulled away from her camera and smiled, letting her desire show through. "I like to watch."

Lindsey leaned back. "Do you? And what do you like to watch?" She moved her legs apart; the silk robe split along the inside of her thighs. Rebekiah's eyes followed the move, her desire pooling much lower.

"Hmm…Lots of things."

Lindsey's hand drifted across her stomach and played with the knot at her waist. "Can you be more specific?"

Rebekiah turned the focus a little tighter and said, "Sure. Can you follow directions?"

Lindsey looked right in the camera and said, "I'll do whatever you want."

Rebekiah felt a rush of warmth. "Okay. Then let's move your legs apart a little bit more."

Lindsey pulled her knees up. "Like this?"

"Like this." Rebekiah moved her hand along Lindsey's thigh. Lindsey jumped, and Rebekiah smoothed her hand along the soft skin. "It's okay. I've got you." She knelt on the bed and wrapped her hands around the belt, loosening the knot. Lindsey's chest rose and fell as Rebekiah pulled the belt through the loops and let the robe hang open. She smiled and leaned back. "Perfect."

Lindsey's body leaned toward her before pulling back. Her eyes drilled into Rebekiah. She felt their pull and almost put aside her camera, but she had waited months for this opportunity, so she stepped behind the tripod and took a couple more shots.

Rebekiah moved her head back from the camera and came forward again. "Okay. Lean back." She placed a few pillows behind Lindsey's body and positioned one of her legs up against a pillow. She took the other one and spread her legs. Lindsey closed her eyes and shivered. Rebekiah leaned over her and whispered, "This turns you on."

Lindsey opened her eyes. She swallowed. "A little."

"Me, too." She pulled away and returned to her camera. "I want you to touch your breasts. Gently at first. Make them hard for me."

Lindsey's hands came up and cupped her breasts. She moved her fingers across her nipples, scissoring her index and middle finger around the hard-soft peaks.

"Good, good," Rebekiah murmured. "Now move your hand down. That's great. Oh, nice. Yeah, touch yourself." Rebekiah's smile widened when Lindsey's fingers dipped into her wetness and brought it up to her breasts. "Very nice."

Rebekiah sank into her photographer persona, surprised by how quickly Lindsey responded to her requests. She'd expected a little more resistance. Lindsey was more of an exhibitionist than she'd let on. She wondered how far she'd go.

"Now move your hands; take your nipples and pinch them." She focused on her breasts and took a few more shots. "Harder, harder, harder."

Lindsey gasped and arched off the bed.

"Excellent. You're doing just fine."

And there it was. That piece of Lindsey she'd seen under the work façade. That still passion moving just under the surface.

"Okay, let go."

Lindsey sagged back against the cushions for a moment, brushing her nipples back into her chest to ease the soreness.

Rebekiah smiled and said, "That's good; ease them into feeling okay. Make them feel loved." Like she wanted to love them. She took a few more shots and then thumbed the camera out of the tripod to move closer. "Now, do it again."

Lindsey moved her hands and pinched them again.

"Harder, yeah, that's good." Sweat dripping down her neck, she held her camera up and took a few shots without looking while she leaned in. "You're doing great." She centered Lindsey in the viewfinder and started clicking off another round of shots. "Just great." She adjusted for light, focus, and distance, getting a range of long and short shots. "Move your hand. Right there." Her hands shook with the effort to stay on task and not join her on the bed.

She stood on a stool to get some distance, but it did little to alleviate her desire. "Okay, now a little higher. Right there. Catch your nipple...yeah, you got it." Stepping off the stool, she circled the bed. She crouched next to her and Lindsey rolled toward her. Rebekiah smoothed her hand along her arm. "Shh. Stay right there." Rebekiah kept her hand on her until the tension left her body, and then she leaned over and whispered, "Are you ready?" Extreme close-up on her eyes, open mouth.

"Oh God, yes." Lindsey moaned.

"Go ahead. Touch yourself."

She moved her hand and dipped into her wetness. She moaned and closed her eyes for a moment and then snapped them back to Rebekiah's face. Her voice husky and raw, she said, "Put the camera down."

Rebekiah started to pull away. Not yet. They weren't done. Just a little more.

Lindsey grabbed her free hand and, wrapping her fingers around it, brought their hands to her inner folds. "If you want to watch, I want to see you." Rebekiah closed her eyes at the first touch. So wet and ready. She shifted position and took control, swirling their hands together up and down her labia and around her clit. Lindsey gasped and arched. "Or I put my clothes on and walk out the door."

Rebekiah lowered her camera. She wanted to shove her fingers inside. But unwilling to relinquish total control, she pulled back from Lindsey's wet grasp and knelt at the edge of the bed. She kissed Lindsey's foot. "Okay, it's just you and me here. No camera."

Lindsey smiled and stared, never breaking eye contact as her left hand slid across the dip in her hip toward the dark patch of hair. Her other hand opened her vulva to Rebekiah: pink, red, and wet.

Rebekiah eased back. "You're gorgeous." Lindsey's hands moved quickly. Her eyes snapped shut, and her hips arched into the air.

Rebekiah's hand itched for her camera even as she shot the scene with her mind. A series of pictures taken in her head. "So good, so good," she murmured, resisting the pull to move closer.

Lindsey's face twisted, her body bucked, and her hands moved faster and faster.

Giving into the urge, Rebekiah leaned down and picked up her abandoned camera. Looking through the lens, she urged, "That's it. Let it come to you."

Lindsey opened her eyes at the sound and gasped. "Rebekiah…"

"Don't stop, keep working yourself. I want to see you let go." She slid her hand along her thigh and whispered, "Come for me, Lindsey. Show me."

Lindsey's eyes opened wide, and her hips rose off the bed. Her legs splayed open, and her inner folds were exposed to Rebekiah's lens as the pull of her orgasm rolled through her. Rebekiah captured her gasp of pleasure and moment of extreme openness as she came. It was more exquisite than she imagined. And left her wanting more.

CHAPTER THIRTEEN

Lindsey's whole body went boneless. She had no idea that she'd carried so much tension until it just flowed out of her. She threw an arm over her eyes and just lay there.

"Talk to me. Tell me how you feel."

Lindsey's hands moved up her stomach and across her chest in a big stretch. "Good." She smiled. "Relaxed." She closed her legs and laughed. "Exposed."

Rebekiah laughed with her.

Lindsey pulled her hands away and saw the camera. She rolled over and crawled, her open robe flapping around her. Reaching out, she pulled the camera down and leveled a look at her. More curious than annoyed, she asked, "How much of that did you shoot?"

Rebekiah shrugged. "Just the end."

Lindsey leaned back on her heels and pulled the robe around her with one hand and held out her other. "Let me see."

Rebekiah pulled back and shook her head. "They're not ready."

Lindsey waggled her fingers. "Come on."

Rebekiah frowned and scooted closer. But she held on to the camera. The first picture appeared on the screen. Lindsey was stretched out naked with her hand across her eyes, the robe splayed out, her legs spread, her breasts falling to both sides and her stomach drooping to the left. Slightly mortified, she made a noise and tried to take the camera. "I look terrible."

Rebekiah held it out of reach and said, "No, you don't." She got up and put the camera back on the tripod. Turning, she faced her with her arms crossed. "I told you they're not ready."

"I can't let you keep those." Lindsey looked around and found the robe's tie. She'd let her libido do the thinking, something she always regretted. After alcohol, it was the second biggest cause of poor decisions in her life. She said, "They're too…"

"Raw?"

"Real."

Rebekiah dropped her arms and stepped forward. "That's the point. It's what I look for."

Lindsey paused. She stared at Rebekiah standing there so open and so sincere. A strange mix of honesty, confidence, and hurt. And everything clicked into place. This dance that they had been doing since the beginning. Every moment between them had been about trust. But if Rebekiah wanted her trust, she was going to have to give it, too.

Grinning, she pulled Rebekiah toward her. Then she spun her around and walked her backward toward the bed. Rebekiah's face switched from consternation to delight. She reached for Lindsey, but Lindsey swatted her hands away. "My turn."

Rebekiah raised her arms. Lindsey worked the buckle of her belt and slipped the leather through the loops. She held the belt to her side and let it drop. Her fingers made quick work of the button and zipper, and she yanked Rebekiah's pants down to mid-thigh. She found the hem of Rebekiah's T-shirt and tugged it up and over Rebekiah's head. It got caught in her hair before pulling free. Rebekiah wore no bra. Lindsey smoothed her hands down the slope of her breasts and gently palmed them in both hands. She wanted to pinch them into hardness, giving Rebekiah a taste of her own torture.

"Oof." Rebekiah's knees crumbled against the bed, and she landed with her legs trapped in her pants.

"Allow me." Lindsey knelt down and pulled her free, removing her underwear in the process. She dropped them to the side and looked right up into the V of Rebekiah's legs. The curls were damp. A fresh wave of arousal coursed through her, centered in her core.

"Did watching me turn you on?" Lindsey crawled up. She dipped her hand between their bodies, along the length of her vagina and around her clit. She smiled at the moisture she collected. "Hmm?"

Rebekiah jumped at her touch and clamped her hands around Lindsey's face. Lindsey pulled back before she could kiss her. Rebekiah followed, and Lindsey slipped farther back. "No touching." She was in control here, not Rebekiah. She felt her robe sag open but didn't bother to fix it.

Rebekiah's eyes stared at the gap, and Lindsey shrugged out of it. She smiled and ran her hand down her torso. "Better?"

Grinning, Rebekiah leaned forward again, and Lindsey scooted to the edge of the bed.

Rebekiah groaned and flopped back down.

Lindsey drew her fingers back through Rebekiah's wetness. "Now, I asked you a question."

Rebekiah hissed and put her hand on Lindsey's hand. Lindsey let her touch her. She moved her fingers again, and Rebekiah moaned.

"Did watching me turn you on?"

Rebekiah nodded.

Lindsey swirled her fingers through Rebekiah's vulva and up past her clit. "I didn't hear you."

"*Yes.*"

Lindsey smiled. "So responsive." Laying her fingers on top of Rebekiah's, she manipulated their joined hands up and down and along her inner folds. Taking time to sweep past her clit and then down to tease her opening. Again and again until Rebekiah started to move on her own.

Lindsey slipped her hand away and whispered, "Good. Now,

I want you to come." Any lingering feelings of vulnerability vanished as she watched Rebekiah's internal struggle play out across her face. She'd played the aggressor before, but she got the feeling that Rebekiah rarely relinquished the lead.

Rebekiah shook her head and locked eyes with her. "I can't."

Lindsey laid her hand back down. "Yes, you can." She pinched her clit.

Rebekiah gasped and arched her back. "Jesus."

"Do you like that?" Lindsey did it again to the same response. She grinned. "Yes, you do."

Rebekiah's hand moved frantically after each pinch until she finally pushed Lindsey's fingers away and took over. She came with a shuddering gasp and a long groan, her body bowing up and then slamming back down.

Her momentum pulled Lindsey toward the bed, and she tumbled into her. Rebekiah laughed and steadied her, their faces inches from each other. Rebekiah smiled and tucked a strand of Lindsey's hair behind her ear. "Hi."

Lindsey returned her smile. "Hi."

It was the closest that they'd come to each other since the kiss, and it felt almost too intimate. Rebekiah leaned in, and Lindsey met her halfway. Their mouths joined in a gentle caress that became more and more heated. Rebekiah shifted, and Lindsey moved with her. Their legs wrapped around one another, and the whole length of their bodies touched, skin on skin. Lindsey's arousal started to ramp up again.

A big bundle of dog wormed its way between their bodies and licked Rebekiah's face. "Ugh. Sera." She flopped back, wiping her face with her arm.

Moment over, Lindsey laughed and rolled over. Sera settled between them. Lindsey scratched her head, and Sera tilted into the touch. "Does she always do this?"

Rebekiah lifted her arm off her face and raised an eyebrow. "Cock-block for me?"

Lindsey smacked her. "Really?" She made a show of looking between Rebekiah's legs. "I don't think that term applies here."

"Well, what's the female equivalent?"

Lindsey laughed. "I don't know."

"Where's urban dictionary when you need it?"

"Across the room in my pants."

Rebekiah laughed and started to move Sera off the bed. She would not budge and cuddled closer to Lindsey instead.

Lindsey chuckled. "Maybe that's a sign."

Rebekiah stared at her. "Of what? Entitled pet behavior?"

Lindsey shook her head and sat up. "No. That I should be going."

She was starting to have second thoughts about sleeping with a client, regardless of who they were. And she still had a mountain of work to do before the end of the year. Now that her arousal had been taken down a few notches, reason had returned, and this seemed like the easiest way out.

"Oh." Rebekiah's face shifted, and her features went blank.

It was subtle, but Lindsey saw it. Rebekiah expected more. Lindsey hid her dismay. This was precisely the reason she avoided relationships. They always wanted more from her than she could give.

A shrill ring stopped her thoughts. Rebekiah rolled out of bed and padded across the room. She disappeared around the corner and the ringing stopped.

Lindsey stood, and Sera rolled over into her warm spot. She shook her head and leaned down to pick up the robe. She felt like a chicken for wanting to come and run.

Rebekiah appeared around the corner, naked, and all thoughts of leaving evaporated. She might avoid relationships but she still needed—no, wanted—sex. Her expression must have given her away because Rebekiah said, "See something you like?" and sauntered back to her.

Lindsey grinned. "I think so."

Rebekiah's phone rang again, and she glanced at it. "Shit, I have to take this."

Lindsey sighed and sat on the edge of the bed. Sera inched over and put her head in her lap.

❖

Rebekiah stepped away and turned toward the reception area. Collette had called her twice in five minutes. "Hey, Collette, what's up?"

"Hi." Her voice sounded tired and flat. Totally off.

Rebekiah turned around. "What's happened?"

"It's Thea."

Rebekiah walked back to bed and started to pull on her clothes. The need to get dressed to deal with whatever was happening was powerful. "Is she…" She stepped into her underwear.

"No, but she had a heart attack." Collette added, "She's in the ICU."

"What does that mean?" She pulled on her pants. Sensing Lindsey's concern, she squeezed her shoulder.

Collette sighed. "It means you should come home and see her."

Rebekiah sat down and clutched her T-shirt to her chest. "Is she going to die?" Lindsey's hand went to her knee.

"I don't think so. But she's got Alzheimer's. She's had it for a while."

She let her T-shirt drop and reached for Lindsey's hand. Lindsey squeezed it and put her other hand on top. "When? Why didn't you tell me?"

"I tried to tell you. In person. But you were too stubborn."

Rebekiah remembered the hard sell to see Thea's show in October, and a twinge of guilt ran through her. "Oh. I didn't know. For how long?"

"A few years." Collette choked back a sob. "But it's getting worse."

A few years. She felt a pang of regret for keeping Thea at a distance. Tears pooled in Rebekiah's eyes. "I'm sorry."

Collette cleared her throat. "Just come home."

"Does she really want me there?"

Collette sighed. "Of course she does. She won't say it, but she misses you."

Rebekiah glanced at Lindsey. Her face expressed empathy and support. She took a deep breath. "Let me see what I can do." Not a commitment but not a no. It was the best she could do without saying, "I'll think about it," which was not what she wanted to say.

Collette said, "Don't take too long. Love you. Talk to you soon."

Rebekiah hesitated for a half second before she said, "Love you, too," and hung up.

"Are you okay?" Lindsey touched her shoulder.

Rebekiah squeezed her hand and then stood. "Yeah. Fine."

"That didn't sound fine."

Rebekiah looked down at her with Sera curled up beside her. For a moment, she wanted to share it all with her. The hurt, the anger, the pride, the confusion, all the bullshit that was her relationship with Thea. "It's complicated." Stuffing her phone in her pocket, she snagged the shirt and shrugged into it. "You've got to go."

Lindsey stood. "Are you kicking me out?"

Rebekiah shook her head. That did not come out like she meant it. Talking about Thea always messed with her head. "No. No, you said you needed to go."

"Work can wait." She nodded toward the dressing area. "Let me put some clothes on, and then we'll talk."

She wasn't sure what kind of talk she meant, but Lindsey didn't leave her room to disagree so she waited. She glanced around the room and the clock on the wall. 9:17 p.m. No sense staying here. Somewhere else then. A neutral setting sounded like a good idea. She didn't trust herself to be alone with Lindsey because she didn't want to fuck her feelings away. Especially with Lindsey. She switched off lights and left the tripod and other equipment where they were—it could wait until the morning—and called, "I need to take Sera for a walk. Do you want some coffee?"

Lindsey swept the curtain back and said, "Sure."

Looking down at her chinos and tee and then back at Lindsey's tailored work clothes, Rebekiah smiled. "I might be underdressed."

Lindsey shook her head. "It's Providence. You're fine."

CHAPTER FOURTEEN

Snow glowed orange in the city's ambient light, and the street was relatively empty in front of her studio. Providence was home to several colleges, and its nightlife dwindled over the holidays. Lindsey walked with them while Sera sniffed along the sidewalk, finding a particular tree with minimal snow piled in front of it. "Where do you want to get coffee?"

"I was thinking the Point Street Café. It's on the way home. And dog friendly." Which really meant that the owner let Rebekiah bring her dog inside on cold nights, health codes be damned.

Rebekiah's phone dinged. She glanced at the name. Collette. *They're putting in a stent. Surgery scheduled for tomorrow.*

She texted back. *Okay.* With a sigh, she put her phone back into her pocket.

"Who's Collette?"

Rebekiah chuckled. "That's a good question." She glanced at Lindsey. "Sorry. She's Thea's 'companion.'" She used air quotes. "I don't know what Thea calls her, but they have lived together for ten years."

"And Thea?"

"My mother's 'friend.' After my father died, she moved in. She lived with us until my mother died. Took care of my mom after she got sick." Thea's relationship to her family had never been defined but always assumed. As a teenager, Rebekiah hated that ambiguity, and they fought constantly.

"Were they together?"

Rebekiah shrugged. Her mother had relationships with both men and women. Thea remained the constant. "I don't know. But Thea loved her."

"What happened?"

She answered for the present and not the past. "She had a heart attack."

"Oh, I'm sorry." Lindsey touched her hand, and Rebekiah grabbed it and squeezed. Lindsey did not let go.

She drew comfort from the touch as she spoke. Her gentleness made it safe to share, and she opened up. "She wants me to come home."

They walked down Westminster. The light brightened; most of the street was shut down, but ghost lights shone through the plate glass displays. Amid the closed stores, a restaurant or bar stood open with a few customers outside smoking. "And you don't want to?"

"Thea and I have a difficult relationship. Collette says it's because we're too much alike. I don't know about that." She shifted her hold on the leash, and Sera moved toward the middle of them. "We had a fight. A few years ago. We're not speaking right now. And it's Key West. Even if I wanted to go, there's Sera. I don't know who's around for the holidays, and I can't put her in a kennel. She hates sleeping alone."

"I'll take her," Lindsey said.

Rebekiah paused and pulled Lindsey to a stop. She had heard the excuses roll out, knowing full well that her pride was holding her back. A pride that had replaced her anger and hurt over the years. "You would?"

"Yeah. I'm back for a week and a half." She held up her hand. "Barring any catastrophes. I could take care of her for the week."

Rebekiah stared. Lindsey held her gaze. The whole night

was surreal. She finally got her to agree to pictures only to have her turn the tables and want something more. Then Collette called and opened up all her old wounds. And now she was offering to dog sit. Without understanding the baggage with Thea, Lindsey had effectively removed the last barrier and forced her into acknowledging her real reasons for avoiding the trip. She was going to have to go or risk looking like an asshole in front of Lindsey, which was more important to her than she realized.

"Rebekiah?" Lindsey squeezed her hand.

Rebekiah offered a grateful half-smile before they resumed walking. "Thanks. I'll think about it."

Point Street Café stood out among the dark windows of a boutique clothes shop and a children's toy store. Lindsey ordered a latte, Rebekiah bought a mocha, and Sera got an oatmeal bone laced with peanut butter, which she devoured.

They settled into a table near the window where Rebekiah watched the snowfall before turning back to Lindsey. "What are your plans for the holiday?"

"My mother usually holds court at the Barrington house, and we're all expected to show up."

"We?" Rebekiah realized she didn't know anything about Lindsey's personal life, and she wanted to.

"My sister and me. And the rest of the Blackwell clan."

"Sister? Older or younger?" She tried to imagine an older version of Lindsey and couldn't. She had oldest child written all over her.

"Grace. Younger. She's Coast Guard. She rarely makes it home anymore." She sipped her coffee. "What about you? If you don't go to Key West, then what?"

Rebekiah stirred her coffee. "Christmas was never a big deal for us. Thea prefers the solstice. I usually spend the day with my friend, Elena, her family. They're my chosen family." Rebekiah went into detail about Elena and her various relatives. As she described them, she thought about bringing Lindsey along and how they'd react. She'd never purposely brought a woman home to them. Through the years, they had met many of her lovers as friends because Rebekiah slept with her friends. But introducing Lindsey that way felt wrong, and if she did bring her home, she'd do it a different way.

When Rebekiah wrapped up a few minutes later, Lindsey smiled and said, "They sound…normal." Her tone conveyed her delight.

Rebekiah paused and thought about Elena's family in contrast to others, including her own. "Yeah, they are."

"You met in college?"

"Yep. Junior year. Elena was a senior at Brown. Emma picked her up at a bar, and they had this torrid affair for like, four weeks, some ridiculously short time. But she clicked with the rest of us and stayed. Emma went to New York, Europe, all over. Elena finished law school, worked for a federal judge downtown until she went into private practice."

"Were you ever together?"

Rebekiah laughed. "Elena and I? Oh, no." She didn't think a couple of threesomes counted. It was only sex, and she wasn't sure how Lindsey felt about multiple partners. It was too soon.

"How did you get into photography?"

She shrugged, unfazed by the change in topic and willing to let her ask anything. She didn't feel like hiding tonight. "I was a shitty painter. Easily bored illustrator. No patience for the final product. Cameras were always around. It was easy; I was good at it." Thea had bought her first camera.

"Just like that? No starving artist phase?" Lindsey turned her cup in her hand.

Rebekiah laughed. "Well, not starving but definitely working hard at low-paying jobs. I did commercial jobs to make ends meet before my own work took off. For a few years, most of my work showed up in corporate brochures. What about you? How'd you get into wealth management?"

Lindsey laughed. "Sort of the same way. I was good at it. My mother's social circle always had money even if we didn't. I learned to navigate that world. I've got a head for numbers and an eye for patterns. It's a combination that can make you a lot of money."

"Where'd you go to school?"

Lindsey smiled. "As far away from my mother as I could get. A liberal arts school in Portland. Reed College."

"That doesn't exactly sound like Wall Street."

Lindsey laughed. "No, it doesn't. I majored in economics and East Asian studies. After graduation, I spent a year abroad in Beijing and Hong Kong, working for a boutique investment firm translating financial documents. By the end I was doing research analysis. I loved it."

"Lindsey?" a voice interrupted.

❖

Lindsey looked over Rebekiah's shoulder and covered her dismay. Of all the nights to run into a fellow AA member, she had to be with Rebekiah. There was no way to avoid him. "Rory?" She stood up as a huge man crossed the room and wrapped her up in a bear hug. He was six-foot-four, rail thin, and sporting the biker look without a motorcycle.

He held her at arm's length and looked her up and down. "You look good." He glanced at Rebekiah and reached out his hand. "Rory Lynch."

"Rebekiah Kearns."

"I haven't seen you around in a few months." He narrowed his eyes. "You're okay?"

Lindsey nodded. "Yes." She sensed a deeper question there, but Rory didn't push it.

He nodded toward the woman behind him. "I just wanted to say hi. Don't be a stranger." He looked at Rebekiah. "Nice to meet you."

Rebekiah smiled. "You, too." Rory left, and Rebekiah turned back to Lindsey. "He's not your usual buttoned-up type, is he?"

Lindsey smiled. "No."

"AA?"

She felt an obligation to protect his privacy, so she hesitated.

Rebekiah held up her hands. "I'm sorry. I have friends in recovery. It's none of my business."

Lindsey glanced around the coffee shop. Rory was at the counter, and a few patrons were scattered around the room. She leaned in. "Not many people know about me." She thought of Li Jing, Jen, and every other alcoholic she met and added, "Almost no one."

"But isn't that part of the twelve-step process? Making amends?"

"That's not the kind of drunk I was." She shifted, not at all comfortable with this conversation. She clutched her cup and frowned at Rebekiah's skeptical look. "It would look bad for my clients to know. I make amends in my own way. I don't need to shout it from the rooftops."

Rebekiah placed her hands on top of Lindsey's. "I'm not judging."

Lindsey held her stare and tried to think of what she wanted to say. "Everyone else does."

"I'm not everyone else."

That was an understatement that she was just starting to unravel. Lindsey took a deep breath and let it out. "I got sober on accident. A colleague recognized me for who I was and called me on it. He challenged me to work the program." She shook her head, remembering the fits and starts of that first year. "I had no idea how much alcohol impacted my life until I quit. It was not easy."

"Why do it alone?"

Lindsey chuckled, bitterness rising in her throat. "Is there another way?"

Rebekiah frowned.

Lindsey waved her hand. "Sorry. It's not funny." She blew

another breath. "Vulnerable is hard for me. It's not something I like to do."

Rebekiah smiled. "Me either."

Lindsey glanced away; Rebekiah was staring at Sera. She felt relieved that she didn't have to make eye contact. It was weird how adept Rebekiah was at sensing her moods. She knew just how far to push and when to pull away. Lindsey didn't like feeling so transparent.

Rebekiah shifted.

Lindsey took the last sip of her drink and stood. "Let me take you home."

Rebekiah stood, and Sera lumbered to her feet. "I can walk. It's not that far."

"I know, but I'll feel better knowing you got home safely." Back on the street, Lindsey asked, "Are you going to go?"

Rebekiah sighed and took so long to answer that Lindsey thought she was going to ignore her question. "I think I should."

They arrived at Rebekiah's building, and Lindsey reached out. "The offer's still good. I can take her."

Rebekiah paused with her hand on the door and nodded. "Okay, I'll text you with the details."

"Great." She stood there for a minute, trying to figure out how to end the evening after the physical and emotional intimacy they'd shared. Was it a date? It felt like a date. But did it feel like a date to Rebekiah? Was she the only one who came on to Rebekiah after the pictures? Or did those other women experience similar feelings? How could they not?

Rebekiah took the lead and cut through her doubts. "Thanks." She made eye contact and added, "For everything." She leaned in and kissed her cheek.

Lindsey turned her head and captured her lips with her own. Rebekiah responded immediately, wrapping her hands around her waist and drawing her close. The kiss ignited the passion from before, and if she'd been home, she might have dragged her upstairs. Instead, she pressed her against the brick wall and kissed her with all the pent-up emotions of the night. Rebekiah matched her ferocity. When they finally pulled apart, resting their foreheads against each other, Lindsey said words she didn't want to say: "I should go."

Rebekiah leaned in and nipped her lip. "Are you sure?"

No. But instead she said, "I don't want to rush this." And as those words left her mouth, she wondered what *this* was, but it felt too new and precious to ruin by not slowing down.

Rebekiah tucked a strand of Lindsey's hair behind her ear and said, "Okay." She moved away, and Lindsey felt her loss.

"Good night."

Lindsey managed a smile. "Good night." Sera pushed through their legs, and she scratched her head. "Good night, Sera." She walked away feeling horny but happy.

CHAPTER FIFTEEN

Rebekiah booked a ten a.m. flight for Christmas Eve. Elena had been both shocked and grateful that she'd left Sera with someone else. Elena loved Sera because Rebekiah loved Sera, and Elena loved Rebekiah. Theirs was a relationship born of shared affection. They had moved beyond tolerance toward acceptance, but neither was the other's favorite. She had, however, grilled her over her choice of guardian.

"Doesn't she manage your money?" Elena's tone echoed her disbelief.

Rebekiah regretted answering the phone almost as soon as she picked it up. She should have texted from the airport. After the initial concern for her well-being and Thea's, Elena zeroed in on her dog sitter with an accuracy she'd wanted to avoid.

"Yeah, sort of." Rebekiah switched ears and stuffed a couple pairs of shorts in her suitcase. She palmed the SD chip on her nightstand and tucked it into an interior pocket of her camera bag. "Among other things."

"Other things? Like what?"

"We're friends."

"Friends with benefits?"

"Yes." Rebekiah tossed a few more shirts into the suitcase and realized what she'd said. "No." Elena always caught her off-guard. She wasn't ready to talk about Lindsey just yet.

Elena laughed on the other end of the line.

Rebekiah stared at the mismatched mix of thermal and summer wear. She needed to get off the phone and actually focus on her task before she left for the airport. "It's complicated."

"Sounds it."

Rebekiah sighed. "I'll fill you in when I get back." The doorbell rang, and she said, "I've got to go. I'll text you when I get there."

They exchanged Merry Christmases and hung up. Rebekiah opened the door and ushered Lindsey inside.

Lindsey glanced around and said, "Nice place."

Rebekiah smiled. "Thanks. Let me get her stuff. I really appreciate this." She leaned aside and handed Lindsey a gym bag stuffed with Sera's dog food and other doggie goods. Nodding toward the bag, she said, "I tucked Elena's number in there. Along with her vet." She paused, wondering why it felt so awkward. "I could pay you."

Lindsey pulled back in horror. "You'll do no such thing." Sera butted her hand. She crouched and put her hand back on Sera's neck.

Rebekiah gently ruffed Sera's fur. "Don't be rude."

Sera barked and flopped. Lindsey gave up her half-sitting position and settled on the floor. Sera turned so that she had unobstructed access to her belly.

Rebekiah glanced at her watch. She had to finish up soon, but Elena's conversation still rattled in her head. She wanted to touch base with Lindsey before she left. Lindsey's desire to slow things down had hit home for her. There was something deeper going on between them, and she wanted to talk about it. She stared at the woman lavishing love on her dog and said, "Last night...the pictures—"

Lindsey's shoulders hunched, and she didn't look up. "Please, let's not."

Rebekiah crouched. "Don't be embarrassed. I wanted to thank you."

Lindsey looked up and stared. "Really?"

"That was a gift you shared with me. Don't you see that?" She didn't know the right words to convince her.

Lindsey rolled her eyes.

With a frown, Rebekiah pulled out her phone. Unable to sleep, she'd spent half the night tinkering and touching up the picture until it was just right. "Look."

Lindsey touched the phone. "Is that how you see me?"

Rebekiah smiled and pulled it back. Of all the women she'd shot, Lindsey had been the one she thought would need the least convincing. She was so strong and confident. "Yes."

Lindsey shook her head and took a deep breath. "I'm not very good at navigating between professional and personal boundaries. I like to keep them separate."

"I don't want to." Her stomach hurt at the idea of a purely professional relationship with them.

Lindsey stilled. "What does that mean?"

She settled on the direct approach. "Do you think I signed with you for purely professional reasons? What the hell do I know about wealth management?"

Lindsey shook her head. "I'm bad at relationships."

"Then let's not call it that." The fact that she didn't do relationships the way most people did wasn't the issue. The connection with Lindsey was so much realer than any label. She reached for her, and Lindsey put a hand in her palm. "Let's talk when I get back. Okay?"

Lindsey nodded and squeezed. "Okay."

❖

Lindsey walked to work with Sera in tow. She couldn't stop thinking about that picture. She'd seen it the night before, but it was not the raw shot anymore. The light was softer, the tone richer, the contrast gentle. It was open and sensual, stark in its beauty and strong in its intimacy. Once again, Rebekiah had captured a part of her she'd never seen. But what did it mean? Rebekiah had a gift for seeing people; Lindsey was no exception.

She arrived at her building a little after ten and entered the lobby. She nodded toward the security guard at the front desk, who smiled for her and gave an even larger one to Sera. She pressed the button, and the doors opened. Just as they started to close, she heard someone shout, "Hold the elevator." She juggled the leash and pressed the open button.

"Thanks." A slightly rumpled woman ducked in carrying a coffee cup and discreetly shaking her hand free of spilled liquid. She glanced up and her eyes widened. "Ms. Blackwell."

Lindsey smiled. "We meet again." Six months ago, Vanessa had flirted with her and also asked for a job before knowing who she was. She'd studiously avoided eye contact since. "Alone at last."

Vanessa groaned. "Great." She took a deep breath. "About that. I wanted to apologize. If I'd known…"

Lindsey chuckled. "You might want to stop right there. Either answer hurts my professional or personal ego."

Vanessa's shoulders sagged. "I think I'd rather you didn't remember me."

Lindsey laughed. "It's okay, Vanessa. If I had an opening, I'd encourage you to apply."

She straightened and said, "Thank you." And that recovery—coupled with her honesty and earlier confidence—was the reason Lindsey would hire her, provided the references checked out. Lindsey valued all of those traits in her staff.

Sera nudged her leg, and Vanessa looked down. "Oh, what a gorgeous dog." She held out a hand, and Sera sniffed it before giving a tentative lick. She gently petted her. "How long have you had her?"

Lindsey shrugged. "About an hour."

Vanessa stopped petting. "Oh."

"It's okay. She's not mine. She's my..." She pursed her lips. Girlfriend? Not really, but... "Friend's. I'm dog sitting."

"Hmm." Lindsey watched a part of Vanessa wall off and knew that a door with her had closed. She felt a momentary pang of regret, and then it passed.

Vanessa's floor opened, and she stepped off. Glancing over her shoulder, she said, "It was good to see you."

Lindsey winked and smiled. "You, too." Just as the doors closed, she spoke without thinking. "Don't be a stranger."

Vanessa nodded. "Understood."

Lindsey and Sera stepped into a mostly empty office. Most of the staff took the day off, but that didn't mean the financial markets slowed or end of the year stock sell-offs and buybacks didn't happen. It just meant that there were fewer people to do it. As a result, Lindsey worked the holiday week in town and spent most of January traveling.

She wound toward her office, comparing Vanessa and Rebekiah. Vanessa was more her type: a slightly younger version of herself and focused on her career. Rebekiah was outside her norm, less business oriented and more emotionally focused. "Let's talk when I get back." Lindsey wanted to believe her, but she'd heard those words before. A few months later, they were followed by other words, accusing words, hurtful words, words that demanded more time or attention than she could give.

Sabine stood, then crouched, and Sera barked. Lindsey pulled up short, and Sera sniffed Sabine's hand before she surrendered to a head pet. "Hey, you." Sabine cocked her head and smiled. "Did you get a dog?"

Lindsey shook her head. "No, I'm just dog sitting."

Sabine laughed. "Wow, that's very..."

Lindsey wondered where Sabine was going with that. She'd worked for her for many years, and they shared a deep professional trust, but their relationship always stopped short of the truly personal details. Lindsey suspected that Sabine was queer, but other than that, she knew nothing about her.

"Domestic of you."

Laughter bubbled up, and Lindsey shook her head. "It is, isn't it?"

Sabine gave Sera one last pet and grinned. "It looks good on you."

Lindsey's face burned, and she mumbled her thanks before heading into her office. Safely buried in her work, she thought about her conversations with Vanessa and Sabine. Both women she'd held at a professional distance until today. Bringing Sera to work had broken the ice, but after that, it was her letting her guard down. Maybe mixing the personal and professional wasn't all that bad.

CHAPTER SIXTEEN

Rebekiah parked her rental car on the street and headed up the front walk to Thea's bungalow in Key West's Old Town. Thea bought the house three years after Rebekiah graduated from RISD, but the bungalow had been in Rebekiah's family for two generations before that. Her childhood was spent playing in the old shell and sand backyard. She felt strange just opening the door, but it felt even weirder knocking, so she did a little bit of both. "Hello?" She turned the knob and stepped into the tiny foyer. A light shined from the far end of the hall. Closing the door, she dropped her carry-on and walked toward the light.

She stepped into the large back living room with its open kitchen on her left and the small dining room tucked in the corner. Not much had changed since her childhood. The bones of the house were the same; only the décor was updated. Holiday decorations were scattered throughout the room with a fake but tastefully decorated tree in the far corner. The entire back wall was a mix of French doors and plate windows looking out to a covered porch and the small L-shaped pool beyond that. Thea had renovated the backyard and put in the pool, surrounding it with heavy foliage and hidden fences to make it completely private. She missed the sand and shell of her youth.

Collette stood up from the couch in the living room. "You should have called. I would have picked you up."

Rebekiah shrugged. "It's okay. I wanted the time to myself."

Collette smiled and nodded. "Of course." Meaning that, as usual, Rebekiah did something just like Thea, and Collette was the first one to notice it. "Are you staying here?"

"If you have room."

Collette smiled. "Of course. Take whichever room you want. I'm heading back to the hospital soon. But the upstairs is all yours. Are you hungry?"

Rebekiah started to tell her no but thought better of it when she had already begun moving toward the kitchen. "Sure."

"Sit down. I'll make you a sandwich." She pulled plastic bags and condiments out of the fridge. Rebekiah settled on a stool and looked out the window. The pink and red sunset was visible over the fence. Collette sighed. "I was just about to go on the back porch and watch the stars come out. Even with all the light pollution you can still see some of them. It gets so hot that sometimes I only go out at night." She unscrewed the mustard and slathered a piece of rye bread. "Did you take a cab?"

"I rented a car."

"Oh, good."

Tired of the small talk, she screwed up her courage and finally asked, "How's she doing?"

Collette took a deep breath. "I told you they put the stent in last night." Rebekiah nodded. She'd called Collette back to get an update. "If she shows progress, she should be out in a couple days."

She watched Collette's movements as they engaged in more small talk about the trip and then the weather. Rebekiah followed her hands as they traveled the path of pastrami to bread, lettuce to bread, bread to bread, and then knife to bread. Putting the finished product on a plate, she put a pickle on the side. "How's your work coming along?"

Rebekiah picked up the sandwich and took a bite. "Okay. I am putting up a show in June at the Cohen Gallery."

"Aldina's gallery?" Rebekiah nodded. "That's great. I'm glad you're showing again." She touched Rebekiah's hand.

"Me, too." Rebekiah swallowed a bite. She couldn't remember the last time she was in Collette's kitchen eating a sandwich. Just after college? She smiled. "This is really good. I didn't know I was this hungry."

"It's Thea's favorite. Pastrami on rye." She looked down for a minute and then back up.

Rebekiah put the sandwich down, her appetite gone. "How's she doing otherwise?" She couldn't bring herself to say Alzheimer.

"Better." She put her hands against the counter. "Sometimes I think she'll outlast us all and then..." She paused, taking a deep breath, and brushed the edges of her eyes. She squeezed Rebekiah's hand. "I'm glad you came."

Rebekiah squeezed back. "I know."

Collette pulled back and nodded at the plate. "Finish your sandwich."

❖

Lindsey extricated herself from the fourth conversation on the same topic with another distant relative and slipped out the sliding glass doors to the rock garden. She smelled the bay's salt water lapping against the docks forty yards away. In the summer, she'd wander those docks and dangle her feet in the water. It was too cold to do either. Her feet crunched on the thin crust of snow as she walked the gravel paths. A small bench stood in a semi-circle, looking toward the dark water but shielded from the wind. She tucked her jacket under her and sat down. Light from the house bounced off the snow and provided her with just enough illumination to see around her.

Every year she felt more and more like a stranger in her own family. She pushed that familiar feeling aside and returned to the conversation that had been on repeat since yesterday, her conversation with Rebekiah when she picked Sera up. She found it difficult to think about anything else. She had surprised herself by texting a Merry Christmas to Rebekiah sometime after brunch and was slightly disappointed not to hear back.

Another set of shoes crunched behind her. Her father stepped into view. His genes dominated her features; both her gray eyes and slight built came from him. He was smaller than her mother; people often underestimated his iron will. "Avoiding your mother?"

She looked up at him and smiled. "Are you?"

"Just getting a little fresh air." He pulled out a cigar and trimmed the end.

"I thought you'd quit."

"Don't tell your mother." He lit up and inhaled. Out of the corner of his mouth, he said, "How's work?"

"Good. You?"

He sighed and puffed his cigar. "Still traveling nine months out of the year. I'm looking forward to retirement."

Lindsey smiled. "Does Mom know?"

He cringed. "Not yet." He cut her a sideways look. "I worry that we might do each other bodily harm if we actually lived together."

"Me, too."

Her father hummed his agreement. He sat down beside her and huddled in his jacket. "Brr. It's cold."

She shrugged. It beat hanging around inside. "You get used to it." Lindsey stared at the stars for a bit, trying to pick out the Big Dipper. She'd always found her parents' relationship to be a bit of a mystery. They existed on two different ends of the emotional spectrum yet somehow made it work. "Do you ever regret getting married?"

Puffing a long line of smoke, he said, "No." He took another drag and finally said, "I regret the choices I made. In particular with you. Especially now."

"What do you mean?" Stung by his comments, Lindsey pulled back, and he reached out.

"Oh, honey, I don't regret having you. Not at all. But I chose career, and so did you. Your mother and I modeled a very specific lifestyle, and you have adopted it as your own. Your work is your life." He squeezed her hand. "But it doesn't have to be."

A little taken aback, she said, "What makes you say that?"

He sighed. "I was hospitalized last month."

"What?" Alarmed and worried, she sat up. "For what?"

"Chest pains."

"Jesus, Dad, and you're smoking." She reached for his cigar. He waved her away. "Relax. I did it to myself. I fell face-first on some ice in Oslo and forgot all about it. When I came back to the States, I had terrible chest pains. I went in, and one of the enzymes to detect heart attacks was elevated, so they kept me for observation." He rolled his eyes. "It turned out to be muscle strain. Silly really, but it got me to thinking."

"Why didn't you call me?" She tried to hide her hurt. If he noticed, he didn't say.

He took another puff. "Not much to tell. Besides, your mother was there. I got an earful about how much I worked from the kettle herself. I didn't need the pot to come along, too."

"Dad…" Did he really think that about her?

"Linds…" He arched an eyebrow, and she relented.

She smiled and nudged his shoulder. He leaned his head against hers. Her chest tightened and refused to let go. "Just remember, there's more to life than work, honey." He kissed her forehead, and the pain eased.

She said, "I know. But I like my life like this." Thinking about Rebekiah and how quickly life could change, she wondered if maybe she wanted more. She rolled her eyes at the thought. The holidays really brought out all these people celebrating ideal versions of their lives. She was not immune to their influence, but it was reality that grounded her and reality that kept her sober.

He finished his cigar while they dished about her mother's guests. They split up at the door to avoid censure for disappearing at the same time. Lindsey snuck in first and spent the rest of the evening in small talk. It was close to ten thirty by the time she left, using the excuse of watching Sera for why even her father's promise of eggs benedict in the morning could not keep her overnight. Besides, her family time maxed out at thirty-six hours; the addition of her extended family cut that time in half. She felt marginally bad leaving her father behind, but not enough to stay or neglect Sera on his behalf.

CHAPTER SEVENTEEN

Lindsey took Sera out for a quick walk and unloaded her pockets before getting ready for bed. Rebekiah's reply text from an hour ago stared up at her.

You, too. How's the family? How are you doing?

She crawled into bed and felt Sera jump up and settle next to her. She ruffled her head. Sera snuggled in tighter. Lindsey hummed and pulled her phone over and texted back, *I have achieved escape velocity. You?*

At the house.

How's Thea?

Better. Surgery went well. The stent appears to be working. Colette thinks she'll be home in a few days.

How are you doing?

Okay. Miss Sera.

Lindsey glanced over at the sleeping dog and took a quick selfie with her. *She misses you.*

Is that your bed?

Lindsey smiled, thinking about what it would be like to have Rebekiah in it. *Yes.*

Ugh. I should have brought her doggie bed.

She doesn't sleep with you? Lindsey looked down at the dog and said, "So you're not supposed to sleep with the humans. I thought you might be fibbing." She bent down and scratched her ears. "You little sneak."

Oh, hell, no. She snores.

Lindsey laughed. Sera's eye popped open. "Is that true? Do you snore?" Sera closed her eye again and sighed.

Rebekiah was texting back. *Tell me a secret.*

Lindsey smiled at the abrupt topic shift. *Why?*

Honestly? Too much introspection here. I want to hear about someone else's life.

Lindsey didn't trust her curiosity. *Someone else or mine?*

Yours.

Okay. She came up with the least personal secret she had. *I didn't vote for my mother last election.*

LOL. OMG. Are you a Republican?

Lindsey could see where she might get that, but she was quick to reply. *No. But I thought her policies at the time were not serving my interests.*

Cold. But kind of awesome.

Lindsey chuckled, oddly pleased by her approval. *Your turn.*

I hate ice cream.

Lindsey smiled. An equally fluffy detail. *Really?*

Too cold and not a big fan of dairy.

Cheese? Lindsey tried to remember if she'd seen her eat it.

Rebekiah replied with *Meh*.

How could she not like cheese? She went all in on the banter. *I don't know, that feels like a deal breaker.*

Deal breaker?

I'm not sure we can be friends, Lindsey teased.

Friends? Is that what you call us?

Lindsey paused in her reply. She couldn't tell what she was asking. With no emoticon or tone, it was hard to tell if she was teasing or seriously asking. Suddenly, the conversation felt less playful. She wished she could see her face or hear her voice. *Why? What do you call us?*

Friends...friends with benefits?

Lindsey responded with a smiley face. She wasn't sure how to react. Did Rebekiah have a lot of friends like this?

What would you call us?

Lindsey groaned. She so did not want to have this conversation over text, but now that they were, she did not want to call her either. The anonymity of not seeing her face made it feel easier. *I don't know. I've never done this before.* Rebekiah immediately started texting back, and Lindsey palmed her forehead before she added, *Mixed business with personal.*

Ah. I see. Do you want it to stop?

They'd skirted this conversation before she left, but they hadn't gotten this specific. She felt a twinge of disappointment at the thought of stopping whatever was happening between them. *No.*

Neither do I.

Lindsey smiled and cuddled her phone closer to her chest. The next statement from Rebekiah shifted the subject again. *Not looking forward to tomorrow.*

Somewhat relieved, Lindsey rolled with the subject change and typed back, *Why?*

Not sure what to expect with the medication. She's been a complete asshole the last few times we've seen each other. I'm not sure who I'll be dealing with.

At least her parents were civil, even when they were distant. She wished she could make it better for her and was surprised by that thought. She'd never really cared to fix her ex-girlfriends' problems. Perhaps because she didn't know that much about them. Their lives existed outside her own, and that was probably why.

That sucks. How long have you known her?

All my life. She lived in the same commune as my parents.

Lindsey laughed. It totally fit with Rebekiah's bohemian past and alternative artistic pursuits. *Of course?*

?

Explains your open attitude toward sex. She knew that she was taking the conversation in a different direction.

Ha...you don't know the half of it.

Oh, but she wanted to. Desire moved through her. She reached over and switched off the lights. *Then tell me.*

What do you want to know?

She turned down the brightness on her phone and snuggled into the bed. A pleasant warmth spread through her body. *What's your biggest turn-on?*

Lindsey waited while Rebekiah typed, *Submission as willing consent.* Lindsey puzzled over that one until Rebekiah added, *I like to push boundaries, that moment of submission and surrender is a total turn-on for me.*

That warmth turned wet and moved toward her core. *And how would you get that from me?*

Three dots appeared immediately, but no text came through. What was taking so long? What if all she wanted was the photos? What if she lied, and she didn't want this and was trying to find a way to let her down? Wet and wanting, she struggled to stay calm. Finally, Rebekiah's reply arrived. *I would overwhelm your senses. You're cerebral, so I'd need to ground you in the here and now. The physical. Maybe a blindfold? But you like control, and that would unnerve you. So I'd need your trust. We would talk every step of the way until you finally felt comfortable with my lead.*

Lindsey sighed and closed her eyes; her hand slid down her stomach.

Her phone dinged. She glanced at the screen, and her sister's name popped up. *Merry Christmas!*

All the arousal left her, and she pulled her hand back. *You, too.*

How are Senator Blackwell and Dad? Grace asked.

Good. I left early.

Bummer. No eggs benedict.

Lindsey laughed. *We all make sacrifices. Where are you?*

Miami. Grace sent a picture of her standing on the deck of her ship in her duty uniform.

Rebekiah texted back, *Too much?* She wrote to Rebekiah, *Sorry, sister just texted.* Then she asked her sister, *When are you back in town?*

I've got another three months.

Rebekiah's text showed up right after Grace's. *Ah. I'll let you go.*

No.

No? Grace texted back.

Shit. *Sorry, texting another person.* She texted no to Rebekiah.

Work?

Lindsey considered her response. Grace's timing could not have been worse. A half answer would only get her more questions, but a real answer would draw their conversation out. *Not exactly.*

Grace sent a big smiley face. *Not exactly. Lol.*

Lindsey typed back, *It's complicated.*

Isn't it always?

She smiled and typed *Good night, Grace.* And hoped it ended there for the night.

Love you, too.

Back, Lindsey typed to Rebekiah, but the moment was gone.

Rebekiah asked a couple questions about Grace, which ended with Lindsey sending her the picture she'd just received. *She looks like you.*

Lindsey smiled and typed, *Only younger.*

Any other pictures?

Lindsey rifled through her Dropbox. A few years ago, she had all her pictures digitized and cataloged in an effort to purge excess junk from her life. She guessed the year and scrolled through a few pictures before she found the one she was looking for. She was in her late teens sitting on a wooden boat with Suzie's legs wrapped around her, half turned in the V of her legs and smiling. They looked so young. She hit send.

Aww…

First girlfriend. Parents hated me. Staunch conservatives and very very rich. Her boat. Not mine.

What happened?

Lindsey smiled at the memory. *College. Married a man. Had kids. Lives in Greenwich, CT.*

LOL.

I know. Tragic. You? She suspected that Suzie was still trying to live up to her parents' expectations.

?

First girlfriend?

Hmm. Official or first woman I slept with?

Lindsey laughed. "Oh, Rebekiah, why am I not surprised?" *There's a difference?*

Yeah. For me at least. You?

Lindsey considered her early relationships, Suzie and Monica. *No. I slept with my first girlfriend.* She grinned. *I did sleep with my second boyfriend.*

Lol. No men for me. So, yeah, there was an older girl in high school. Alex. Sigh. She broke my heart.

Lindsey saw a young Rebekiah, all awkward and earnest, and she sent a sad face emoji.

You? First heartbreak?

Monica immediately came to mind. The longest relationship she'd ever had that spanned college, grad school, and New York City. Monica's leaving took Lindsey by surprise, although in hindsight, the last two years of their relationship had seen a steady increase in late nights, constant travel, and binge drinking. By the time she sobered up and left New York, Monica had moved on. She was her first and last heartbreak. After Monica, she settled for brief affairs abroad or longer relationships in town often involving her current lover moving in and then out citing neglect or emotional distance. Neither of which felt particularly off base to her.

The conversation lost its fun, and she typed a quick follow-up. *Sleepy. Talk tomorrow.*

Rebekiah's response was instantaneous. *Sure. Ttyl.*

Sleep came quickly but was filled with dreams of Monica and their life together. She woke up the next morning sad and lonely. She cuddled with Sera and cried before she nudged her awake to go for a run.

CHAPTER EIGHTEEN

The day after Christmas, Rebekiah woke up before dawn and left the house in search of coffee. Her conversation with Lindsey the previous night had ended abruptly and left her kind of unsettled. At five a.m., traffic was thin as she took US 1 along the water. Unwilling to head to the hospital yet, she kept driving, ending up in the parking lot of the White Street Fishing Pier.

Coming home always stirred up the past. White Street Fishing Pier was no exception. Whenever her father brought her down to visit, her grandfather would pick a day and wake her just before sunrise. Armed with poles and tackle, they'd drive down to the pier and spend the morning watching the sunrise and catching fish. After college, the place took on another meaning.

The pier was also the site of the Key West AIDS Memorial, and it was the only physical place where her mother was memorialized. She wandered down the length of black marble before stopping at the second to last set of names and finding the one she was looking for. She never knew until her late twenties that Thea had paid to put her mother's name in the stone, and it was only after another argument that she told her.

She struggled for years to understand both her parents. Anger and bitterness fluctuated with acceptance and understanding. Memories of her father were wrapped up in childhood and tinged with nostalgia. He was a distant and loving figure gone before she really knew him. But her mother had been present until adulthood. She'd encouraged and loved her, but she'd always held back a part of her life, the one she shared with Thea.

She stared at the name for a while, letting the sound of the ocean fill her ears and wondering what her mother would think of her life now. If Thea was any judge, she'd be proud of her art. She liked to think that she would've understood her commitment to Emma, but she'd never know. There were too many blank spaces in her life with unanswered questions. Finally, she turned and walked along the concrete pier amid the fisherfolk with a nod and a smile if they looked up from their lines. The salt spray covered her forearms, and the waves washed away her maudlin thoughts.

Her phone dinged, and she almost didn't pull it out, but she figured it was Collette. She saw a picture of Sera sprawled out on a puffy quilt, fast asleep. Lindsey. Any lingering feelings about her mother and Thea faded into the background.

Four-mile run and she's out like a light.

Rebekiah smiled and typed, *Four miles. So early…*

Did I wake you?

Nope. Just heading to the hospital.

Rebekiah looked for a place to sit. Finding none, she headed back to the parking lot and moved to the beach. Walking down to the edge of the tide line, she sat on the sand to watch the sunrise.

Actually, I'm avoiding it. She took a picture of the rolling waves and sent it.

Lindsey pinged back. *Nice avoidance location.*

Their conversation last night had been equal parts flirtatious and serious before Lindsey had ended it. It was hard to tell over text if she'd been sleepy or ducking the question. She didn't want to pick at an old wound, but she wanted to know more about her. She asked again. *Never told me about your first heartbreak…*

Three dots showed up on her phone, but nothing arrived. She waited and waited, then sat on the beach, tucking her phone into her pocket, hoping Lindsey had gotten sidetracked and that she hadn't pushed her too far. She cursed the fragility of texting until her phone dinged again.

Monica.

Rebekiah waited, but nothing more was forthcoming. Figuring that was all she was going to get, she filed that name away for later and started thinking about a safer topic.

We met in college. We were together for seven years.

Or maybe Lindsey would talk about it now. *Wow. What happened?*

I did. Work, booze, other women.

Rebekiah did some math in her head, and unless Lindsey was with someone right now, Monica had been the longest relationship she ever had. *Ouch. Been there, done that.*

When I was drinking, I was much less selective with my choice of partner. Sobriety made me more risk averse.

Rebekiah thought about her own early sexual history with its random hookups and short-term affairs and the precautions she'd taken in the years that followed. Taking a deep breath, she typed, *Can I ask a personal question?*

Lol...What are these then?

Rebekiah chuckled. *Getting to know you questions. Well?*

Go ahead.

Have you been tested? Rebekiah realized that her question was a little late in their relationship. They'd already touched each other intimately. But she had more plans for them, and given their collective histories, she needed to be sure going forward.

There was a pause before Lindsey texted back. *HIV? Yes. Every six months. I'm assuming this line of questions has a purpose.* Three dots were followed by a smiley face with a wink.

Rebekiah laughed, any sting the comment might have had erased by the emoticon. *What do you think?*

Lindsey replied right away. *I got tested two months ago. You?*

HIV negative. A month ago. Just after their time in New York City. *Also, no STDs.*

Lindsey reported a clean bill of health as well. *What happens next?*

Relief washed through her. Previous partners were either offended or confused when she asked these questions. After Emma died, she'd been less rigorous with her precautions, engaging in unprotected sex with a variety of women, up to and including her most recent photo subjects. Rebekiah smiled. *I come home and do those things I told you about.*

Feels like we're doing this backward.

Rebekiah stared at her text. *How so?*

Having sex first. Getting to know you second.

Rebekiah chuckled. She forgot how her approach differed from most people's. *You know me. Besides, that wasn't sex—it was foreplay.*

Lindsey sent a smiley face back. *If you say so.*

I do.

Okay.

Rebekiah couldn't get a read from her comment. *Are you really okay?*

A smiley face came back. *Absolutely.* More dots. *Hate to run, but I gotta get ready for work.*

Their conversation wrapped up after that. She felt better for having the talk. She didn't know what she'd do if Lindsey had balked at the topic of getting tested. Sitting so close to her mother's memorial made her acknowledge just how important it was to her and how little she'd cared to follow her own heart the past few years. She steeled herself for the next part of her day by taking a couple shots of the sunrise before she got back into her car and headed toward the hospital.

❖

Rebekiah stood at the edge of the room and watched Thea sleep in the early morning light. She stared at her features, so gaunt and unlike the woman who dominated her past. She'd spent alternating years admiring, despising, ignoring, and finally acknowledging the significant role Thea played in her professional and personal life. They never talked about any of it. Instead, they danced around the edges, attacking and surrendering when the other least expected it.

"Sasha, is that you?" Thea's voice rasped across the quiet room.

Rebekiah pulled away from the wall. "No, it's Rebekiah."

"You look like your mother." Her eyes scanned the room and focused. A slight shake of her head and a twist of her lips preceded her words. "You didn't have to come."

"Collette called me. She's worried about you." She took a deep breath. It wasn't easy to say this. "I'm worried about you."

Thea flapped her hand and patted the bed. "Did you see the show? Collette said you were out of town."

Rebekiah hid her irritation at Collette's white lie and sat on the edge of the bed. "Not yet."

"Pfft. Doesn't matter. It's stuff you've seen before." She touched her knee. "What are you working on?"

Rebekiah shrugged. "Not much."

"Bullshit. We're artists. We're always working on something. What is it?" She made a face. "Not that death stuff with that model."

Rebekiah stiffened. Aldina was not the only critic of her work with Emma. "No, that's done."

"Good. Good." She patted her knee. "Don't get me wrong. The intersection between life and death is worth exploring. But those shots were devoid of commentary. Look at your father's picture. Now there's a scene rife with emotions."

The image of Rebekiah's mother standing next to her father's open casket popped up, followed by the memory of that picture. Her mother had whirled on Thea and slapped the camera out of her hands. "Didn't she break your lens?"

Thea chuckled. "She did. We didn't talk for a whole year." She sighed and closed her eyes. Her hand grasped at Rebekiah's knee. "You're just like her, you know?"

Rebekiah scoffed. Her mother floated in and out of people's lives. She was always moving, never stopping. And yet people loved her. Just like Emma. Intimacy with them had vacillated between fleeting and intense. She was nothing like that.

Thea opened her eyes and clutched Rebekiah's leg. "You always take everything head-on. Sure, you made mistakes, but you never cried about it. You moved on. She did that, too."

Rebekiah absorbed this piece of information.

A slight smile touched Thea's lips. "Your grandfather hated her."

Rebekiah remembered his face at her mother's funeral, one of the only times she ever saw him cry. "He did?"

She barely nodded and yawned. "These damn drugs make me so sleepy." She slurred the last words. "You're going to be here when I wake up?"

Rebekiah smiled and held her hand. "Yeah."

Thea's eyes fluttered, and Rebekiah waited for a minute to see if she'd say anything else. She didn't, and Rebekiah watched while she fell asleep. The conversation unsettled her. Thea rarely talked about the past and even less about her mother.

Collette arrived while she was still sleeping, and Rebekiah went to get coffee. When she came back, Thea was awake and disoriented. She helped Collette calm her but suffered a few well-placed barbs during the argument. Collette didn't stop her when she left the room angry and hurt.

Over the next two days, Rebekiah helped move Thea back to the house and arrange medical services for her. But they never talked about her mother again. A particularly grueling day with Thea was followed by a quiet conversation with Thea's in-home nurse about the need for a long-term solution in the not so distant future. And another conversation with Collette that laid bare how little savings they had.

Equal parts overwhelmed and emotionally drained, her text conversations with Lindsey provided some relief. They consisted of brief check-ins and candid shots of Sera lounging in Lindsey's office or house. But after her talk with Collette, she finally called Lindsey to discuss setting up a trust for Collette and Thea.

Lindsey was all business at first. "I'll have our retirement expert pull something together for you." She paused and her tone switched. "How's it going otherwise?"

Rebekiah sighed. "We had a moment, but that's done." Thea's homecoming heralded the return to their adversarial relationship. She didn't elaborate, and Lindsey didn't push. She asked a few follow-up questions around the trust and then hung up.

Throughout the week, Collette and Thea's friends drifted in and out of the house, bringing food and company. Rebekiah caught up with childhood friends and spent New Year's Eve with her uncle and his kids, all of whom were ten years younger than her. Her last two days she puttered around the house, helping Collette as much as she could. On Rebekiah's last day, Lindsey FedExed a packet with all the details, and Rebekiah presented it to them both after dinner. As expected, she was met with stony silence from Thea and tearful gratitude from Collette. She left it at that.

She took a long walk through the neighborhood and considered texting Lindsey, but she didn't want to burden her with any more of her dysfunctional family dynamics. Lindsey had her own family for that. But even thinking about talking to Lindsey gave Rebekiah comfort, and that feeling was both welcome and surprising. She had let so few new people into her life since Emma's death. And before that, she'd had a pretty tight circle. Yet something about Lindsey drew her in.

She came back to a slightly dark house and settled into the living room with her laptop. She heard movement upstairs and assumed that Collette was getting Thea ready for bed.

"She's striking."

Rebekiah glanced up as Collette sat on the couch next to her. She was combing through photos for Lindsey's spread and stumbled on the shots she took in the Philadelphia hotel room.

Lindsey held her hand to her ear with her head slightly downcast but her eyes level with the camera. She had a slight smile on her face that conveyed both annoyance and a you-caught-me look. Rebekiah tilted her head to the side and smiled. It was quintessential Lindsey and made her slightly homesick. "Yeah, she is."

Collette nodded. "Is she the person you've been texting?"

Rebekiah smiled. "Sorry. I tried to be discreet."

Collette patted her hand. "No worries. She's got your attention." She smiled. "That's good for you."

Rebekiah sighed. "I hope so." She closed the lid and put the laptop on the coffee table. "How's she doing?"

Collette rolled her eyes and leaned back. "She's cranky but sleeping. Are you sure you don't want to stay longer?" She smiled. "Thea'd love to have you around for a few days."

Rebekiah snorted but held her tongue.

"Thank you for the trust. I know she won't say it, but she's really grateful for the help."

Rebekiah bristled. "You don't have to speak for her."

"I know. But I do anyway. She's set in her ways, and what's left of her is fading." She sighed. "You know she's proud of your work."

Rebekiah coughed.

Collette squeezed her forearm and turned toward her with a grin. "She is. She brags about you."

Rebekiah rolled her eyes. Knowing that fact only reinforced her bitterness. "No doubt as the prodigal protégé."

Collette shook her head. "No. As her child. It's hard for her to see you as who you are because she still sees you for who you were. But she loves you. She always has."

Rebekiah swallowed, not trusting herself to speak.

Collette patted her shoulder and stood. "It's never perfect. You do the best you can with what you got."

Rebekiah returned to Providence the next day.

CHAPTER NINETEEN

Lindsey turned the corner, carrying her lunch in one hand and holding Sera's leash with the other. Sera pulled up short and barked. Rebekiah sat on the marble steps of her apartment building with her hands between her knees. A warm feeling poured through Lindsey. It was happiness and relief—she'd missed her, even though they texted or spoke almost every day. "You're back."

Rebekiah glanced up and stood.

Lindsey's happiness faded at the look on Rebekiah's face. She moved as if all her energy was gone, and her expression conveyed sadness. Lindsey moved toward her. Was Thea dead? "What happened?"

Rebekiah bit her lip and shook her head as if to say "nothing."

Lindsey's heart clenched. Sera tugged on her leash and barked again. Lindsey let her go. Sera plowed right into Rebekiah, and Rebekiah dropped to her knees and buried her face in her neck.

Lindsey knelt down beside them. She could hear Rebekiah's quiet sobs. Sera squirmed, and Lindsey picked up the end of the leash. Her uneasiness faded, replaced by a protectiveness she wasn't aware she felt. "Rebekiah?" Rebekiah looked up with her arms still around her dog and tears streaming down her face. Lindsey reached out. "Oh, come here."

She put the bag on the sidewalk and pulled Rebekiah into a

hug. Sera stepped aside, still attached to Lindsey and the leash but free of her owner's suffocating grip. Rebekiah tucked her face into Lindsey's neck and continued to cry.

She felt completely out of her depth. It had been far too long since she'd comforted someone. Physical comfort wasn't something her family did. Monica had been the only one she'd done it for, often prompted.

Rebekiah pulled away and brushed the tears from her face, "I'm sorry. I didn't mean to fall apart on you like that."

"Don't be. I think you needed that." Lindsey tucked a strand of hair behind her ear.

Rebekiah sniffed and shrugged. "Maybe."

"Why don't you come inside?" She led her upstairs and sat her on the couch while she made a cup of tea. It felt very domestic and not at all what she thought their reunion would be.

"Thank you." Rebekiah wrapped her hands around the mug and breathed in the scent of Earl Grey. Sera curled at her feet. Lindsey settled next to her.

Lindsey rubbed along her shoulder. "Do you want to talk about it?"

Rebekiah shook her head and sipped her tea.

"When did you get back?"

"An hour ago." Rebekiah put her mug on the coffee table and, pulling her legs up on the couch, wrapped her arms around her knees.

Lindsey gave her some space. "Why didn't you call me?"

"My cell phone died."

Lindsey gave her a gentle smile. "Did you get any sleep on the plane?"

Rebekiah shrugged. "A little."

Lindsey stood and held out her hand. "Come on."

Rebekiah took her hand and followed her upstairs. Lindsey let go and walked toward her bed. When Rebekiah didn't follow, she turned and saw her staring at her wall. Centered above her bed hung a painting with swirls of red and black that looked reminiscent of native totem carvings. "Oh, do you like it? I picked it up in Vancouver about four years ago."

Rebekiah turned her head to the side. "It's two women."

Lindsey grinned. "Yes. I know. Isn't it great? Not many people see that right away. It usually takes the fourth or fifth time to figure it out." Lindsey saw the spark of attraction light up.

Rebekiah's lips quirked. "You have many repeat visitors to your bedroom?"

"Uh…" Lindsey blushed, slightly uncomfortable but a little relieved that she felt good enough to tease her.

But the moment passed quickly, and Rebekiah's smile faded as she moved toward the bed. Sera followed, leaping up beside her. "What are you doing up here?" She pointed at the floor. "Down." Sera glanced at Lindsey. With a slight groan, she jumped to the ground and parked her butt next to her owner. Rebekiah's eyes narrowed. "Did you sleep on the bed the entire time?"

Lindsey answered for her. "Yes?" After the second time Sera had jumped into her bed, Lindsey didn't have the heart to kick her off, and besides, she liked her warm body curled next to her.

Rebekiah looked at Lindsey. "She did, did she?"

As if sensing her owner's annoyance, Sera trotted past her and walked to Lindsey, who changed the topic. "Here." She flipped back the covers. "Lie down."

Rebekiah shook her head. "Lindsey, I can go home."

"Let me take care of you."

Rebekiah's shoulders slumped, and she exhaled, "Okay."

"Here. I'll get you some clothes." She went to her closet and heard Rebekiah kick off her shoes. She turned around and held out the items only to see Rebekiah crawl into her bed naked. A tiny gasp escaped, and she dropped her arms. "Or not."

Rebekiah gave her a sleepy smile and said, "Don't let me sleep the day away."

Ignoring the fact that she was naked and in her bed, Lindsey tucked her in.

Rebekiah snuggled down and rolled over. The blanket slid, and Lindsey tucked it back. She rested her hand along Rebekiah's back until she fell asleep. Then she pulled away and gently closed the door.

While Rebekiah slept, Lindsey worked downstairs on her couch with Sera nestled beside her. As evening approached, she ducked in and checked on her guest. Rebekiah still slept soundly. Lindsey didn't have the heart to wake her. She couldn't remember the last time she took care of someone. She had no idea what to do or how to act so she waited, hoping Rebekiah would give her a clue when she got up.

She ate dinner on the couch, watching the news before returning to her laptop. An hour after dinner, she looked up when Rebekiah padded into her living room wearing sweats and a T-shirt. "I slept the day away."

Lindsey smiled and put her laptop to the side. Sera slid off the couch. "I know. You were sleeping so soundly."

Rebekiah stroked Sera's head and then straightened. She ran a hand down her clothes. "I hope you don't mind. I found them on the dresser."

"Not at all. You look good in my clothes." She patted the cushion next to her. Sera jumped up next to her.

"Down." Rebekiah tapped Sera's ass and took her place. Lindsey raised her arm and curved it around Rebekiah's shoulders. She leaned in and sighed.

Lindsey craned her neck to the side. She didn't know where to begin. "Long week?"

She nodded.

Lindsey combed her fingers through her hair and marveled at the easy intimacy. "Do you want to talk about it?"

She groaned. "I feel like all I've done is talk all week."

Lindsey eased back. "Okay. Are you hungry?"

She shook her head.

What else did people do when they didn't want to talk? Should she just hold her? She'd already done that. Did she need more? Lindsey leaned forward and grabbed a remote. "Want to watch a movie?" Rebekiah's hand wrapped around hers, and Lindsey admitted, "I'm not sure what to do."

"Just sit here."

Lindsey nodded and leaned back again. Rebekiah lay down and put her head in her lap, her hand stretched across Lindsey's legs and cupping her waist. Lindsey inhaled.

Rebekiah rubbed her hand along her waist. "Is this okay?"

Warm tingles moved up her body along all the points Rebekiah touched. "Yes."

Rebekiah spoke so quietly that Lindsey almost missed it. "You can keep combing my hair."

Lindsey smoothed her hand across Rebekiah's forehead and back again and again. The rhythm relaxed her mind, and she drifted in that half-conscious, half-asleep state until Rebekiah's grip grew slack and her breathing evened. Trapped, Lindsey couldn't reach the remote, her phone, or her laptop. If she moved, she'd wake her, and somehow, she couldn't do that. So she sat and finally fell asleep.

CHAPTER TWENTY

Lindsey picked up the phone on the second ring. She answered, not sure which Rebekiah she'd be dealing with this morning. "Hey."

"Hi, I got your note." Her voice was raspy and low, all traces of last night's vulnerability gone.

Lindsey glanced at her phone. Almost noon. "Did you just wake up?"

A warm chuckle. "No. I've been at the studio for a couple of hours." How did she make a simple statement sound so sexy? A pause and then she said, "Thinking about you."

Her tone left no doubt as to what she was thinking about. Lindsey got up and closed her office door.

"What are you doing tonight?"

"Working," Lindsey replied without missing a beat. But now she was interested in a much different activity.

"When you're done, come over."

"It could be late." She wanted to see her but knew that her schedule was erratic. Former lovers had complained enough that she felt compelled to put it out there.

Rebekiah didn't take no for an answer, and Lindsey thanked her for that. "I'll wake up."

"Okay. I'll let you know when I'm on my way." She felt the heat rising in her face. She glanced around to make sure no one could see.

Rebekiah's voice was a low whisper. "Just show up."

Lindsey hung up and exhaled. After a week of explicit flirting on text, she'd expected their reunion to be more sexual and less emotional. Although, after Rebekiah's week, she wasn't surprised by her needs, only that it was her who Rebekiah turned to. She still wasn't sure how to deal with the complications Rebekiah represented. She liked her life and how she lived it. Still…

An email from Li Jing appeared in her inbox, and she almost breathed a sigh of relief when she realized that work would soon take her out of town for more than a week.

She got up and leaned out her door. "Hey, can you book me a flight to Hong Kong?"

Sabine looked up and nodded. "Sure. When and what time?"

Lindsey considered her options. "Next Tuesday should work. Something really late or early morning."

"No problem. I'll get back to you with some possibilities."

"Great." She paused. "Can you get the trust paperwork for the Kearns account over to Amy's desk today?"

"Sure." She scribbled a note on a Post-it and turned. "Are you still pursuing the foundation approach with her?"

"Yeah, Rebekiah and I need to reschedule the New York trip." The thought of going anywhere with Rebekiah right now filled her with anticipation.

"Did you want me to schedule that for you?"

Lindsey shook her head. "Not yet."

She cocked her head to the side. "Do you want me to take over the account for you?"

Lindsey stared, wondering how obvious her connection to Rebekiah was.

Sabine coughed and stammered. "I mean, I know that she's not your usual client…"

Lindsey smiled and shook her head. She was overworked. "I'm good. Thanks."

"There's something about her. She's got this…pull." Sabine reached out with her hands to mirror her words.

She said it in such a way that Lindsey asked, "Did you know her before?"

Sabine shrugged. "We travel in the same circles. She's hard to miss." Her smile said there was so much more to the story.

"Oh." She wanted to know what circles, but she'd have to work up to that. Instead, she tapped her hand on her door and said, "Well, I've got to get back to work."

She sat down at her desk both intrigued and confused at Sabine's revelation. She was right; Rebekiah did have a pull, and Lindsey was not immune to it. She doubted if she ever was.

CHAPTER TWENTY-ONE

Lindsey stood on the threshold of Rebekiah's apartment and took a deep breath. Her invitation left little doubt about what she wanted them to do tonight. And she wanted that as well. That was not the issue. It had more to do with the way Rebekiah wanted to have sex. What did she call it? Willing submission. The idea of surrendering to someone else's will left her excited and nervous. In some ways, she'd already done it. She had allowed Rebekiah to control her movements while she took pictures. And that had gone well. But this was taking it a step further, and she felt a little anxious. She swallowed her nerves—she'd slept with women before—and knocked.

Rebekiah opened the door and swung it wide. "Come in." She leaned in and kissed her cheek.

Somewhat surprised by the casual affection, Lindsey stepped inside and smiled. "Sorry I'm late."

Rebekiah closed the door behind her. "There's no late. I told you to come whenever." She brushed Lindsey's neck as she took her coat and asked, "Did you eat? Are you hungry?"

"No, I grabbed something earlier. How are you feeling?" She wanted to check in about last night.

"Better. Sorry, I don't usually fall apart like that."

"It's okay." She squeezed her hand. "I'm glad I was there to help."

Rebekiah squeezed back but averted her eyes and pulled away.

"I really like your place." She'd only gotten a glimpse of the entryway when she'd picked up Sera. Even more than her studio, the apartment was all Rebekiah. The open floor radiated warmth and style. Hardwood floors were burnished a bright gold, inset track lights created a soft glow, and comfortable furniture divided the space into a relaxed living room, a small but efficient galley kitchen, and at the far left, a bedroom.

"It's a little messy."

Odds and ends were scattered around the apartment; tiny stacks of papers sat on the kitchen island and coffee table. It looked lived in. Bending down to take off her boots, Lindsey looked up at her and said, "If you say so."

Rebekiah maneuvered them into the living room. Curled up on her dog bed, Sera raised her head and scrambled over. Lindsey leaned down and scratched her head.

"Can I get you anything to drink?" Rebekiah nodded toward her kitchen.

"Do you have club soda?" Lindsey and Sera moved toward the living room.

"Sure."

She missed the weight of Rebekiah's hand on her back as she wandered toward the living room. A set of three pictures hung on the wall. Shots of bridges. She paused at the middle one. "I love the Brooklyn Bridge shot from the East River. Yours?"

"Yes. All of them are mine."

"Were you on a boat for that one?"

Rebekiah walked over, weaving between her dog and the coffee table. Handing Lindsey a glass, she said, "Sort of. A friend of mine works with the NYPD, and I was out on one of the marine boats."

"Cool." Sera butted her legs.

Rebekiah frowned and pointed to her bed. "Go lie down."

Sera glanced up at Lindsey, and she shrugged. "I'm sorry, girl." Sera moved away, and Lindsey focused on several black books and photo boxes in a corner cabinet. Nodding, she asked, "Is that your portfolio?"

Rebekiah nodded and sat down on her couch. "More or less."

Lindsey glanced at her. "Do you mind?"

Rebekiah gestured with a go-ahead motion.

She pulled a book at random and joined Rebekiah on the couch. Taking a quick sip, she set her glass on the coffee table. Then adjusting the book on her lap, she slowly flipped through a series of black-and-white BDSM photos. "These are good."

Rebekiah moved closer and ran her hand along the photo. "I've been blessed with good moments."

"Good moments?" Rebekiah's face was much closer than she thought. She could just lean in and—

"Photography is really just having the camera ready for the right moment."

Lindsey's mind came back to the conversation. "And what's the right moment for these?" She swept her hand across the open book.

Rebekiah smiled. "I wanted to capture moments of humanity. People use sex to explore. The BDSM community is no different. They take pain and transform it into pleasure. It's a concept that mainstream society just can't wrap their minds around. They see the whips, the chains, and the leather and think pornography."

Lindsey looked at the pictures and understood. The pictures were done in a pinup style, but the people were not objectified.

Rebekiah tapped one of the pictures. "This woman is the CFO of a multibillion-dollar insurance company in Hartford. She spends her life being on top, and at the end of the day, she can no longer step out of that persona. She doesn't need therapy; she just needs to reconnect with herself. Her dom helps her do that."

Lindsey stared. It was not the first time Rebekiah had talked to her about domination and submission. Lindsey's other lovers enjoyed power play, but none of them spoke so directly about it. Lindsey touched Rebekiah's jaw. "What about your needs?"

Rebekiah kissed her palm. "I get what I need."

Lindsey closed the book. Rebekiah put it on the floor with a slight thud. Lindsey held her face and kissed her, openmouthed and hungry. Rebekiah returned the ferocity of the kiss while their hands roamed over and under their clothes. Lindsey hissed as Rebekiah's hands brushed against her breasts. Rebekiah moaned into the kiss.

Coming back to her ear, Rebekiah whispered, "I should have fucked you that night."

Lindsey sucked in a breath. She wasn't sure which night, but she didn't care. With just a few touches, Rebekiah had brought her arousal to the forefront of her thoughts.

Rebekiah made quick work of her shirt and bra. She kissed her bare breasts. Lindsey's breath hitched at the first touch of tongue on her nipples.

"Do you like that?" Rebekiah breathed into her ear, planting kisses along her jawline.

Lindsey nodded.

Rebekiah tweaked one of her nipples and said, "I asked you a question. Do you like that?" She squeezed again. Lindsey arched into her hands as Rebekiah worked her breasts and nipples.

"Yes." Her voice broke.

Rebekiah kneaded her nipples, bringing them up to points and squeezing them. Again and again, alternating between each nipple, each breast. Lindsey's breaths deepened, and her gasps came quicker with each pinch.

Finally, Rebekiah twisted both nipples at the same time and nipped at her neck. "I want to push you into places you never thought you'd go."

Lindsey groaned, and Rebekiah squeezed them again. She gasped, and Rebekiah whispered, "Do you want me to do that for you?"

Lindsey moaned. "Yes."

Rebekiah let go again and smoothed them back down. "Then I'm going to need a safe word for you."

Lindsey opened her eyes, the mood temporarily dampened. She was familiar with the term and its usage but confused by why she needed it. "Safe word?"

Pulling away, Rebekiah looked her in the eyes and said, "Do you know what I mean? It's important that you know you can stop this at any time."

Lindsey nodded; curiosity coupled with desire ran through her as she tried to imagine what Rebekiah had planned that might need stopping. "How about 'stop'?"

She frowned. "Something you're less likely to say in the heat of the moment. Like 'red' or 'apple'?"

Lindsey laughed. "iPhone."

She grinned. "Exactly. So, 'iPhone' when it's too much and you need to stop. We should have one for 'you're getting close to my boundaries, but keep going.'"

"Laptop."

"Great."

Lindsey pulled her in. "What about you? Do you have safe words?"

Rebekiah leaned in and whispered, "We'll use yours." She caught her mouth in a searing kiss, and Lindsey's arousal returned full force.

"Stay here."

Lindsey groaned and opened her eyes to see Rebekiah getting up. Her body ached to be touched. She shifted on the couch, aware of how wet her underwear was. The constant push pull of pain and pleasure had her soaked. Loosening her belt, she slid her hand down her pants. Her eyes closed as her finger brushed past her clit.

"Tsk, tsk. Starting without me."

Lindsey opened her eyes and smiled up at her. "You were taking too long."

Rebekiah grinned and said, "Well, I wanted to bring toys." She held up a silver chain that looked a lot like nipple clamps and a blindfold.

Lindsey smiled and increased the motion between her legs. "Then by all means, come back."

Rebekiah put her toys down and knelt in front of Lindsey. "Let's get rid of these." She tugged on her pants. Lindsey pulled her hand out, and Rebekiah pushed it back. "Oh, don't stop."

Lindsey kept circling her clit while she let Rebekiah remove her pants and underwear. "What about you?"

Rebekiah spread her legs. "Let's worry about you first."

Lindsey didn't argue and asked, "Is this how you want me?"

"Almost." She reached behind her and brought back the silver clamps. "Here. Hold out your hands." Rebekiah passed her the clamps. She smiled and chuckled. "Used these before?" she asked as she moved her hands up Lindsey's body and began to twist and pinch her nipples like before but with more pressure.

Lindsey gasped and nodded. "Once or twice."

"Good, put them on." Rebekiah twisted hard on one and then the other. "I'll help."

Lindsey moaned as Rebekiah ran her tongue around her breasts again and again, ending each time with a sharp pull and tiny bite at the tip. Lindsey struggled with the chain and the clips, trying to attach them while Rebekiah sucked her breasts. She managed to get one on and then it slid off before she could tighten it.

Rebekiah held it in place. The first one sent bolts of sensation—neither pain nor pleasure—throughout her body, and she gasped. Rebekiah eased in front of her and held her face. "It's okay. I've got you."

Still panting, Lindsey locked eyes with her, and the feeling faded. She was ready for the next one and rode the sensation with a breathy moan. She opened her eyes and saw Rebekiah smiling up at her.

"You look beautiful." She gathered the chain and tugged. Lindsey groaned and writhed at the contact. Rebekiah adjusted the tightness. Then she leaned in and purred, "How's that feel?"

Lindsey groaned. She curled in to lessen the tension, but Rebekiah tapped her chin and smiled. "None of that. You're supposed to feel it."

Lindsey wanted to please her. Taking a slow breath, she embraced the pain while it flowed. Pinpoints of pleasure mixed with pricks of pain. Her entire body lit up with its intensity.

Rebekiah settled between her open legs. "Such a gorgeous body. So strong and soft. I bet you have women hitting on you all the time."

She shrugged, and the chain pulled tight. Amid a fresh wave of pleasure pain, she struggled to concentrate. "Yes."

Rebekiah put her finger to her lips. "Shh…but you're too busy, aren't you?"

She relaxed at her touch and nodded, entranced by her voice and the words she was saying.

"Close your eyes."

She took a deep breath and closed her eyes. A soft cloth covered her head, and she opened her eyes to the blindfold's darkness. Stripped of her sight, all she could do was concentrate on Rebekiah's voice and her touch.

Fingers traced along her stomach. "You never slow down, do you?"

Lindsey shook her head, more aware of the pull on her breasts and the touches on her body.

"That's why you run. That's why you travel. You don't ever have to slow down. Nothing to ground you."

With the blindfold on, what was an electric hum along her nerves burst into a kaleidoscope of sensation. Rebekiah's words touched at a core truth. She did run. She did hide. Blinded and forced to look at the truth, she stopped fighting and let go.

Fingers moved along the inside of her thigh. Her breath caught and ended in a moan.

"I'm going to ground you, Lindsey. I'm going to pin you in this moment, in this space, and you're going to feel every minute of it knowing that you've stopped and that you're actually here and present. Are you ready to do that?"

She managed a breathless "Yes." Rebekiah was right; she'd never been more present in a moment of her life than now.

Rebekiah took one of her hands and moved it back between her legs. "I want you to keep touching yourself."

Lindsey moved her fingers. She was so wet. She felt the air shift, and Rebekiah's tongue ran over her fingers and into her wetness. Her tongue teased along her inner folds and rubbed up against her clit and then back again, running up and over her fingers. Her breath came quicker and quicker and hitched for a moment as Rebekiah's tongue pressed inside her. She lost herself to the sensations of Rebekiah's mouth until far too soon she pulled away, and Lindsey blindly reached for her. "Don't stop."

Rebekiah's hand smoothed along her thigh. "I'm still here. Keep touching yourself."

Her face grew hot. Not seeing Rebekiah made the act of masturbating much more intimate than before.

The cushion shifted, and Rebekiah whispered, "How close are you to coming?"

Lindsey groaned. "Pretty close."

"Then I want you to come."

She doubled her efforts, settling right on her clit and flicking it repeatedly.

"Let go. You look so ready. Your lips are so red and full. Everything's so wet, and I can hear you every time you move your fingers. Come for me." Rebekiah's words talked her toward her climax, and she felt it wash over her, coming in fast and then ending languid.

Before she could recover, Rebekiah's fingers slipped inside her. Her body arched, and she moaned. "Oh…" The fingers shifted, and a deliciously full feeling rolled over her. Her hand slipped against her clit, and she howled her second climax.

Fingers opened first one and then the other clamp. She yelled as the blood shot straight to her nipples. She grabbed them, hoping to relieve the pressure. And then Rebekiah's tongue dove into her center, licking and lapping all around her clit. She licked her again and again as she felt her third orgasm coming.

"Can you feel me?" Rebekiah's words spoken against her body.

"I can feel you."

The licking stopped, and she felt more fingers poised at her entrance.

"What can you feel?"

Fingers pushed inside, and she bucked against them.

"Tell me."

The blindfold made her feel desperate for visual connection, so she pulled it off. Blinking against the sudden brightness, she stared down at Rebekiah. "I feel you everywhere."

Rebekiah's hair was plastered to her face, and she grinned. "Where? Tell me where."

The fingers twisted inside Lindsey, bringing another wave of wetness.

She closed her eyes and gasped. "In my cunt."

Without losing a beat, Rebekiah reached up and pinched her left nipple. "And where else?"

Her eyes snapped open again, and she covered her breasts with her arms. "In my breasts. My fucking nipples."

"That's right. I'm right there in all those places and so are you. Now come." Rebekiah's fingers kept moving, a relentless push pull inside her. Her tongue lapped faster and faster. And her nipples—fuck, that was not fading. Her whole body stiffened for one long moment, held at the edge of her orgasm before she crashed.

She slumped against the couch and lay there for a minute while the aftershocks ran through her. It was the second time Rebekiah had reached past her walls and pulled her out. It was unnerving, comforting, and arousing. She opened her eyes. Rebekiah knelt at her feet with a satisfied smile on her face.

Bleary and sex drunk, Lindsey reached out. She needed her closer, much closer. "Come here." Rebekiah crawled up her body and kissed her. She cradled her face and deepened the kiss. They crashed sideways on to the couch and broke apart. She felt both light and heavy.

She touched the rough fabric of Rebekiah's clothes and asked, "Why are you still dressed?" Her words came out sleepy and slurred.

Rebekiah chuckled. "Don't know." Her hand rubbed down her back. She drew circles with her palm, and Lindsey sagged into her. "Shh...it's okay to go to sleep."

She shook her head and tried to muster energy to wake up. Somewhere in her lassitude, she felt a need to reciprocate, but her body resisted. "Don't wanna. Y'r turn."

"Shh." Rebekiah brushed another kiss at her temple and whispered, "Let it go...shh." She continued rubbing circles down her back and whispering nonsensical words until she fell asleep.

CHAPTER TWENTY-TWO

L indsey opened her eyes and smiled at Rebekiah. "Hi."
Rebekiah cupped her cheek and smiled back. "Good morning."

She raised her head slightly from Rebekiah's chest and took in the slight gray tint to the room. "I guess it is. I fell asleep on you, didn't I?" She had a vague memory of moving into the bedroom.

Rebekiah kissed her forehead. "I wore you out."

Lindsey groaned. "Yes, you did." She had coaxed orgasm after orgasm from her that left her completely relaxed and content. She just wanted to lie there and soak it all in. But her work brain stirred, and she sighed. "What time is it anyway?"

Rebekiah glanced at her alarm clock. "Five fifty." She brushed back her hair. "What time do you work today?"

Lindsey hid even farther in her chest. "Ugh…I don't know. Depends on my appointments." She popped her head up. "You didn't hear an alarm go off, did you?"

Rebekiah shook her head. "No. Should I have?"

Lindsey leaned back down, grabbed her hand, and turned so that Rebekiah spooned her. "No. If you did, then I'd be worried I missed a call or something." She squeezed the hand wrapped around her belly and snuggled closer. "Thank you."

Rebekiah leaned her head against Lindsey's shoulder. "For what?"

Lindsey poked her hand. "For last night. For knowing what to do." She brought the hand to her lips and kissed it. She felt grateful, and it made her affectionate.

Rebekiah kissed the edge of her ear. "You're welcome."

Lindsey leaned back into her kiss and just basked until a buzzing ringing sound invaded their quiet space. So much for no work. "That's my phone." She rolled away.

❖

Rebekiah groaned as Lindsey slipped off the bed and headed toward the living room. From the bottom of the bed, Sera gave a short, sharp bark. Rebekiah raised her head and looked down. Sera barked again. "What?"

Rebekiah yawned and stretched. Several vertebrae popped into place as she did so. She got up and took a shower.

Lindsey's responsiveness last night had surprised her, and her willingness to submit excited her. She wasn't sure if Lindsey would agree to her terms and had been ready to back down, but she'd consented. Now Rebekiah's mind started to play at other boundaries they could explore together.

"Can I buy you breakfast?" Lindsey called from the bedroom.

"Sure. Let me get dressed." She got out of the shower and walked to her dresser without looking up.

A hand ran down her back, and she straightened. Her desire returned full force as Lindsey wrapped her arms around her and nipped her ear. "Not yet. It's still my turn." Before she could react, she kissed her with an intensity that stunned her mind into silence. Her hands, her lips, her tongue, Lindsey was everywhere at once, and she struggled to follow her lead. Then Lindsey's hand pinned her against the wall, and she froze.

"Stay." It was not a request. Rebekiah swallowed her resistance and relaxed against the wall. She could do this.

Lindsey grinned as she slid down her body. She nipped and sucked, kissing her way down. Rebekiah gasped at the first swipe of Lindsey's tongue against her clit. She groaned at the sight of her on her knees, remembering the clone at the Christmas party.

Wrapping her hands in Lindsey's hair, she pushed her center toward her, and Lindsey pushed her back. Rebekiah tried a couple times but finally relented when it became clear that Lindsey set the pace, not her. Frustrated and turned on, she let her take control. After that, her orgasm came quick and fast. But Lindsey did not let up. Rebekiah twisted in her grip, fighting against the second wave that overtook her. When Lindsey pulled back—her wetness on her face—Rebekiah crumpled to the floor.

Lindsey caught her and held her. "I've got you." Unable to think, Rebekiah sagged in her arms. She could feel the sweat rolling down her face and into her lips. Lindsey peppered kisses around her face and said, "I'm sorry. I didn't mean to hurt you."

Rebekiah looked up, confused. "Hurt me?"

Lindsey wiped Rebekiah's face, and what she thought was sweat were actually tears. She pulled back and swiped at her cheeks. This was the second time she'd cried with her. "Damn it."

Lindsey loosened her grip and leaned back.

Rebekiah sighed. "You didn't hurt me." She exhaled and struggled for words. "I just…It's hard for me…" She rarely allowed women to top her like that. She liked to dominate, not be dominated. It wasn't the act itself—she had no problem orgasming with women—but the switch in power dynamics threw her for a loop. She should have stopped it, but she didn't, and that unsettled her.

Lindsey put two fingers on her lips and nodded. "It's okay. I wanted to reciprocate. I should have asked." She wiped her mouth against her shirt and leaned against the wall.

Rebekiah felt Lindsey's eyes on her but refused to make contact. Instead, she mirrored her position against the wall, their shoulders just touching and their breathing the only sound in the room.

Maybe this was a bad idea. Something about Lindsey had

been different from the start, and now she had physical proof. She felt exposed in ways that hadn't happened since childhood, and the urge to run and hide overwhelmed her. She could do this. It was scary but not unwelcome. Besides, it felt too good to push away.

Lindsey's hand wrapped around her fingers, and her voice soothed her. "I get it."

"Do you?"

"You like to give, not receive." She squeezed her hand. "I'm okay with that." She grinned. "Who doesn't like to be a pillow princess?"

Rebekiah laughed. "Pillow princess?" She rolled her head along the wall and gave Lindsey a look. "That's not what I had in mind."

She trailed her fingers down Rebekiah's arm. "Then perhaps you should show me."

Rebekiah answered her grin with a growl and lunged toward her.

CHAPTER TWENTY-THREE

While Lindsey showered, Rebekiah took Sera for a quick walk. Back at the apartment, Lindsey emerged from the bedroom wearing a borrowed button-down and yesterday's dress pants.

Rebekiah stood and smiled. "I like the look."

Lindsey waved a hand. "Well, nothing says 'I just got laid' better than wearing the same outfit the next day. The shirt's always a giveaway. But I can make this work today."

Rebekiah laughed and helped her into her coat. They walked to an upscale diner off Snow. The January wind stripped the warmth away from their bodies, and they walked to their destination without a word. Unbundling and stomping snow from their boots, they stepped inside a faux 1950s interior done up in dark red vinyl and chrome. A young hipster waiter called from another table, "Just pick a spot, and I'll get you some menus."

The waiter came with coffee, and after they ordered, Lindsey reached for the creamer. She hissed as her hand brushed past her bra.

Rebekiah feigned a wince. "A little sore?"

Lindsey ripped the top off the creamer and poured it into her cup. "Just a little."

Rebekiah leaned in and whispered, "I might have been a little aggressive."

Lindsey leaned in and whispered, "I don't mind." She draped

a napkin across her lap. "So do you bring all of your conquests to breakfast?"

Rebekiah choked on her coffee. "Conquests? You invited me."

"True. But you didn't answer my question."

"Well, first of all, I don't consider them conquests." Rebekiah thought about her previous lovers. The majority of her sexual partners had been friends and occasional lovers.

"So there have been a few?"

"Not that many to qualify as conquests. I tend to sleep with my friends."

Lindsey's expression was hard to read.

"Here we go, ladies." They pulled apart, and the waiter deposited their breakfast on the table before asking, "Anything else?"

Rebekiah shook her head and Lindsey said, "All set."

They ate quietly, stealing glances between bites but not really saying much. Something unsaid hung between them. Rebekiah finally put her fork down and said, "Not all of my friends."

Lindsey stopped eating as well. "It's none of my business."

Shaking her head, she said, "But it is. If we're going to keep doing this," she gestured between them, "then you have a right to know."

"Are we?" Lindsey fixed her with a look.

Her heart sank. "Oh, this was a one-time deal."

Lindsey reached for her hands. "No. No. I'm just trying to get my bearings."

Rebekiah exhaled. Sometimes she could see through Lindsey's armor, and other times, she got nothing. She squeezed. "You don't give much away, do you?"

Lindsey gave her a sheepish grin. "Sorry. Habit."

"Well, this just brings back all sorts of memories." Rebekiah looked up as Elena neared their table. Rebekiah frowned, and Elena just smiled as if daring her to state the obvious. She was having breakfast with someone she'd slept with the night before.

Rebekiah shifted and stood when Elena reached their table. "Well, this is a surprise." They hugged, and Elena stepped back. "You remember Elena?"

Lindsey half stood and shook her hand. "Of course."

Elena's eyebrow raised. "It's awfully early for a business breakfast."

"Elena." Rebekiah's voice held a note of warning.

Lindsey resumed her seat and gave a half-smile. "Yes. Well…"

Elena waved Rebekiah off. "Relax. Rebekiah's told me about you."

"She did?"

"*Elena.*" Elena just couldn't resist teasing, but Rebekiah was not about to let it spill over toward Lindsey.

"Mind if I join you?" Elena nodded at the empty space.

Rebekiah glared. The last thing she wanted was Elena giving Lindsey the third degree.

Elena rolled her eyes. "Fine. I'll behave."

Rebekiah slid her plate across the table and settled next to Lindsey while Elena sat across from them. She exchanged a look with Elena, who just shrugged, called the waiter over, and ordered coffee and an egg white omelet.

She thanked the waiter as he set a cup in front of her. She picked up a sugar packet and smacked it against her hands a couple of times before ripping it and pouring it into her cup. Nodding toward Rebekiah and Lindsey's plates, she said, "Eat. Before it gets cold."

"What are you doing up so early? Do you have court today?" Rebekiah shoveled egg into her mouth. Elena was not an early riser.

"Yes." She closed her eyes at the first taste of coffee.

Lindsey sipped her own and asked, "What kind of law do you practice?"

"Criminal defense, and before you ask, yes, some of them are guilty."

Rebekiah rolled her eyes. She'd heard that one before.

Elena's breakfast arrived quickly. She cut into her omelet and asked, "How's your show coming?"

"Almost done. I've got mounting and framing on the last set." She slipped her hand under the table and rested it on Lindsey's knee. She didn't want her to feel disconnected.

"It's next month, right?"

"Yeah. Aldina's gallery. Which reminds me…" She took out her phone and typed a few keys. "I need to send you the link for those pictures." She almost dropped her phone when Lindsey's hand slid past her knee and up her inner thigh.

"The holiday ones?" Elena smiled. "I'm curious to see how they turned out."

Rebekiah shot a quick look toward Lindsey, who continued eating without looking up. "I think you'll be pleased. Let me know which one you want, and I'll get it framed for you."

"No. I can get it done."

Rebekiah shook her head. Lindsey's fingers started a swirling pattern on her leg. "No. I'll do it." Elena opened her mouth, but Rebekiah cut her off. "It's a present."

Elena acquiesced with a curt "Fine." She turned toward Lindsey. "How goes the wealth management business?"

Lindsey moved her fingers upward, the tips just brushing along Rebekiah's inseam. She swallowed her last bite and replied, "It's good."

Elena nodded at Rebekiah. "Have you convinced her to keep the money yet? She's earned it." Rebekiah started to protest, but Elena held up a hand.

Rebekiah glanced at Lindsey, who looked as if nothing was going on while her fingers brushed along Rebekiah's core. She wanted to be anywhere but here for this conversation. "Elena, stop. We're having breakfast." She squeezed her legs closed, trapping Lindsey's hand.

Lindsey escaped and glanced at Rebekiah's watch. "Actually, speaking of work, I should get going."

Rebekiah felt her loss and wanting nothing more than to head back to her apartment for another round. "What about…" She trailed off, not wanting to ask about the clothes in her apartment. Elena's arrival had tanked their breakfast. Lindsey's work mask was back in place. Rebekiah wanted more time alone to get a sense of what she was thinking and feeling.

Lindsey pulled a card from her wallet. "I'm all set." She waved the waiter over and handed him the card. "All of them." Elena started to protest, but Lindsey shook her off. "Think of it as a courtesy breakfast for sending me new clients."

When the waiter came with the check, Lindsey signed it with a flourish and stood.

Rebekiah stood but stalled at a hug or a kiss. It was all so new, and they hadn't worked out the public aspect yet. Lindsey reached out, and Rebekiah took her hand. Lindsey's lips quirked in a half-smile, and her finger traced the inside of Rebekiah's wrist before pulling away. "We should get that trip to New York on the books this week."

Rebekiah nodded. "Yeah. Send me the details, and I'll see if I can make it work." She sat down and stared after her. Lindsey waved through the window heading downtown. She should have kissed her good-bye or at least hugged her. Having Elena show up had totally thrown her off her game. Elena was family, and Lindsey was…she didn't have a name for it yet. Not friend, not fuck buddy, a little of both and something more.

Elena tugged on her sleeve. "I'm still here."

Rebekiah frowned. "Yes, you are. Did you need to bring up Emma?"

Elena rolled her eyes and laughed. "She should know what she's getting into. Emma really fucked you up. That last year was hard. And not fair to you."

Rebekiah threw up her hands. "I'm not dating her."

"Really?" Elena cradled her coffee cup and leveled a look at her. "She was totally feeling you up under the table."

Rebekiah sagged under her gaze. Elena always saw through

her bullshit. It made her a good lawyer and an irritating friend. "Okay, we're something."

Elena sipped her coffee and waited.

"She was so hard to read. But I'd got these glimpses, and I wanted more."

Elena smiled. "Sounds like you got it."

Rebekiah grinned thinking about last night.

Elena laughed.

"What?"

"When you talk about her, you look happy. It's been a while."

"I do?" Rebekiah glanced at her empty plate and then back up. Elena didn't say it, but she knew what she meant. Before Emma. Before her death. Before her money. Before Lindsey showed up and challenged her thinking by making her feel things she thought were lost.

Elena scooped up the rest of her egg whites and said, "Yes. So tell me about her."

Years of friendship made her capitulation a foregone conclusion. Elena was in cross-examination mode, and she'd get to the truth eventually, so Rebekiah gave her the broad strokes first. The meetings, the texts...

"You went to Philly together?"

"Not together." Then taking care of Lindsey in New York.

"I bet that felt familiar."

"Not exactly. I get the feeling that no one takes care of her." She frowned. "It was kind of sad." And painful to see that she was so emotionally isolated that it never occurred to her to ask someone for help.

"Hmm." Elena's lips puckered.

"What?"

"You like to rescue women."

Rebekiah moved her head side to side. A couple of women came to mind. "Yeah, I do. But it's not like that." She told her about the pictures and then Key West—the parts with Lindsey; Elena had already heard about Thea and Collette.

Elena pushed her plate to the side when Rebekiah paused. "Tell me."

Rebekiah ran her fingers through her hair and rested her palms against her temples. "I broke down. It was too much." She could count on one hand the times that she'd cried in front of Elena. She had struggled to identify it at the time, but with Elena sitting across from her, she recognized it for what it was; she'd felt safe. Not so much physically but emotionally safe. Even with Elena or Collette, she felt like she needed a degree of protection, not because they'd deliberately hurt her; she just didn't feel safe with people. But with Lindsey, Rebekiah knew she could let down all her defenses, and it would be okay. Something about Lindsey made Rebekiah trust her.

"Ugh. I hate this shit."

Elena burst out laughing.

Rebekiah lifted her head and glared. "It's not funny."

"It is. You call me emotionally stunted."

Rebekiah frowned. "I do not."

Elena looked at her.

She relented and moaned. "Okay, I'm sorry. What am I going to do?"

Elena rolled her eyes. "What do you want to do?"

"I don't know." She leaned in. "Can't we just be fuck buddies?"

"I think you're way beyond that."

"Why do I talk to you?"

"Because I'll tell you the truth."

"Well, that's overrated." She glanced at the clock on the wall. "I've got to go to work." She stood and slipped into her jacket. "Dinner next week?"

Elena grabbed her coat and stood as well. "Yes, but bring Lindsey."

Rebekiah paused. Was she ready for that? Did Lindsey want that? Rebekiah shoved those thoughts aside and opened the door.

She ignored Elena's request and asked, "What's going on with your sex life?"

Elena smiled and breezed past. "Oh, it's not nearly as complicated as your tête-à-têtes. We meet, we fuck. She's usually a hot submissive."

Rebekiah laughed as she let the door close. For one moment, she wished her relationship with Lindsey was that simple, but what she had with her now was so much better.

CHAPTER TWENTY-FOUR

*I*have your shirt.

Halfway through her three-hour conference call, Lindsey glanced at her messages and smiled at Rebekiah's text. She replied, *I'm sorry. Who am I speaking to?*

LOL. Nice.

It had been only two days since she'd spent the night at Rebekiah's apartment, and she couldn't stop thinking about her. But thoughts of Rebekiah had always been at the edge of her consciousness for months, and now she was front and center.

Lindsey chuckled and typed back, *Is this your way of getting me to come over?*

You betcha. I want to do unspeakable things to you. Again. And again.

Lindsey smiled. *Like what?*

Come over, and I'll show you.

Lindsey shifted in her seat. *Too bad I'm in Hong Kong.*

I could always walk you through it.

Lindsey's body warmed. *Intriguing. I'm trapped on a conference call.*

So?

Lindsey laughed. *So it's hard to concentrate on the subject if you're sexting me.*

Rebekiah sent her a smiley smirking emoji before she said, *Ttyl.*

PROVIDENCE

Over the next few weeks, their texting continued with the playful banter interspersed with random topics and more personal details. They discovered a shared love of history. Rebekiah liked to read biographies; Lindsey liked to read social histories. As the conversation grew more substantial, the texting moved to phone calls that spanned the international dateline. Lindsey talked about college and the early years of her career while Rebekiah talked about Emma and her first shows. They spoke during the off times of their days. Sometimes Lindsey would call at six a.m. her time to talk to Rebekiah at four thirty p.m. her time or vice versa.

In Vancouver, their conversations switched to video. Although their previous texting often veered into sexual innuendo, it wasn't until the video talks that it morphed into masturbation. In the afterglow, Lindsey traced her finger along the edge of her phone and said, "Come to Vancouver." Inside, she cringed. What was she doing? She never brought her lovers on business trips.

Rebekiah brushed sweat off her face. "Really?"

Unable to rescind the offer without looking foolish, she tried another tack. "If you don't have the time—"

"I can be there tomorrow."

Lindsey swallowed her fear and smiled. "Great." She yawned. "I should…"

Rebekiah smiled. "Me, too. I'll send you the details."

Lindsey ended the call and stared up at the hotel ceiling. Why did she ask her to come? Was she so lonely and horny that she needed to have an international booty call? The sex was great—fantastic—but she was drawn to Rebekiah for other reasons. Reasons that had a name she didn't want to consider just yet. Rebekiah was right. She did overthink everything. She laughed at both the acknowledgment and the irony that Rebekiah was the reason she was overthinking in the first place.

Rebekiah texted her the next morning with an evening arrival time. *Where should I meet you?*

I'll pick you up.

Lindsey spent the day in a series of meetings ending at a

• 185 •

coffee date with Adam. He handed her a drink and sat opposite her. "You should come to dinner tonight. Carrie would love to see you."

Lindsey sipped her café au lait. "I can't. I'm picking someone up at the airport."

"Someone I know?"

Lindsey struggled for a term to define Rebekiah. "No. She's a...friend."

Adam put his drink down and grinned. "A friend? Or a friend-friend?"

She had learned long ago to just tell him straight up what was going on. "A friend-friend. I asked her to come."

Adam leaned in. "You did?"

"Is that so hard to believe?"

"In all the years that we've worked together, you've never mentioned a friend-friend."

Lindsey folded her arms. "I've had girlfriends since we met." Was that what Rebekiah was? A girlfriend? She'd had girlfriends before; Rebekiah didn't feel like one of those women. She felt more like...Monica. She brushed the implications of that thought aside.

"None that you brought on a business trip."

"True."

"What's her name?"

"Rebekiah."

"How'd you meet?" He reached out. "Please tell me she's not part of the program."

Lindsey patted his hand. "No. She's a client."

Adam covered his mouth. "No."

Lindsey rolled her eyes. "Don't look so scandalized. She was one of Roger's people."

"Have you heard from him?"

Lindsey shook her head. "No. He's left a bit of a mess behind. I'm not sure what I'd do to him if he came back."

Adam shrugged. "You'll figure it out. So what does she do?

Where does she live? How did you move from client to something else? Is she rich? I want to meet her."

"Whoa." Lindsey pulled back. "Slow down. She lives in Providence. She inherited a large trust from her best friend, and she's a fine arts photographer." She omitted the boudoir photographer part; no need to get into all that.

Adam grinned. "An artist. Nice. And how did she transition from client to friend-friend?"

"Well, that's a longer story." She took another sip. She wasn't sure how to begin or what to share. She trusted Adam without reservation, but this thing with Rebekiah was beyond her experience.

He wrapped his hands around his cup. "I've got time."

She leaned in and told him about that first meeting and the subsequent studio visit. "Something clicked. And then she took pictures of me." She regretted speaking as soon as the words left her mouth.

His eyes narrowed. "What kind of pictures?"

She felt the heat rise in her cheeks. "Artistic."

He burst out laughing. "Yeah. Artistic. And you agreed?"

She swallowed. She was not going to tell him about the masturbation pictures. "Yes."

He kept smiling and shook his head.

A need to defend her connection to Rebekiah emerged, and she said, "It's not what you think. Well, it is, but there's something more. I've never been with anyone quite like her."

Still smiling, he reached across the table and held her hands. "Good. You need someone like that. Now tell me more." She did.

All the way to the airport, she mulled over their conversation and his parting words. "Bring her to dinner tomorrow night." Introducing Rebekiah to Adam meant integrating two worlds she worked hard to keep separate. But Rebekiah already straddled both of her worlds. And having Adam meet her might not be the worst idea Lindsey ever had.

CHAPTER TWENTY-FIVE

Lindsey opened her hotel suite and found Rebekiah sitting by the windows, looking at the London skyline. The sex in Vancouver was still fresh in her mind, so she smiled and dropped her work bag by the door. "Hey. Sorry I'm late. How was your flight?"

Rebekiah looked at her and smiled. "Good."

Lindsey took off her jacket and hung it in the closet. She was beginning to enjoy coming home to someone and the domesticity of it. "Did you eat yet?"

When Rebekiah didn't answer, she glanced over. Rebekiah's expression was hard to read, and Lindsey worried that she'd done something wrong.

Rebekiah leaned back and crossed her legs. "Do you remember your safe words?"

The words sent shivers down her spine, and desire settled low, wet and waiting. Her night spread out before her. "Yes." She moved toward her, eager to touch.

"Stop." Rebekiah held up her hand. "Take off your clothes."

Her tone brooked no argument, but because she evoked the safe word, Lindsey knew she could stop it at any point. Giving in to her wishes, Lindsey shimmied out of her pants.

"No, slowly."

Surrendering all control, she swallowed and adjusted her pace to the command.

Once the last article of clothing hit the floor, Rebekiah said, "Go to the bedroom and wait for me on your hands and knees facing away from the door."

Lindsey left her in the living area. While she waited on the bed, she listened to the soft sounds of changing clothes and the jangle of buckles. When Rebekiah finally walked in, Lindsey saw her through the window's reflection—naked with a strap-on dangling between her legs. Her heart raced knowing it was for her. The bed dipped, and her body tensed for the anticipated touch.

"So you like it when someone tells you what to do."

"Yes." Lindsey's voice came out higher expected. She cleared her throat.

"Hmm. Does it make you wet?" Rebekiah's fingers brushed against her and dipped inside to test her theory. Wanting to hold them where they were, Lindsey clenched, but Rebekiah slipped her grasp and ran wet fingers down her back.

"Yes." Lindsey groaned as those fingers gripped her ass before pulling away.

She heard the snick of a lube bottle opening and felt her ass being spread. Cool gel dripped down her crack, and Rebekiah worked it around her anus, pushing against the tight orifice.

Lindsey arched her back, excited and apprehensive. It wasn't the first time Rebekiah had touched her there, but the intent felt different, a good different.

"You like that?" Rebekiah withdrew her finger and slid it back until Lindsey's body gave way.

Lindsey gasped and dropped to her elbows.

"Hmm...you do. I wonder what you would do if I just stuffed this dildo straight up your ass?" She pulled her finger out and pressed the dildo against the hole.

Lindsey moaned and pushed back. She'd dabbled in anal play but never had anything bigger than a finger. It aroused her. The thought of that thick silicone inside her...

"Laptop, Lindsey?"

Lindsey struggled to understand. She was on all fours with a dildo lined up against her ass, and Rebekiah was asking about a computer? Oh. Right. Safe word. "No."

Rebekiah stayed still. "You got awfully tense on me."

Lindsey willed herself to relax and said, "I got lost in the moment."

Rebekiah kissed the back of her neck. "Is this something you want?"

"Yes. Maybe." What if it didn't fit? What if she couldn't do what Rebekiah wanted?

Rebekiah rubbed her back. "It's hard, isn't it? Making decisions. You like to take charge of a situation. Show them who's boss. But tonight, you don't have to decide. I will."

Relief poured through Lindsey as she shed her responsibilities. She could just be, and Rebekiah would take care of her.

More lube, and Lindsey willed herself to relax as Rebekiah's finger slipped back inside. It felt different having Rebekiah behind her and inside her ass. Once again, Rebekiah had figured out how to shut down her brain. She felt controlled and more vulnerable but also free. She moved into Rebekiah's thrusts with less thought and more feeling.

When Rebekiah added another finger, the pressure increased, and Lindsey worried about the dildo's size. *Would* it fit? But the rhythmic thrusting never slowed, and after Rebekiah began rubbing her clit, she stopped paying attention to those details.

Lindsey groaned continuously, each breath coming faster and faster. She no longer cared about fingers and size; she just wanted more. "Please."

Rebekiah didn't make her beg, just pulled her fingers out and moved the dildo against her. "It's up to you to take this, baby." Her hand rested on Lindsey's shoulder and gently pulled while her other hand continued the assault on her clit.

Lindsey's sphincter tightened against the larger intrusion. But the fingers on her clit proved relentless. She almost pulled back, but then a wave of arousal opened her up, and the dildo was inside her.

"That's it. Take it, baby. Take it all in." Rebekiah's hand slid down her arm and palmed her breast. Her body enveloped Lindsey, one hand at her clit, the other at her breast, and her body against her back. Grounded in her arms, Lindsey felt her orgasm grow while more of the dildo slid inside.

Rebekiah rode her movements. "You can do it. Just let yourself go. Feel me inside you."

Lindsey bucked at her words and groaned. Her pants grew harder and harder, her need to come hitting its peak as Rebekiah murmured in her ear, "Fucking your ass."

Lindsey's arms pushed straight, and her body went rigid. Her orgasm pushed up and over her, and she pulled Rebekiah down on top of her when she finally came.

Her whole body trembled when Rebekiah pulled out.

Lindsey turned her head to the side and muttered, "Jesus, what the fuck did you do to me?" She lifted her head and stared at Rebekiah lying next to her.

Rebekiah smiled and wiped a damp strand of hair from Lindsey's face. "Thoroughly fucked you."

Lindsey buried her face in her hands. "Yes, you did."

❖

Later, sore and satiated, Lindsey collapsed on the bed with the taste of Rebekiah still on her lips. Rebekiah lifted an arm, and Lindsey scooched closer. "I could get used to this."

"Which part?" Rebekiah asked.

Lindsey thought for a minute and realized she wasn't sure. It had been surprisingly easy having her around in Vancouver. Lindsey had shown her the sights and even introduced her to Adam and his family. And now that she was here in London, it felt natural to have Rebekiah by her side. She didn't say any of that but instead said, "Fucking you in hotel rooms across the world."

Rebekiah chuckled. "That could get expensive."

"I could always expense it." She smiled. "I wonder how I'd justify it."

"Client relations?"

Lindsey laughed. "Among other things."

Rebekiah rolled over, put her head in her hand, and said, "I meant to tell you I had a good time in Vancouver. It was nice meeting Adam."

"Me, too. Adam liked you." She didn't tell her that Rebekiah was the only woman she'd ever brought to him.

"How long have you known him?" Rebekiah touched a strand of her hair.

Lindsey closed her eyes at the touch and thought for a minute. "About seven years." She debated how much she wanted to share but finally opted for the truth. "He's my sponsor."

"He's in AA?"

"Yes. We met at JP Morgan. We were both living in New York City but traveling extensively."

"Sounds like you."

Lindsey chuckled. "It does, doesn't it? We were friendly colleagues. He didn't do the party circuit at night, so I didn't know him that well."

"There's a party circuit for wealth management types?"

Lindsey smiled at the memory of all the privilege and excess that came with unchecked wealth. "It's the original jet set. Anyway, we were in Bangkok on a deal, and I missed an important meeting. Adam found me blacked out with some woman in my hotel room and a tourniquet twisted around my arm."

"Shit."

Lindsey shuddered. "Yeah, that was new. I'd never blacked out on a business trip, and I stayed away from needles. Adam cleaned me up and covered for me. Then he told me his story and offered to help." She chuckled. "But I was stubborn, and when we got back to New York, I stayed sober for six months before I went back to it. It wasn't until Monica left me that I realized how far things had gone, and I called him." She stopped, a bit surprised that she'd revealed so much so easily. Only Adam knew her so well.

She glanced over, not sure what to expect, and was surprised when Rebekiah said, "Thank you."

"For what?"

Rebekiah pulled her into her arms. "For trusting me."

Lindsey swallowed hard. Trust. That was what she had now that all her previous relationships lacked. Physical trust and now intimate trust. Maybe she wasn't bad at this. Maybe she'd had the wrong partners. Maybe Rebekiah was the right one. She was willing to find out.

Something shifted inside her, and she said, "Want to come to Berlin next?"

CHAPTER TWENTY-SIX

Lindsey watched the first rays of sun peek over the New York City skyline while she listened to the British diplomat rattle off the historic barriers associated with working with the Chinese. She avoided rolling her eyes at his prejudices and voiced her counterpoints. She tried not to laugh as Li Jing, the fifth person on the Skype video call, succinctly put him in his place with a concise history of British imperialism in China and the ill will that had brought to the region. His face bulged with suppressed anger that gradually softened by the time Li Jing finished talking.

Lindsey's email dinged, and Li Jing's one-line subject, *Is this idiot for real?*, made her smile.

The call wrapped up ten minutes later, and Li Jing stayed on the line to check in. After a quick debrief of the call and their business, she got right to the point. "I had an interesting conversation with someone from the US Embassy last week. They showed up at my office."

A muted alarm from the bedroom reminded her that Rebekiah was there. Images from last night flashed through her head, and she actively suppressed them to reply, "Really? Regarding?"

Li Jing leaned in. "You. Our business dealings. An organization called the Kharitonov Group." She glanced aside and lowered her voice. "I pulled a few strings. They have ties to the Russian mafia. If you're connected with this group, you need to be very careful."

Lindsey leaned back. Rumors always surfaced with flashy Russians, that they were working for the mob. What disturbed her more was the fact that the government was starting to contact her business colleagues. It represented a threat to her livelihood. If word got out that her company was under investigation, she could lose credibility and business deals. She rubbed her face. She'd need to let Cathryn know. "Thanks."

Li Jing nodded. She switched to Cantonese. "Let me know if I can be of service. I am not without resources. I have many pockets, and they are deep." Her eyes narrowed, and she grinned. "I see I'm keeping you from a more pleasurable morning."

Lindsey turned; Rebekiah had walked out of the bedroom in a robe. Lindsey faced Li Jing with a chagrined look. "She just woke up."

Li Jing chuckled. "Happiness looks good on you." The video window winked out as the call disconnected.

Rebekiah leaned down and kissed the back of her neck. "Sorry. I didn't mean to disturb you."

Lindsey closed her eyes. "You didn't." Reaching up, she pulled Rebekiah in for a kiss. Light caresses gradually turned more purposeful. She slid her hands into the robe and loosened the tie. Rebekiah shrugged out of it. Standing, Lindsey traced a line of kisses up her neck. She wanted to touch, make her come apart in her hands, her mouth. But Rebekiah had been resistant to sharing power, and it was starting to bother her. Rebekiah demanded trust without giving it back. She still held all the cards, and Lindsey wanted to change that. With a groan, she wrenched her head away and pulled back.

Rebekiah kissed her collarbone. "Why'd you stop?"

Lindsey tilted her head back and moaned, her body giving in before her mind. "I should get to work."

Rebekiah slipped under her T-shirt and pushed it up. Her

fingers fanned across Lindsey's stomach and moved up to her breasts. "I've heard that one before…"

She groaned and arched into the touch.

Rebekiah whispered, "Are you sure?"

Lindsey captured her mouth in a searing kiss and, then, stepping back, tugged Rebekiah's hand toward the bed. "It can wait."

She took her time, kissing along the length of Rebekiah's body and using her own body to say the things she couldn't say with words. A kiss that said *trust me*, a touch that said *I'm here for you.*

Rebekiah seemed to sense her desire and changed the way she touched as well. They moved together until Rebekiah came with a deep groan, and Lindsey followed with a shuddering gasp. They lay wrapped in each other's arms while Lindsey's mind wandered and Rebekiah's fingers ran along her back in a haphazard pattern. In the hazy post-sex bliss, Lindsey struggled to give voice to her underlying frustration with their power imbalance; its importance had faded with the intensity with which they made love.

Rebekiah spoke first. "Do you really have work?"

"I always have work." She sighed, and all her relationship thoughts dissipated in the wake of that question.

"I'm thinking about bumping my flight. I've got a few things I want to do in the city."

Lindsey glanced up. They'd been in New York for two days, meeting with foundations and talking about the creation of Rebekiah's foundation. She was on the cusp of passing her along to a colleague. This was the last business trip she had planned with her, and even though they'd met in other cities for other reasons, she worried their connection would fade. The feeling of intimacy was so fragile right now. "Anything I can help with?"

Rebekiah smiled at her. "Want to see an art show?"

❖

Vancouver, London, Berlin: they were Lindsey's world. She'd had no idea how much fun it would be to have Rebekiah with her. Her presence did not detract from work; in fact, it made work more enjoyable. But New York was Rebekiah's domain, and she was vague about the artist they were seeing.

They ate a late breakfast in Soho. Rebekiah told stories about her time in New York, and Lindsey added her own escapades. But Li Jing's parting words rolled around in her head. *Happiness looks good on you.* Was that the feeling she experienced around Rebekiah? It felt so different that it was hard to define.

After brunch, Rebekiah took her to the Whitney Whitaker Gallery. Lindsey suppressed her surprise when she read one exhibit from a list at the door—*Thea Devore: A life in photos.*

"Is that your Thea?" she asked even though she knew the answer. She'd drawn up paperwork two months ago for their trust.

Rebekiah nodded and held the door. "It opened in October."

The space was filled with a vast amount of light considering the solid gray February outside. White walls with gray accents provided a sterile background for the art. The women moved along the first exhibit before Thea's, taking their time with each picture.

Rebekiah chuckled. "She's really rather good. Thea would hate her."

Lindsey glanced at the backdrop of kids on a playground underneath a billboard advertising adult entertainment. "Why?"

"Its themes are too obvious. Innocence in the face of reality."

They moved to the second floor via a metal staircase—complete with see-through rivets—that looked like its own version of modern art. Rebekiah paused at the top, and Lindsey looked toward the two adjoining rooms. Pictures hung on the wall of various shapes and sizes, a mix of color and black and white. The line of Rebekiah's shoulders tensed.

Somewhat surprised by that reaction—she did bring them

here on purpose—Lindsey stepped around and held out her hand. "Come on. Show me."

Rebekiah took her hand, and she squeezed it and pulled her along. The first few pictures were striking. Shots from the seventies with lots of butches and drag queens interspersed with other people and drug paraphernalia. And then it changed.

A curly haired tomboy with a blue and white striped collared shirt stared at the camera while perched on the lap of a woman in profile rolling a cigarette in her hands. A white picket fence stood in the background with street traffic behind it. *Sasha and Rebekiah, Key West, 1989*. The eyes were definitely Rebekiah's. Something about the slope of the older woman's shoulder made Lindsey ask, "Is that your mother?"

"Yes," was so soft she almost missed it.

She needed to tread lightly. Of all the art galleries in the city, she chose this one. There was something here that touched deeper than Emma, an older hurt. Strange how Lindsey could see that so clearly now. She squeezed her hand again, and Rebekiah relaxed. "How old were you?"

Rebekiah stared at it. "Five or six. If it's summer, then six." She let go of her hand.

Lindsey wandered down the aisle. "I didn't know she took so many pictures of you."

Rebekiah followed at a slower pace and shrugged. "Thea took pictures of everyone."

They stared at a picture of a twentysomething Rebekiah kissing another girl while tucked into a corner behind a bookshelf with the camera leering at an angle. *First Kiss, 2001*. Lindsey wandered, seeing Rebekiah at various ages. So open and innocent. Then more pictures of her mother and more drug culture.

She paused at another still with Rebekiah's mother standing next to an open casket. *Sasha and Martin. Providence, 1984*.

Rebekiah came up behind her. "My dad."

"Is this staged?" She stared at Sasha's expression and realized it couldn't have been staged. The grief was too raw.

Rebekiah shook her head. "No, it's his funeral." She chuckled. "My mother broke her camera after that shot." She got quiet and stared for a minute longer. "I don't think she ever really got over him."

The photos of Rebekiah tapered off after college. At the end, Lindsey turned and shook her head. "All these pictures of you."

Rebekiah stood in the center of the room with her arms spread. "All these pictures of me."

Lindsey tilted her head. This was how Rebekiah did it, how she got women to have sex on camera. How she saw through Lindsey so easily. She had spent her entire childhood and early adulthood on display. She knew how it felt to be exposed. Like Lindsey growing up as a child of a politician, Rebekiah's private life had been subject to scrutiny. She knew how to maintain privacy in the face of publicity. They were two sides of the coin. Rebekiah exposed; Lindsey hidden. But together, they could put their barriers down and let themselves be seen. She walked over and took Rebekiah's face in her hands. She kissed her softly, gently. "Thank you."

Rebekiah smiled. "For what?"

"For showing me this."

Rebekiah shrugged. "I wanted to see the exhibit."

Lindsey let her have that lie and took her out to dinner, but the mood had changed. She tried not to take it personally but she mourned the loss. Rebekiah closed off, and when they got back to the hotel, Lindsey pretended to be too tired for sex and offered to sleep on the couch to avoid any awkward cuddling.

"Why would you do that?"

Lindsey shrugged. "You seem like you need some space."

She stared. "I'm not making you sleep on the couch in our hotel room. If you want me to, I can get another room."

Lindsey shook her head. "No, I'm not...yeah, stay." So much for avoiding awkward.

Rebekiah rolled her eyes. "I think I can sleep next to you without having sex." She raised an eyebrow. "Can you?"

Lindsey tossed a throw pillow at her.

Rebekiah caught it and laughed. "Come on. Let's cuddle."

Lindsey groaned, but when they crawled into bed together, Rebekiah opened her arms, and she slid into them. They lay together in the dark for a few minutes before Lindsey spoke. "It was hard for you, wasn't it?"

Rebekiah shifted but didn't pull away. "Mmm."

Lindsey knew she wasn't asleep. She'd never felt more connected *and* distant from her. "Talk to me."

"I've been in a fishbowl all my life. Since I was a baby."

Lindsey smiled at the memory of that particular picture. "And what a cute baby you were."

"Photography was my way of stepping out of the limelight. And I was good at it. And then Emma calls me up."

Lindsey tightened her hold. Rebekiah squeezed back.

"We haven't seen each other in years, and she wants to come home. She's dying. And she's angry. She wants me to help her make something of her life, so I spend the next year photographing her decline one day at a time."

Lindsey waited, determined to be here for her. No more ducking away from the hard stuff.

"She broke me."

Lindsey shifted up on her elbow and looked down at her in the dim light. "You're not broken."

"I know. But for the longest time, I couldn't connect without the camera. You changed that. You saw me."

Tears welled in Lindsey's eyes. She was glad it was dark. It had taken Rebekiah this long to open up, and she was scared that so much emotion would make her run away again. She swallowed and asked, "Why did you take me to the show?"

"I wanted you to know who I was before Emma." Even though her body language said it was hard, Rebekiah had deliberately opened a door. Lindsey had figured that out earlier but did not understand what door she was opening. It wasn't about Thea; it was about Lindsey. She felt the weight of the relationship shift, and rather than run away, she embraced it. She finally allowed herself to acknowledge the feeling that had been growing since December—love.

She could do this, and she would. "Can I hold you tonight?"

Rebekiah shifted and said, "That would be nice."

CHAPTER TWENTY-SEVEN

Two weeks before her show opened, Rebekiah stood outside another hotel room in another city—Hong Kong—waiting for Lindsey to answer the door. It had been almost two months since she'd hopped a flight to Vancouver. Despite the near-constant jet lag, Rebekiah was beginning to see the allure. It wasn't just the work that pulled Lindsey in; it was the travel. It was so easy to step outside herself in a distant place. Each trip opened a new window into Lindsey's world, and Rebekiah experienced a freer version of her. She liked that.

She'd almost passed on this trip—both her show and the constant shuttling of Sera to different sitters was starting to wear on her—but it was Hong Kong, a place that had significant meaning to Lindsey, so at the last minute, she booked a flight.

The door opened, and all her thoughts dissipated with Lindsey's smile. "Hey."

"You're here." Lindsey pulled her in for a searing kiss against the door.

Rebekiah smiled into the kiss and nipped at her lips.

She grinned and let her tongue play with the edge of Rebekiah's mouth. "I have wanted to do this since New York." She drew her into a deeper kiss.

Rebekiah grabbed her waist while they moved together, kissing and sucking. She fumbled with the tiny buttons on

Lindsey's blouse; Lindsey just pulled it over her head and threw it aside. Rebekiah worked her belt, button, and zipper in a matter of seconds. Lindsey bucked against her when Rebekiah slipped into her underwear and toward her opening. She groaned and stepped back with her hands on Rebekiah's shoulders. "I'm so wet."

"I can tell." Rebekiah grinned and moved the hand still in her pants.

She stilled Rebekiah's hand between her legs and looked at her. "I want to fuck you."

Rebekiah swallowed. Lindsey wasn't asking about the actual act; she wanted to take charge. As the months had gone by, Lindsey had become more assertive in their physical relationship. Instead of pushing her away, the change in power dynamics turned Rebekiah on.

"Will you let me do that for you?" She circled Rebekiah's body and licked her earlobe. The tips of her nipples grazed Rebekiah's back. "I'll take care of you, you know that." She slipped her hand into Rebekiah's waistband.

Rebekiah tilted back and groaned when Lindsey brushed her clit. It would be so easy to let her take control. She already trusted her with so much. Taking a deep breath, she let go of her fear and said, "Okay."

"You're so wet. And ready for me."

She closed her eyes and leaned against Lindsey, whose fingers moved at a leisurely pace in her wet folds.

Lindsey pulled away and held out her hand. "Come on."

She let Lindsey direct her toward the bedroom. Lindsey crawled up the mattress to straddle her thighs with a feral grin on her lips. She worked Rebekiah's belt off and cinched it over both her hands. "My turn."

Lindsey pulled Rebekiah's pants off, along with her underwear, and pushed her legs apart. She continued pushing until Rebekiah bent her knees, heels touching her ass. Open and exposed, she knew what she looked like. She'd taken this picture before, and the voyeuristic aspect thrilled her, especially on the other side of the lens.

Lindsey leaned down and brushed a series of light kisses along Rebekiah's inner thighs. She touched between her legs with a kiss before she looked up. Grinning, she said, "You like to watch?"

"Yeah, I do."

Lindsey trailed a line of kisses up her hip across her stomach to her breasts, which she licked until the nipples pebbled, and then she bit each one in succession. Rebekiah arched in response. "A little pain before pleasure. Too bad I don't have those clamps with me. Those really hurt."

She traced Rebekiah's chest and up to her bound arms, then crawled off the bed. She cupped her own breasts for a minute while Rebekiah watched and strained against the belt. She could move if she wanted to, but she didn't. Even though Lindsey was calling the shots, she could still stop it, and that helped her accept the power shift.

Lindsey pushed her own pants off. She wasn't wearing any underwear. Coming back, she slid down Rebekiah's body, kissing her way down. "You're awful quiet. Let me change that."

She licked Rebekiah's opening from top to bottom, twirling down around her perineum and then back up to her clit. Rebekiah jerked at the touch, and Lindsey clenched harder around her thighs and said, "That's it, stay with me."

Rebekiah writhed as Lindsey repeated the motion again and again. Her frustration grew with each touch; Lindsey's tongue always just missed the right place to make her come. She finally gave voice to her desperation and whispered, "Please…"

Lindsey stopped licking and trailed her fingers against Rebekiah's opening. "Please? Please what?" She pushed two fingers inside, and Rebekiah bucked. Lindsey pulled out, and her hips slumped back down. "What do you need?"

Rebekiah closed her eyes and shook her head. She knew

what Lindsey wanted, but the words would not come. She had already given so much and heard the begging in her voice as she asked again, "Please." It was too hard to give in. She couldn't do it. She started to sit up, struggling with the belt.

Lindsey crawled up her body, and Rebekiah lunged forward to kiss her, determined to take back control. She tasted herself on Lindsey's lips. Lindsey's tongue twirled and twisted inside her mouth just like it had been doing between her legs moments before. She lost herself to the feeling as Lindsey continued to kiss her.

Lindsey pulled back, and Rebekiah chased her. Leaning back, she put a hand on Rebekiah's chest—the same place Rebekiah always put her hand—as if to calm her. "Shh. It's okay."

She took a deep breath and stared into Lindsey's face. It was almost too much, letting her have this power.

Lindsey smoothed her skin. "You need to trust me. Do you trust me?"

Rebekiah nodded.

Lindsey smiled gently. "I need you to be here. You're going to have to let go. Can you do that for me?" She held Rebekiah's hand.

Rebekiah squeezed her hand and closed her eyes. She took comfort in the touch and tried to give in to the intimacy she wanted. Just like in New York, when she realized how emotionally closed off she'd been, how she had been the same in all their sexual encounters. Even now, she was trying to maintain control. She needed to let go. Taking a deep breath, she opened her eyes and said, "Yes."

Lindsey squeezed her hand "Thank you."

She closed her eyes when Lindsey's lips touched her again. She opened herself to the sensations, letting them overwhelm her and turn off her defenses. No longer needing to be in control, she let herself feel.

Her climax started slow, matching Lindsey's strokes, and

then it changed. Her body grew charged and twitchy until her breath hitched. She bucked once, twice, then stiffened and collapsed on the bed as she came. Her orgasm rushed through her, leaving her hollowed out and exhausted.

Lindsey slid back up her body and loosened the belt. Rebekiah wrapped her arms around her. Hands roamed each other's bodies, gentle caresses and soothing touches. Tracing Lindsey's eyebrow, Rebekiah started to come back to herself.

Lindsey murmured, "That feels nice."

Rebekiah continued her slow exploration until her energy returned. Then she shifted and moved on top. She slipped her leg between Lindsey's and grinned at the wetness from earlier. "How about now?"

Lindsey gasped. "Yes."

"And now?" She cupped Lindsey's sex and started to play with her lips.

Lindsey leaned up and kissed her. Then she shifted and rubbed her leg against Rebekiah's center. "It's good. But this is better." She rocked her leg for emphasis.

Rebekiah groaned and increased her speed in response. Lindsey pushed her fingers inside her and started a slow rhythm. Rebekiah pushed two fingers in, and Lindsey came back with an unexpected thrust. Rebekiah captured her mouth in a searing kiss. Using their knees for leverage, they pumped into each other as they kissed harder and harder. She felt herself getting close again when Lindsey wrenched her lips away and hissed, "I want you to come with me."

She inhaled sharply and redoubled her efforts. They pushed and pulled against each other. Lindsey came with a shout, Rebekiah with a long moan. She held Lindsey tight to her for a minute before Lindsey withdrew her fingers. Rebekiah pulled out, too, and flopped back on the bed staring up at the ceiling. She felt like liquid.

The bed shuddered, and Rebekiah looked over. Lindsey looked at her and laughed.

Smiling, Rebekiah brushed against her hair. Her heart opened, and she wanted to scoop Lindsey inside. "What?"

"That felt fantastic."

Rebekiah chuckled. "Really?"

Lindsey rolled back over on top. "Really." Rebekiah pulled her close. Lindsey kept her hands free and stroked the hair from Rebekiah's face. "You know why?"

Rebekiah kissed her lips with a gentle touch. "Tell me."

Lindsey spoke the words against her lips. "Because you came with me."

The words resonated. How long had Rebekiah been playing cat and mouse with people? Since Emma or was it before? Had she always kept a part of herself separate and alone? And what had she gained from that behavior? A safe secure existence with no real intimacy. Regret bubbled inside her, and she said, "I'm sorry."

"For what?"

Rebekiah caressed her cheek. "For keeping you at a distance." Slowly, she worked her way down Lindsey's body, tracing contours and curves with hands and lips, saying in touch what she couldn't express in words. Lindsey spun her around so that their mouths worked each other at the same time. They moved from soft and languid to hard and fast. When Lindsey finally came, Rebekiah followed.

Turning, she crawled up and collapsed to the side, her body draped across Lindsey's. She lay for a while, enjoying the taste of Lindsey on her lips and the aftershocks rocking through her; Lindsey caressed her hair. She was just starting to drift off to the sound of Lindsey's heartbeat when she heard her whisper, "I love you."

Rebekiah's breath hitched. Did she feel the same way? Maybe. But she wasn't sure, and she didn't want to lie. Fear gnawed at her voice, keeping it silent.

Lindsey kept brushing her hair and whispered, "It's okay. I just wanted you to know. It doesn't have to change anything."

But it did, and Rebekiah didn't know how to say that, so she pulled Lindsey closer and pretended to fall asleep. The next day, Lindsey showed her the sights, and then they fucked all night before Rebekiah hopped a plane back to Providence.

CHAPTER TWENTY-EIGHT

Rebekiah sat and watched Neil lock the gallery doors with a mix of satisfaction and disappointment. He turned to her with a bright smile. "That went really well."

She returned his enthusiastic grin. "I know."

Aldina sat next to her on one of those round couches seen throughout the world in hotel lobbies and Victorian sitting rooms. This particular one did not suffer from an excess of red velvet but reflected the gallery's open space with stark white fabric. She tapped Rebekiah's hand. "You should be proud." She yawned. "I don't know why I'm so tired. It's early. Do you have plans this evening?"

Neil flopped next to Rebekiah and leaned his head on her shoulder. "She's coming out with me. Right?"

Rebekiah glanced at her watch. "I don't know." She didn't tell them that the person she wanted to see all evening was a no-show. It wasn't as if she was expecting Lindsey to be at the opening. She was still in Hong Kong. Lindsey's declaration of love still surprised her. She didn't know what to do with it. Did she feel the same way? She wasn't sure. Love didn't feel this way. Love carried a burden and a barb. It was fierce and critical. It soothed and then hurt. Her feelings toward Lindsey were none of those things. And when Lindsey hadn't mentioned it the next day, she never brought it up again. Their texts hadn't suffered, but something was different.

Neil nudged her. "Come on." He looked at her with his best puppy dog eyes.

She groaned. She just wanted to go home to bed. "Okay."

He slapped his knees and jumped up. "Let's go." He paused and looked at Aldina. "You coming?"

She shook her head and pushed off the couch. "There are a couple of flower arrangements in the office if you wanted to take a look."

"Sure."

"I'll pull the car around," Neil volunteered.

Rebekiah tossed him her keys and followed Aldina upstairs. She surveyed the various bouquets in vases and gift baskets scattered across the table, a box of chocolates, a crate of oranges, and a package from Harry and David in their midst. "Wow."

Aldina smiled. "More than you expected?"

She nodded and glanced at the cards. The Harry and David package was from Elena, the chocolates from Nicole, and the box of oranges had the note, *Thea wanted you to have something practical instead of flowers.* Other well-wishers from the artist cooperative and the BDSM community had sent bouquets. She paused by a large glass vase of pale violet orchids interspersed with a white and red spotted variety and pulled the card. *I can't wait to see it. Love, Lindsey.*

Love. Her fingers brushed the delicate petals. That was what Lindsey had said to her in Hong Kong, and yet Rebekiah had said nothing. It wasn't that she didn't feel it, but saying it…

Aldina paused beside her. "Oh, those are my favorite. So delicate and elegant."

Rebekiah grabbed the vase. "I'm taking these home tonight. I'll come back for the rest." She kissed her on the cheek. "Thanks."

Aldina wrapped her in her arms and said, "Anytime. I'm proud of you."

"Are you in tomorrow?"

Aldina shrugged. "Call me, and I'll swing by for you."

Rebekiah nodded and bundled into her coat. On her way out,

she switched off the critic inside and did a last circuit of the room. The comments had been positive and enthusiastic. Her work felt like hers for the first time in years.

She slowly made her way through the pictures, thighs, hips, backs, vulvas exposed in the act of intimacy—sometimes alone, sometimes with another, and sometimes in a group, but all in the same light with the same feel, same poses. It was elegantly staged. Each picture, each shot, that intimate moment captured over and over again. Picture after picture: Renee and Dawn, Meghan, Nicole and Jae, and the memories of those shoots. And how she'd only opened herself afterward both physically and emotionally. They were the bright spots in her life. Vivid memories captured amid the gray day to day. When did the color seep out of her existence?

Aldina and Elena were right—Emma did hurt her work, just not in the ways they thought. She skewed Rebekiah's lens and severed her connection to her subjects. She'd been so disconnected since Emma's illness—living her life, dealing with her death, settling her estate. She'd spent so much time gradually numbing out that it wasn't until she started connecting again that it became obvious what had happened.

She came to a line of three pictures printed in landscape and bounded by two huge pictures blown up to three feet by three feet. Lindsey stared back at her—half-lidded, legs spread, fingers splayed, mouth open, and features twisted in pleasure. Lindsey had been a part of her professional return but more accurately, a reflection of her returning emotions.

Everything was different with Lindsey. The connection, the sex, the feelings. Standing in front of her work, she could finally say it back. She loved Lindsey. And not the ephemeral kind associated with infatuation and obsession, which had fueled her earlier drive to connect with Lindsey. It was a deep, abiding feeling of connection and commitment that came after allowing herself to be vulnerable to someone else.

Rebekiah didn't really do love. She did connections and

friendships but not relationships. At least in the traditional sense. Her models—her parents, Thea, Collette, and the other artists in their community—approached relationships more amorphously. And yet, they made lifelong commitments to each other. Lifelong, was that what she was looking for with Lindsey? She wasn't sure, but the alternative was unthinkable.

She pulled out her phone and shot off a quick text: *Got the flowers. Private showing when you get back?*

Neil honked the horn.

She stuffed her phone back in her pocket, then ducked outside, cradling the flowers and protecting them from the cold. She slid into the passenger seat and tucked them on to the floor behind the driver's seat. Buckling in, she banged her hand against the console and swore.

"You okay?" He glanced over and pulled away from the curb.

She nursed her hand and nodded. "This damn car." Emma's car.

He shrugged. "I don't know. It drives smooth."

Rebekiah narrowed her eyes and made a decision. "Do you want it?"

"You're serious?"

She glanced at the leather interior and too wide dials. She'd been in such a fog that she'd ignored her own discomfort and held on too long. "Yeah. I hate this car. I want a Jeep."

He laughed, and Rebekiah joined him. She felt much lighter.

❖

The flight attendant woke Lindsey up half an hour before they landed in Providence. The flight from Hong Kong to LA to Providence had been over twenty-three hours. She had slept fitfully for the last six. Taking an earlier flight, she'd hoped to be on time for Rebekiah's opening. She wanted to surprise her.

Everything was perfect until she went and said *I love you*. She had replayed and edited their last night together, trying to find a way to take it back. Sure, she wanted more. The truth was that she'd always wanted more in all of her relationships, but she'd never had the time to give it. Not even with Monica.

Monica, who'd become the standard by which all other women in her life were judged. Lindsey hadn't made time for her and lost her. She didn't want to make the same mistake twice. Whether Rebekiah loved her or not, she was determined to make time for her.

Her stomach rumbled as the plane touched down. She looked out the window. Winter's brown, black, and white had given way to spring's green and blue. Hoisting her carry-on to her shoulder and starting down the concourse, she barely swiped her phone off airplane mode before it started a series of pings.

She stopped before the secure glass wall and read the last text from Sabine. *Locked out of our office*. She scrolled down farther. *Cathryn arrested*.

Bile rose in her throat, and an intense desire to turn and run made her shift toward the runway. All her planning and traveling felt useless in the sight of Agent Travers waiting up the walkway. She looked over her shoulder and spotted a couple of TSA agents approaching.

"Lindsey Blackwell?"

She nodded and held up her phone. The first agent took it and stripped her bag off her shoulder. The second one wrapped a hand around her elbow. "We're taking you into custody."

Panic clawed at her mind and she willed herself to stay calm. "What for?" she asked, even though she suspected. She needed time to think.

The first agent nodded toward the glass barrier. "There's a warrant for your arrest, and we're to hand you over to the DOJ once past the security gate."

People stopped and watched. She caught one person holding

up their phone as if were recording. They unlocked a glass door to the left of the revolving door and marched her to Agent Travers and the other DOJ agents. Panic became dread; this was bad.

"Hello, Lindsey." Agent Travers smiled. "You don't stay put, do you?" She nodded to the TSA. "We've got it from here." She held up a set of handcuffs. "Please hold out your hands."

Lindsey listened through her Miranda rights and nodded. She swallowed the wave of nausea rolling through her as Travers locked the cuffs in place. Taking her elbow, Travers turned her toward the exit and marched her to the escalators.

"I'll need to speak with my lawyer before I answer any questions," she called over her shoulder with a calm she did not feel.

"Of course." Travers didn't even bother to hide the weary sarcasm in her tone.

Travers helped her into the back seat of a Dodge Charger while the other agent put her bag in the trunk. Lindsey leaned forward. "What about the rest of my luggage?"

"We'll pick it up." The front door slammed, and the other agent settled behind the wheel.

Lindsey leaned back and watched the familiar landmarks roll past. Her fingers itched to text and get more information. She leaned forward twice to ask a question but pulled back before she opened her mouth. Cathryn's advice ran through her mind. "Speak when spoken to." She was surprised when they pulled into the same public parking garage that her firm used for its staff and clients. The Providence office of the US Department of Justice was less than a block away from her own building.

Inside, a middle-aged white man with a buzz cut and tight dress shirt confiscated her belongings and dropped them into a giant evidence bag before sealing it shut. Then he swung around an electronic reader. "Sign here." Her entire life was locked in that bag—laptop, phone, passport. What the fuck was she going to do?

Another agent—this one a woman a few years older—ushered

her into an adjoining room where they took her fingerprints. Then she brought her to another counter where they took her picture. She was no longer being detained, her possessions seized for an indeterminate time; she was being arrested, complete with mug shot. Her stomach churned, and she tasted bile at the back of her throat.

The agent took her into a windowless room with a table bolted to the floor and a D-ring on the table. "Here." She gestured toward Lindsey's hands. Lindsey was surprised when the agent took the cuffs off and nodded toward a chair. "Have a seat." She turned and left.

Lindsey spotted cameras in each corner of the room. *Keep it together.* Sitting, she flexed her hands and rubbed her wrists. They hadn't shown her the warrant; she had no idea what charges she was being brought up on. But Cathryn had been arrested, so it was something to do with their business. What had Roger gotten them into? His leaving had never felt right, but she'd been so distracted by the work—his work, her work—and then by Rebekiah.

She'd never been good at balancing work and personal stuff, and now she was paying for that. Nauseous and tired, she replayed all the interactions she'd had with Roger, wondering what she'd missed. Disheartened and despondent, she finally gave up. For once in her life, she'd put her personal life before work by coming back early. But instead of being at Rebekiah's show, she was sitting in an interrogation room waiting for the other shoe to drop.

CHAPTER TWENTY-NINE

Rebekiah woke up slightly hungover to someone banging on her front door. She threw on some clothes and stumbled into the hallway. Sera sat next to the door. The knock sounded again.

"Hold on, I'm coming." She threw it open, and Elena breezed in. Sera barked once and followed her into the living room.

Rebekiah plodded after her. "What time is it?"

"A little past four. I called."

Rebekiah glanced at her coffee table and saw her phone sitting there.

"Lindsey's been arrested."

"What? When?" Her mind struggled to catch up. She'd never heard back from Lindsey after she texted last night but dismissed it as time delay.

"Last night when she flew back into Providence. Her assistant called me. They're still holding her. I haven't been able to see her. I'm heading downtown, and I thought you'd like to come." She folded her arms, and it was then that Rebekiah took in her outfit. She was dressed for work, courtroom suit and expensive accessories, a far cry from Rebekiah's current shorts and T-shirt.

Afraid and worried, she shook herself awake. "Yeah. Let me throw something on." She ducked into her bedroom and tossed off her shirt before she yanked on a pair of jeans and scooped up a bra.

Elena called, "We'll drop your mutt off at my sister's. The kids love her."

Rebekiah walked back out, pulling a fresh T-shirt over her head. "Do you think we'll be gone that long?"

Elena stood up from clipping Sera's leash. "I've no idea. Ready?"

Rebekiah grabbed her wallet and phone, then followed her dog and best friend out the door and into the car. "What are they charging her with?"

As Elena drove, she said, "With conspiracy to commit fraud and violating the FCPA. I'm trying to get her arraigned so we can post bail."

"How long will that take?"

"I'm not sure. I don't want to wake up any federal judges this early, but I'm going to have to get on someone's docket soon." She exhaled. "This could take some time."

"Is she going to jail?" Rebekiah's voice cracked. The thought made her heart hurt. She couldn't lose her now.

Elena held her hand. "Not if I can help it."

Rebekiah squeezed back. "Elena, I love her."

Elena glanced at her and shook their joined hands. "You think I don't know that? Why am I picking you up at the ass crack of dawn to go wait in a federal office for the next sixteen hours?"

"Sixteen hours?"

"Give or take eight hours if I pull the right strings."

"What do you need me to do?"

"Be there to pick her up."

They dropped Sera off in Fox Point without any hassle, Elena's sister waving in her housecoat and slippers. They got to the federal building a few minutes later.

Rebekiah followed Elena and took a seat in the beige waiting area while Elena went through the secure door. She proceeded to wait, her stomach in knots as she imagined all the worst possible scenarios.

❖

Lindsey looked up as the door opened. Gail Travers and another agent walked in. "Sorry to keep you waiting. Are you thirsty?"

Lindsey's voice was hoarse when she spoke. "Yes."

"Grab a couple waters." Travers nodded out the door, and the other agent left. She pulled out a chair and sat. "Are you comfortable? Need to eat, pee?"

Lindsey knew she should ask for food—she'd been in the room for what felt like hours—but the acid in her stomach was making her ill.

The agent came back with two cups and a pitcher. Travers poured her a cup and said, "How long have you know Cathryn Wexler?"

Lindsey drank it in one gulp. Travers filled it again. She cleared her throat. "Twelve years."

"And in all that time, did you ever question her judgment?"

Lindsey laughed, which did nothing to alleviate her anxiety. What kind of questions were these? What had happened with Cathryn?

A loud knock sounded at the door, and Travers scowled. "Find out what they want."

The agent opened the door. Elena stood outside. Lindsey's heart soared at the sight. She could hear her mid-argument. "…like hell. She's got a right to see me…"

The door shut, and Travers leaned forward. "This is your chance to tell me what happened before your lawyer comes in and tells you to shut up. Cathryn's already fingered you for the payments—"

The door swung open, and Elena swooped in. "Not another fucking word." She pointed at Travers. "You, out." She held the door and waited for Travers to leave. She pointed at the cameras and said, "Off." She waited until the red light flicked off and then turned to Lindsey. Holding out her hand, she said, "Now we can talk. Hi, it's good to see you again. I'm your lawyer."

The relief Lindsey felt from those three words dissipated twenty minutes later. The news was grim. "Did you know that Roger was working for the DOJ as an informant?"

Lindsey's jaw dropped. "What?"

Elena tapped her hand on the folder containing a copy of the arrest warrant. "Cathryn must have gotten wind of it and fired him. There was something in your accounts that they wanted. Something that tied your company to the Kharitonov Group."

"I had nothing to do with them. They're Cathryn's clients."

"She's saying otherwise."

"What?"

"You need to be prepared. She's trying to pin this on you."

Lindsey shook her head. Outrage and a sense of injustice poured out of her. "But I didn't do anything."

"We're talking jail here, Lindsey. If she was my client, I'd advise her to shift as much blame as possible to you. Her lawyers will be doing the same." Elena fixed her with a look. "And trust me, she has lawyers."

Lindsey rocked back and took that in. She knew Cathryn. Cathryn would take her down or let her hang alone. It was the cutthroat part of Cathryn that she'd always admired and respected. It made their business a success, but it was also the trait that could end her career and her freedom. "You're right. What do you suggest?"

"Let me have one of our corporate people look at your partnership contract. Let's see what we can do to minimize the fallout. But first let's get you out of here." She laid out the rest of her legal strategy and left with assurances that she'd see her at the arraignment.

Elena moved quickly to have Lindsey arraigned and released on bail. Tired, hungry, and wanting nothing more than to take a shower, Lindsey shuffled into the waiting area.

Rebekiah stood with her hands in her pockets and a half-smile on her face. She opened her arms, and Lindsey was in them before she even realized she was walking across the room, she was so tired and happy to see her.

She buried her face in Rebekiah's shirt and whispered into her collar, "What are you doing here?"

Rebekiah kissed her forehead. "Where else would I be?"

Lindsey tightened her grip, grateful that of all the people she expected to have waiting for her, it was Rebekiah who showed up.

Chapter Thirty

The doors opened, and a bevy of reporters stood on the steps. They surged forward.

"Ms. Blackwell, did you know that your partner was working with the Russian mafia?"

"What does Senator Blackwell think about these allegations against you? Did you keep her in the dark?"

Rebekiah positioned herself between them and Lindsey. She pushed past and ushered her into her car. Lindsey leaned her head against the headrest and said with almost no inflection, "My mother's going to be pissed."

Rebekiah glanced at her. "Do you want to go home?"

Lindsey rolled her head to the side and said in that same monotone, "Hell, no. Can I crash at your place?"

This affect worried her. She touched Lindsey's cheek, hoping to give physical comfort if not emotional. "Always."

At her apartment, Rebekiah made pasta that they ate in silence before Lindsey took a shower and went to bed. Rebekiah joined her, wrapping her arms around her from behind. Lindsey didn't even move.

Rebekiah slept fitfully, one ear open, but she must have dozed off because she woke up in the pre-dawn hours alone. She wandered into the kitchen and jumped when a shadow moved on her couch. Her heart rate spiked and then calmed as soon as Lindsey's features became clear. "You scared me."

"Sorry." Her tone was flat.

Rebekiah frowned. "I thought you might have gone home."

"I almost did." Her voice was so soft that it took Rebekiah a few seconds to hear the words.

She rounded the kitchen island and walked over. "But you didn't." Smoothing Lindsey's hair away from her face, she kissed her cheek. "You should have come back to bed."

Lindsey's eyes closed at her touch. "I couldn't sleep."

"How long have you been sitting in the dark?"

"Literally or metaphorically?"

Rebekiah smiled and brushed a strand of hair behind her ear. "I meant literally, but I wouldn't be opposed to the metaphorical answer either."

Lindsey scoffed. "Too long." She turned back to the window and shook her head. "She fucking did it."

"Cathryn?"

Lindsey nodded. "She laundered money through our company and blamed me."

"Wow. That's cold."

Lindsey sighed. "Shit. I keep thinking, what did I miss? How could this have happened? I've been so distracted." She laughed. "I trusted her."

Rebekiah put a hand on her knee. "What are you going to do?"

Lindsey choked on another laugh. "Damage control." She groaned. "I don't know. We're so fucked."

Rebekiah pulled her into her arms, and Lindsey buried her head in her shoulder. She just held her and tried to think of something, anything, to comfort her. "Did I ever tell you how I met Elena?"

Lindsey shook her head but didn't move. Rebekiah grabbed a blanket from the back of her couch and flung it over them. She settled and tucked Lindsey into her. "I played rugby in college, and so did she…" She told her a couple more stories about her college years until Lindsey laughed so hard that tears streamed down her face.

Glad that she'd taken her mind off her troubles, Rebekiah laughed with her and kept talking until the conversation petered out.

After a few minutes of silence, Lindsey turned toward her. "How was the show?"

Rebekiah smiled. "Good. Nice turnout."

"I wanted to be there. I came back early." She teared up.

Rebekiah framed her face. "Hey, it's okay."

Lindsey shook her head. "It's not. I have always done everything in a certain way with one goal in mind, my career. All I've ever done has gone toward that goal. Every person I socialized with—hell, sometimes the people I slept with—helped my career." She made a face. "That sounds bad."

Rebekiah smiled. "I know what you mean."

"You know the only reason I'm sober is because of my career."

"I kind of assumed that."

"And tomorrow morning…" She paused. "Today I'm going to walk into a federal office and destroy that career."

Rebekiah's heart sank, and she put a hand on Lindsey's shoulder. "Oh, Lindsey, I'm so sorry."

"But the only thing I can think about is you."

Rebekiah's breath caught. Her stomach fluttered.

"I know I freaked you out saying I love you, but I can't help it. I'm not going to lie to you or myself."

Rebekiah closed her eyes and tried to summon the words. It was so much easier to communicate with pictures.

Lindsey whispered, "Say something."

Opening her eyes, Rebekiah held her hands. "You know it's more than sex for me, right?"

Lindsey tilted her head. "Is it?"

She frowned. "Yeah, I thought you knew."

"You've never said anything either way. I could only guess."

She shook her head. "I think I knew that, but I didn't know how to tell you. I'm kind of fucked up. Functionally fucked up, but still."

Lindsey smiled. "Me, too."

She knew Lindsey needed to hear something more. The words clawed up from inside and gave voice to the feeling she'd been running from since New York City. Taking a deep breath, she said, "I love you."

The tears on the edge of Lindsey's lashes started to fall.

"Come here." Rebekiah leaned in and kissed her. It was delicate and chaste, but she felt it to her toes. She pulled back, but Lindsey held her, leaning her forehead against hers.

"I love you, too."

Rebekiah's breath caught. She wrapped her arms around her and just held her. Happiness and hope filled her.

Lindsey shifted and looked up. "What does this mean?"

"I don't know. I'm not a traditional person. I'm not looking for a traditional relationship. I think it's okay to make it up as we go along. But for now, it means that I'm going with you to that federal office and waiting until you're done."

Lindsey tried to pull away, but Rebekiah held her. "You don't have to."

"Yeah. I do."

"Why?"

Rebekiah sighed. "Because you should have someone who cares about you—" She swallowed. "Loves you—be there."

Lindsey's eyes glistened. "You tell me this now." She kissed her hard.

"I know, bad timing."

Lindsey sagged. "Is there any other kind?"

Rebekiah's thoughts went to Emma and how the last year of her life stunted her own. She shook her head. "Not in my experience."

"I told you, I'm bad at this."

Rebekiah tilted her chin and looked in her eyes. "That's a lie you've been told." She kissed her forehead. "Don't believe it."

Lindsey opened her eyes and smiled.

CHAPTER THIRTY-ONE

Lindsey woke up to an empty bed in her own apartment. Well, mostly empty. Sera was curled at her feet, snoring softly. Stepping out of the bathroom, she smelled coffee. Rebekiah, the one bright spot in her life right now, stood at the kitchen counter, cracking eggs into a bowl.

She glanced up and smiled. "Good morning."

"Are those eggs?" Lindsey walked into the kitchen and wrapped her arms around Rebekiah. They shared a kiss. Lindsey pulled away, smiling. "You taste like coffee."

She tilted her head. "It's over there."

Lindsey fixed a cup and perched on the kitchen stool. "I didn't even know I had eggs."

She finished whisking and poured them into the pan. "You didn't. I picked them up yesterday."

Lindsey watched her cook. The past two months had been a blur. True to her word, Rebekiah had gone with her to the DOJ office. Elena had met them, and Rebekiah had waited for hours while Lindsey gave her statement. The fallout was almost instantaneous; they lost four major clients in one day. She braced herself each day she went to work. Habit was the only thing keeping her work together. Habit and Rebekiah. Knowing she'd be waiting at the end of the day made getting up so much easier.

"What?" Rebekiah set a plate in front of her and leaned on the counter.

Lindsey pulled her thoughts back to breakfast. "Have I told you how much I love you?"

Rebekiah held her hand. "Several times. Why? What's happening?"

Lindsey looked at her plate. An omelet with chives and cheese. Neither of which were in her fridge yesterday. "How many groceries did you buy?"

"Enough for a few meals. If I'm going to be spending more time here, I'm going to need some ingredients. We can't eat takeout every day. I don't care how much money I have."

Lindsey took a bite and sighed. She just wanted to curl up on the couch with Rebekiah and Sera and watch TV all day. "How can the best and worst things be happening at the same time?"

Grabbing a second plate, Rebekiah came around the island and sat next to her. "Please tell me I'm the best."

Lindsey rolled her eyes. "Yes."

Rebekiah chuckled and cut into her omelet. "Do you want to quit?"

"Every day." Her business profits were down thirty percent, and she was facing layoffs in the next month. She was not cut out to be the managing partner. Cathryn's arrest had damaged their business processes as well as their reputation and financial resources.

Rebekiah put down her fork. "Why don't I take you out to lunch today?"

Lindsey leaned against her shoulder. "That would be wonderful."

❖

Sabine knocked on Lindsey's door and ducked inside her office. "Li Jing is here to see you."

Lindsey stood. "Here?" Li Jing didn't come to Providence. She glanced around. Papers covered every surface; white banker boxes were lined up against the wall. "Now?"

Sabine straightened. "Do you need to be unavailable? I can run interference for you."

"No." Lindsey answered without thinking. She hadn't heard from Li Jing since her arrest, and if Li Jing was here, it was important. She could not brush her off. She glanced at her watch, scooped up her phone, and rounded her desk. "No. Bring her in." She hooked a hand around her suit jacket and shrugged into it.

Li Jing wore a cream Armani pantsuit with a pair of Jimmy Choo heels and a Louis Vuitton handbag. She was dressed to impress and intimidate. She moved toward Lindsey and held out her hands.

Lindsey took them and spoke Cantonese. "What a pleasant surprise. What brings you to Providence?"

She replied in English. "You do." Letting go, she gestured around the room. "I heard about your business partner. Terrible business, that."

Lindsey exhaled. "Yeah, but it's not that bad." Only it was, and she didn't have the heart to tell her. Li Jing knew how hard she worked. She didn't want to see Li Jing's face when she told her the truth; it would make it real.

"I see. Have you eaten?"

Lindsey shook her head. She had plans with Rebekiah.

"I'll buy." She turned without waiting, and Lindsey hurried to catch up.

They walked to the elevator, and Li Jing pushed the down button. Lindsey ran through the local restaurants. "There's a farm to table place in the Arcade."

"Sounds delightful."

Lindsey pulled out her phone and texted Rebekiah. *Sorry, something came up. Rain check?*

Li Jing glanced at her as they walked the half block to the Arcade. "Is that the hotel woman?"

Feeling guilty, Lindsey slid the phone back into her pocket. "How can you tell?"

"Your whole face changes."

Lindsey didn't want to consider what her face might look like as they passed through the Arcade's columns and double doors.

Spring sunlight streamed through the glass roof into the central atrium. Cast iron railings topped with mahogany banisters lined the second and third floor mezzanines. Lindsey led the way past a hipster barber shop, a bustling café, a funky boutique, and straight into a restaurant with a wood, sea, and steel décor. Not a pirate or Cape Cod sea look but more like an America's Cup club feel, a nod to Rhode Island's shipping past. It seemed so provincial with Li Jing beside her.

Li Jing glanced at her menu. "What do you recommend?"

Lindsey picked up her own menu and offered a few suggestions but barely paid attention to the choices. Li Jing was here for a reason, but what was it? Word traveled fast, and the news of Cathryn's arrest was already out there. She had no reason to do business with a company like hers. It only brought her dealings under scrutiny. Maybe she wanted to cherry-pick her holdings or buy her outright. Hope bloomed at the brief thought of selling her firm. She tamped down all her hopes and focused on the menu.

They ordered lunch quickly and talked about the weather before Li Jing leaned forward and said, "I want you to come work with me."

Silently cheering but outwardly calm, Lindsey took a sip of water. "I already do."

"Not like this. I'm offering you a job."

Lindsey pasted on a smile. "I have a job." But a little glimmer of hope sparked inside her.

"True." She sipped her water and raised her eyebrow. "But for how long?" She'd seen the office, and she knew. She hadn't survived this long in the business without reading the signs.

Lindsey leaned back and told the truth. "I'm not sure."

"Let me help you before it's too late." She folded her hands and proceeded to lay out her proposal. Lindsey would come on as a full partner, bringing as many clients as she wanted. Her starting salary would be twice what she was making now.

"Would I need to relocate?"

"Is that a deal breaker for you?"

A month ago, Lindsey would have said no. But her relationship with Rebekiah had taken a new turn and felt too fragile to walk away from. For the first time in her life, she felt at home with someone, and she didn't want to risk losing that. She took a deep breath and said, "Yes."

Li Jing took a long look at her. "I see." The server returned with their meals, and Li Jing waited until she left before saying, "Did you know that I've been married three times?"

Lindsey shook her head. She knew Li Jing had been married but not to whom or how often.

"The first one was a mistake. Joseph and I were from two different worlds. And the third I caught cheating on me. But Wen…That one was my fault. I let him slip away. We're difficult women, you and I. Guarded exteriors. We don't let people in." She leaned in and smiled. "But when we do, it's worth it. I'm happy for you."

Lindsey returned her smile.

"Then let's think a bit more creatively."

They parted ways at the restaurant with a handshake and Li Jing's three words: "Let me know."

Lindsey returned to the office and found Rebekiah wandering the reception area, peering at the pictures along the walls. Even though they had spent every night of the last two weeks together, she got a thrill seeing her. Rebekiah paused at the one closest to the elevator and leaned in; a strand of hair flopped forward.

Lindsey stepped forward and tucked the stray curl behind Rebekiah's ear. "Did you get my text?"

"Yeah. I was in the area, so I thought I'd drop in." She pointed at the mix of historic and contemporary Providence photographs. Rebekiah steered her toward the last picture. "I want to show you something." It was a picture of Waterfire from several years ago. She pointed to the crowd. The focus was clear enough to see individuals seated along the wall and on the walkway but not distinct enough to detect facial features. "That's me." She indicated a group of people to the far right of the picture. "And Emma." Her finger moved along the group. "Elena. Neil. And I don't know her. Oh, and Wyatt." She sighed and smiled. "She was my first girlfriend." She turned to Lindsey with a grin and added, "College."

Lindsey stared at a group so indistinct that the only reason Rebekiah recognized anyone was because she'd been there. "That's so funny." She kissed her cheek. Slipping her hand into hers, she pulled them toward her office. "Come on." Rebekiah followed and sat in the seating area. Lindsey took a seat across from her. "I was offered a job."

"Congratulations." Her features dimmed at Lindsey's expression. "Or not."

"It's in Hong Kong." Lindsey glanced at her hands.

Rebekiah leaned back. "Oh." She crossed her arms. "Do you want to take it?"

Lindsey looked up and sighed. "I don't know if I can with everything that's going on with Cathryn and the firm. But it gets me out of the limelight and back to work." She wasn't cut out to run her own firm, and she didn't want to hold on to the reins of a dying horse. Better to be done with it quickly. Li Jing wasn't just offering her a lifeline, she was giving her a way up and out of this mess.

Rebekiah smiled. "You didn't answer the question."

Lindsey reached out. Rebekiah took her hands. Lindsey gently shook her and locked eyes. "I know. Two months ago, I would have jumped at the chance. It's the best career move I can make after all that's happened. But now…" She looked at their joined hands and shook her head. "Now, I don't want to lose what we have by picking up and heading halfway around the world."

"It's not a zero-sum game." Rebekiah smiled. "Besides, I can do my work anywhere."

Lindsey frowned. She didn't want Rebekiah to give up her life. That was no way to start a partnership. "But your studio…"

Rebekiah shrugged. "It's nice, but I can rent space anywhere. You, on the other hand, not so much."

Lindsey shook her head. Rebekiah had always taken her as she was, and even now, Rebekiah knew that to keep her might mean she had to let her go. No one ever understood that about her until Rebekiah. "What about Sera?"

Rebekiah smiled. "You'll have to ask her, but she's got dual citizenship in the UK."

Lindsey smiled. This was what love was. She leaned in and whispered before kissing her, "I love you."

About the Author

Leigh wrote her first story in a spiral notebook at the age of five and she never stopped pretending. She grew up in three of the four corners of the US before heading to college. Despite the warnings that doing so would make her a lesbian, she went to a women's college.

She lives and works in upstate New York with her wife, son, and two Siamese cats, Percival and Galahad. When she's not writing, reading, or parenting, she's tabletop gaming with a crew of like-minded nerds.

Books Available From Bold Strokes Books

Brooklyn Summer by Maggie Cummings. When opposites attract, can a summer of passion and adventure lead to a lifetime of love? (978-1-63555-578-3)

City Kitty and Country Mouse by Alyssa Linn Palmer. Pulled in two different directions, can a city kitty and a country mouse fall in love and make it work? (978-1-63555-553-0)

Elimination by Jackie D. When a dangerous homegrown terrorist seeks refuge with the Russian mafia, the team will be put to the ultimate test. (978-1-63555-570-7)

In the Shadow of Darkness by Nicole Stiling. Angeline Vallencourt is a reluctant vampire who must decide what she wants more—obscurity, revenge, or the woman who makes her feel alive. (978-1-63555-624-7)

On Second Thought by C. Spencer. Madisen is falling hard for Rae. Even single life and co-parenting are beginning to click. At least, that is, until her ex-wife begins to have second thoughts. (978-1-63555-415-1)

Out of Practice by Carsen Taite. When attorney Abby Keane discovers the wedding blogger tormenting her client is the woman she had a passionate, anonymous vacation fling with, sparks and subpoenas fly. Legal Affairs: one law firm, three best friends, three chances to fall in love. (978-1-63555-359-8)

Providence by Leigh Hays. With every click of the shutter, photographer Rebekiah Kearns finds it harder and harder to keep Lindsey Blackwell in focus without getting too close. (978-1-63555-620-9)

Taking a Shot at Love by KC Richardson. When academic and athletic worlds collide, will English professor Celeste Bouchard and basketball coach Lisa Tobias ignore their attraction to achieve their professional goals? (978-1-63555-549-3)

Flight to the Horizon by Julie Tizard. Airline captain Kerri Sullivan and flight attendant Janine Case struggle to survive an emergency water landing and overcome dark secrets to give love a chance to fly. (978-1-63555-331-4)

In Helen's Hands by Nanisi Barrett D'Arnuk. As her mistress, Helen pushes Mickey to her sensual limits, delivering the pleasure only a BDSM lifestyle can provide her. (978-1-63555-639-1)

Jamis Bachman, Ghost Hunter by Jen Jensen. In Sage Creek, Utah, a poltergeist stirs to life and past secrets emerge. (978-1-63555-605-6)

Moon Shadow by Suzie Clarke. Add betrayal, season with survival, then serve revenge smokin' hot with a sharp knife. (978-1-63555-584-4)

Spellbound by Jean Copeland and Jackie D. When the supernatural worlds of good and evil face off, love might be what saves them all. (978-1-63555-564-6)

Temptation by Kris Bryant. Can experienced nanny Cassie Miller deny her growing attraction and keep her relationship with her boss professional? Or will they sidestep propriety and give in to temptation? (978-1-63555-508-0)

The Inheritance by Ali Vali. Family ties bring Tucker Delacroix and Willow Vernon together, but they could also tear them, and any chance they have at love, apart. (978-1-63555-303-1)

Thief of the Heart by MJ Williamz. Kit Hanson makes a living seducing rich women in casinos and relieving them of the expensive jewelry most won't even miss. But her streak ends when she meets beautiful FBI agent Savannah Brown. (978-1-63555-572-1)

Face Off by PJ Trebelhorn. Hockey player Savannah Wells rarely spends more than a night with any one woman, but when photographer Madison Scott buys the house next door, she's forced to rethink what she expects out of life. (978-1-63555-480-9)

Hot Ice by Aurora Rey, Elle Spencer, and Erin Zak. Can falling in love melt the hearts of the iciest ice queens? Join Aurora Rey, Elle Spencer, and Erin Zak to find out! A contemporary romance novella collection. (978-1-63555-513-4)

Line of Duty by VK Powell. Dr. Dylan Carlyle's professional and personal life is turned upside down when a tragic event at Fairview Station pits her against ambitious, handsome police officer Finley Masters. ((978-1-63555-486-1)

London Undone by Nan Higgins. London Craft reinvents her life after reading a childhood letter to her future self and, in doing so, finds the love she truly wants. (978-1-63555-562-2)

Lunar Eclipse by Gun Brooke. Moon De Cruz lives alone on an uninhabited planet after being shipwrecked in space. Her life changes forever when Captain Beaux Lestarion's arrival threatens the planet and Moon's freedom. (978-1-63555-460-1)

One Small Step by MA Binfield. In this contemporary romance, Iris and Cam discover the meaning of taking chances and following your heart, even if it means getting hurt. (978-1-63555-596-7)

Shadows of a Dream by Nicole Disney. Rainn has the talent to take her rock band all the way, but falling in love is a powerful distraction, and her new girlfriend's meth addiction might just take them both down. (978-1-63555-598-1)

Someone to Love by Jenny Frame. When Davina Trent is given an unexpected family, can she let nanny Wendy Darling teach her to open her heart to the children and to Wendy? (978-1-63555-468-7)

Uncharted by Robyn Nyx. As Rayne Marcellus and Chase Stinsen track the legendary Golden Trinity, they must learn to put their differences aside and depend on one another to survive. (978-1-63555-325-3)

Where We Are by Annie McDonald. A sensual account of two women who discover a way to walk on the same path together with the help of an Indigenous tale, a Canadian art movement, and the mysterious appearance of dimes. (978-1-63555-581-3)